Davina lost the battle to retain her newly acquired Trowbridge control. Tears sprang to her eyes. "You certainly made a mistake in marrying me, didn't you?"

"No!" Adam could have kicked himself. Why must she take his statements the wrong way? "Davina, I love you with all my heart. I don't care what anyone else says about it."

"You shouldn't have married a Halderton." A tear slipped down her cheek. "I am not good enough for you, no matter how hard I try!"

"You are perfect for me when you are being yourself." He stepped toward her.

"You already are. You *were!*"

She merely continued to shake her head. Adam closed the distance between them and took her in his arms. For a moment, he thought she was going to melt against him, but she held her reserve.

"I love you, Davina," he whispered.

"I love you, too, Adam."

But why wouldn't she show it as she used to do? He could only reassure her and continue to tell her she was ideal just the way she was. Surely she would come to believe him and be herself again. If only the vibrant, effective woman he married would not become lost along the way. . . .

Books by Cathleen Clare

AN ELUSIVE GROOM
LORD SCANDAL'S LADY
A PRICELESS ACQUISITION
LORD MONTJOY'S COUNTRY INN
A FAMILY AFFAIR

Published by Zebra Books

A FAMILY AFFAIR

Cathleen Clare

Zebra Books
Kensington Publishing Corp.

http://www.zebrabooks.com

ZEBRA BOOKS are published by

Kensington Publishing Corp.
850 Third Avenue
New York, NY 10022

First Printing: February, 2000
10 9 8 7 6 5 4 3 2 1

Printed in the United States of America

For Robert,
with all my love

Prologue

March, 1816

"Good morning, miss," chirped a cheerful voice. " 'Tis early, but you'd best be up and making ready. Weddings won't wait, not even for the bride."

Having slept lightly, Davina roused easily, butterflies immediately assailing her stomach. The servant was right. The dawn might still be gray and foggy when Margaret, Davina's aunt's abigail, pushed back the heavy draperies, but there was so very much to do to prepare for this, her wedding day. In altogether too short a time, she would be gliding down the aisle to join hands with the most wonderful gentleman in all England. Even now, when she was certain of her love for him and his for her, she could scarcely consider it anything but pure good fortune.

Margaret came round the big four-poster and began plumping up the pillows in preparation for setting a tray on Davina's lap.

"No, only chocolate, please, while I dress." Davina swung her legs over the side of the bed. "I shall go downstairs for breakfast."

The maid looked pained. "But, miss, I've already sent for your bath."

"I'm sorry, but I've important business to attend to with my father and brothers. I shall be quick about it, but I must go down." Smiling kindly, she stepped into her slippers and padded into her dressing room to begin her morning ablutions. "Don't worry, Margaret. I have plenty of time to array myself in my bridal finery. Indeed, that is my priority . . . after my little mission."

She paused to gaze at her wedding dress, which was draped carefully over a dressmaker's form in the center of the room. It was so very beautiful. Of white satin and gauze, its simple, classical lines must find favor with even Adam's haughty mother.

Davina took a deep breath. The very thought of the imposing lady made her heart pound uncomfortably. In their brief but only meeting, Lady Trowbridge had warned her it was not easy to be a countess. Her worrisome words had frightened Davina. Until then, she had thought only of being Adam's wife.

Her face scored with lines of concern, Margaret came up beside her with the chocolate. "Please, miss, it will take time to dress. I want you to be the prettiest bride in all Christendom."

"So do I." Davina nodded vigorously. "We shall strive to attain that goal. I want to be absolutely perfect for my lord. But this business with my family is essential to his happiness, too."

The maid had no choice but to assist her mistress as speedily as possible.

Hurriedly attired in a plain blue morning gown, Davina sat down at her dressing table and gazed into the mirror as Margaret began to unbraid her long and silky blond hair. The butterflies again assaulted her. What should she do with her hair this night? Would Adam want it done up in a properly maidenly fashion, or . . .

She blushed. Once, Adam had told her he adored her long tresses. She'd laughed and told him she could sit on them. He'd replied he'd like to see that.

But his family was one of legendary propriety. He might

think her indecent if she wore her hair down. Oh, dear, what would he expect of her?

Margaret swiftly pinned up Davina's hair in a rather haphazard manner. "There you are, miss. Please . . ." She trailed off.

Davina understood the unspoken appeal. "I will hasten. I know you have much to do, what with dressing my aunt as well. I am sorry to be such a trial. Perhaps Mother's abigail could assist."

"Oh, no, miss! I shall attend you. You are a joy! I only wish I were going with you."

"I wish you were, too." Davina had yet to meet the lady's maid Adam's mother had insisted on hiring for her. The new attendant would not begin service until she and Adam departed on their wedding trip. She hoped the servant would be as kind and comfortable as Margaret.

"Yes, I would love to serve you, miss." Her aunt's abigail smiled mischievously. "It is much more fun to dress a young lady, but please do not tattle on me."

"I shan't." Laughing, Davina rose, squeezed the servant's hand, and rushed from the room.

Clattering down the stairs, she caught herself as a footman looked up in surprise, and proceeded more decorously. She must remember to curb her spirits. Running up and down stairs would not do at the elegant Trowbridge mansion. She must behave like a *countess*.

As she passed the open dining room door, she saw the table set as she'd never seen it before. Her aunt was putting on no meager display of fine china, crystal, and silver for the wedding breakfast. Davina hadn't known the lady possessed such treasures. And the effort was all for her benefit. But no, truly it was for the Trowbridges.

With a soft sigh, she stepped inside and approached the magnificent array. Everything looked so very beautiful. When she sat down at this marvelous table, she would be a countess. Moisture blurred her vision. Biting her lip, she clutched the back of a chair.

"I do not want to be a countess," she whispered. "I do not know *how* to be a countess. I only wish to be Adam's wife."

The butterflies in her stomach renewed their quivering. Thinking of being a countess was terrifying. Why, oh, why couldn't Adam have been a mere mister?

"Miss?"

Davina started, whirling to see her aunt's butler behind her, bearing arrangements of orchids.

"I'm sorry. I didn't mean to frighten you," he said in his kindly voice. "How may I be of service?"

"I was merely admiring the table." She smiled. "The room looks so grand. You have created a spectacular scene, Brill."

He bowed his appreciation. "Now, Miss Davina, how may I help you?"

She noticed two footmen behind him, also carrying flowers, and realized she was in the way. "I just stopped to look. I'll go now."

She hurried through the door and turned toward the breakfast room, where her father and brothers were certain to be. No wedding would cause them to lose their gigantic appetites, but hopefully such a ceremony would be enough to restrain their excessive high spirits. With a deep breath, she entered.

Her eldest brother, Seth, spied her first. "Ho-ha! We have the bride in our midst!"

They all looked her way.

"Well, well, daughter, you do us honor," stated her father. "We never expected to see you until the moment was upon us. Joining us for breakfast? By God, I like that!"

Her middle brother, Lionel, rose to escort her to a vacant chair. "I'll even fill a plate for you, sister dear."

"No." She lifted a hand in protest. "Is it coffee you're

drinking? I'll just have some of that. I am far too overset to want for anything more."

They guffawed, elbowing each other in the ribs. "Maybe you'd best have a beaker of brandy!" Lionel cried. "That'd settle you rightly."

"Certainly not," she said primly.

"I can just imagine the earl's face," yelped her youngest brother, Jeffrey, "if his bride came staggering down the aisle!"

"To say nothing of his prune-faced mother!" chortled Seth.

"Please!" Davina said sharply. "Just the coffee."

A footman served her. The male contingent of the Halderton family was too enraptured with descriptive fantasies of drunken brides to remember she was there. It was just as she feared. They would pay no heed to her, let alone agree to her request. They were a batch of aggravating, noxious buffoons.

"Listen to me!" In nervous frustration, Davina smacked her hand on the table at the first sign of the din lessening.

Surprised, they fell silent, gaping at her.

She could scarcely believe it. She had their attention? What a miracle! She cleared her throat and prayed for another godsend.

"I have come to beg a favor of you," she began. "There must be no practical jokes at my wedding or afterward."

They continued to gawk.

"You did hear me, I presume? No jesting, no boisterousness. Nothing but proper gentlemanly behavior."

Her father and brothers came out of their shock and looked at each other, winking and chuckling.

Davina's resident butterflies beat their wings a bit harder. She cleared her throat. "I am very, very serious about this. You can behave yourselves for just half a day."

They continued to grin and nudge each other.

Seeing their capricious response, Davina was reduced to

begging. "Please, *please,* don't do this to me. You know how his family is. It would be perfectly awful for me to set out on the wrong foot with all those high sticklers."

"Au contraire, my dear." Seth half rose and bowed mockingly. "We should baptize Trowbridge into *our* family."

"Not on my wedding day!" she wailed.

Gnawing her lip, she thought of how Seth had lost the young lady he wished to marry when the girl's parents objected to the horrid Halderton family reputation. Because of their misplaced high humor and practical joking, the Haldertons were considered vulgar, and they hadn't enough wealth to be judged merely eccentric. Only because of her aunt's fine repute had Davina managed a modest come out. When she had landed a prize catch, Lord Trowbridge, the *ton* had been appalled. Couldn't Seth remember what had happened to him, and thus take her side in this matter? But she could not be so cruel as to remind him.

"Please," she implored. "I am already so overset that I wonder if I can survive the ceremony without trembling like a leaf."

"Oh, you'll survive it," Lionel roared. "It's what comes after you should be thinking of."

The male Haldertons laughed loud and long.

"That's right, Davina!" Jeffrey bent over, holding his sides. "But then again, maybe not. After all, Trowbridge is *such a gentleman!* Still, he must have an heir."

Her cheeks burning, Davina clapped her hands over her ears. She'd taken a great chance in coming to them and beseeching them to mind their manners. She could have guessed what the result would be. As always, they'd taken delight in needling her.

Tears sprang to her eyes. "No wonder Lady Trowbridge looks down on me and thinks I am not good enough for her son!"

All laughter ceased. "You are just as good as they are,

daughter," her father contended. "They are lucky to have you marrying into their family."

Davina quickly sensed an advantage. "If you do not conduct yourselves as perfect gentlemen, Lady Trowbridge will be convinced she is right, and she will make my life a living hell."

Halderton jaws clenched belligerently.

Her father narrowed his eyes. "Perhaps you'd best think twice about this marriage, daughter. It is not too late. Have you spoken with your mother? Zounds! She should have chaperoned your Season, instead of trusting your aunt to do the pretty."

Davina knew her mother had remained in the country to keep the male contingent from coming to London. To have them present to remind everyone of their outrageousness would have hampered Davina's chances at making a suitable match.

"Father," she said, "I am sure of my decision. I love Adam. Can I not achieve my heart's desire?"

"Of course, my girl. I'll not stand in the way. Trowbridge seems like a nice fellow, but that mother of his . . ." He pulled a nasty face and shook his head. "She acts like she's better than anyone else, and that's putting it mildly!"

"Exactly," Davina agreed, "so please, Papa, Seth, Lionel, Jeffrey . . . can we not show the old witch we Haldertons can be high sticklers, too?"

For a moment, they looked disappointed. No doubt they had planned all sorts of devilish jests for the occasion. They would not like being virtuous.

"Please?" she whispered.

"Yes, by God!" Her father pounded the table, causing a footman to come running. "That's just what we'll do. We'll show that old antidote!"

Davina could have leaped with joy. "Never let down your guard, or she'll swoop upon the situation like an awful bird of prey."

They nodded, then Jeffrey shrugged ruefully. "The wedding won't be as much fun."

"Trowbridge won't receive a proper initiation into this family," Lionel complained.

"Never mind," said their father. "We'll make up for it at our family reunion this summer. Daughter, you must promise not to interfere with *that* fun!"

"I promise," she vowed, feigning excessive laughter.

"Then never you mind. We'll impress your mother-in-law this day," he vowed.

Relief nearly reduced Davina to a puddle of water. They would behave today in exchange for her lack of interference in their fun at the annual Halderton family reunion. Very well, she would not interfere. How could she? She'd take care she and Adam were not present. He would never know the infuriating extent of the Halderton humor, and she would never again know the embarrassment of it.

Thank heavens! Now she could get on with her life as a Trowbridge . . . as Adam's wife. After this day, she need never suffer the indignity of being a Halderton again.

She finished her coffee in high spirits, even laughing at some of their wretched jokes.

"My daughter, a countess," her father marveled, as she rose to return to her chamber. "I scarcely believe it."

"Neither can I." Davina's spirits plummeted. "I wish I could be only Adam's wife. Being his countess—oh, Papa, I don't know how!"

"Certainly you do. You're a Halderton!" he boasted.

Yes, she was a Halderton. And therein lay the problem.

Attired faultlessly in deep blue superfine and looking every inch the perfect gentleman he was, Adam, Lord Trowbridge, descended the stairs with a cool composure few bridegrooms exhibited on their wedding day. Ceremony was one event in which the ancient Trowbridge family had excelled throughout the ages. Drilled from childhood to display exemplary etiquette, the offspring of the clan were never at a loss as to how to behave; therefore, the nervousness that beset many people on such occasions was totally foreign to him.

Moreover, marriage was a state greatly desired by the current earl. He was about to wed the most precious lady a man could wish for. He was shamelessly head over heels in love, and he was anxious to tie the knot before she could change her mind.

Unfortunately, a glance at the tall case clock informed him it was much too early to leave for the church. He'd have to wait another half hour at least. With a sigh, he deposited his hat and gloves on the hall table and strolled toward the drawing room. A footman sprang to open its door for him.

"Well, you are certainly ready early," the sole occupant of the room observed succinctly.

"As are you, Mother." He bowed to the formidable lady in black who sat decorously on the sofa.

"I felt the need of a glass of sherry to bolster my spirits, so I hastened my toilette," she pronounced, then sipped from the delicate stemmed crystal.

With a sinking heart, Adam crossed the room to the sideboard, but instead of wine, he poured himself a glass of brandy. She hadn't needed to say a word in order to tell him he would have trouble with her. Her appearance said it all. He turned to face her.

"Mother, shouldn't you wear something cheerier to my wedding?" he remarked.

"I am in mourning."

Adam arched an eyebrow. "Father died so long ago. You do not wear mourning at other times."

"Oh, what is wrong with black?" she snapped. "One would think I was dripping with veils, mourning brooches, and other sad devices, which I am not. I thought I appeared very stylish."

He fell silent. There was no point in arguing with her. She would always have the last word, and she would not change her dress. Tongues would wag when the dowager Countess Trowbridge appeared in black on what should have been a happy morning. She knew that, and it was exactly what she wanted. His mother did not approve of his bride, and she wanted the *ton* to know it. Why couldn't she accept his choice?

"I wonder what atrocious fantasy the Halderton woman will wear," his mother mused. "Or, worse still, her daughter. If they wear confections of frills and furbelows, I vow I shall expire."

Adam gritted his teeth. "I have only just met Lady Halderton, but I have never seen Davina clad in anything other than becoming fashions. In fact, it seems to me she goes out of her way to dress with simple elegance."

"If so, it is no doubt because they can afford nothing else. Fine jewelry is certainly out of their reach, or they would be inundated with it. Those sort of people always are." She snorted. "Take care the gel doesn't insist on vulgarly draping herself in the Trowbridge jewels. You must watch vigilantly, Adam. In fact, it would be best if she did not wear the gems at all. Common people like the Haldertons always manifest a tendency to ornate display."

"Common!" He was fast running out of patience. "The Halderton family is just as ancient as ours."

"Humph! Common is as common *behaves*. Everyone knows about the wild Haldertons."

"Davina has always been the ideal lady," he defended. "Why will you not trust my judgment?"

She looked down her nose at him. "Through my sources, I have learned much about the young lady. I know she was not invited to Almack's."

"What a blessing! I have never attended a more disagreeable venue than that marriage mart. I am glad I did not have to go there to be with her."

The dowager slowly shook her head. "You cannot be so naive as to discount the importance of Almack's, Adam. You know the patronesses hold the ruling wand of social approval. Because they withheld their sanction from Miss Halderton, she was denied entrance to many prominent homes. You cannot dispute that."

He sighed. "Mother, why are we discussing this on my wedding day? It is ridiculous."

She leaned forward urgently. "It is not too late to cry off."

"Good God!" he exploded. "I cannot believe you would encourage me to such dishonor—you, who have always placed virtue above all."

"People would understand. Oh, yes! Adam, be guided by me. Flee to the country. It is not too late."

He finished his brandy in one swallow and refilled his glass. "Mother, you had best accustom yourself to the fact I am in love with Davina Halderton and am going to wed her today. The Haldertons will be my in-laws, and I must say I look forward to their refreshing light spirits. I have grown very weary of plodding, strait-laced convention."

She groaned. "Oh, Adam, surely you cannot *approve* of those people?"

To spite her, he very nearly said he did, *carte blanche*. But he was too honest to do that, so he told her exactly what he thought. "Davina has never been outrageous, as the rest of her family is rumored to be. She has an open cheerfulness and a healthy informality I find most attractive. *That* is what she has inherited from her family, not the alleged absurdity."

"Mark my words, you will be unpleasantly surprised," she warned ominously.

"Mother, I am wedding Davina, not her family."

"There's where you are wrong." She shook her finger at him for emphasis. "One always marries the kin, too."

"Fustian!" he countered. "Family has nothing to do with it. It is our marriage, Davina's and mine. It's no one else's business. Now there's an end to it."

"Marriage is a family affair," she persisted. "What do you think will happen when your wife plunges you into social disaster? *I* will be forced to come to the rescue." She smiled smugly.

"That's right, Mother," he murmured. "Have the last word."

She cupped her ear. "What did you say?"

"Nothing of importance." He glanced at the mantel clock. "It is time to go."

She moaned. "So soon?"

"For me, madam, it cannot be soon enough." Presenting his arm, he escorted the elderly lady from the room, pausing in the hall to don his gloves and hat.

"Please, Mother," he beseeched. "If you cannot appear to be happy, can you not at least be gracious?"

"I am always gracious," she said sourly and sailed past him toward the door, her nose so high in the air he wondered if she could see where she was going.

One

May, 1816

Davina fell silent as Adam's well-sprung, deeply squabbed, traveling coach—she couldn't yet think of it as being hers, too—entered London on the road from Dover. Previously, she had carried on a sprightly conversation with her husband, each of them relating favorite features of their fabulous wedding trip to Italy and France. Now, however, attaining the city seemed to put a period to those carefree days. She would be commencing a new chapter in her life. In England, she would really take up her role as a countess.

Of course, she had actually become Lady Trowbridge on that day in March when she and Adam had wed. Their personal servants and the French and Italians bowed, curtsied, and addressed her as my lady or Lady Trowbridge, but she didn't *feel* like a countess, and she reasoned it was most important she did. Surely if she felt like a countess, she might have some inkling of how to conduct herself and her concerns. The thought of not knowing what to do made her stomach quiver.

Sighing, Davina slipped her arm through Adam's and rested her head against his shoulder. Though she might not be conversant with the duties of a countess, there was one thing she was certain of. She felt very much a wife. She was more deeply in love with her husband than she had ever thought possible. How wonderful it was that she had him to love and that he loved her in return. In these days of marriages of convenience, a love match was something very, very special.

"Are you weary, darling?" Adam brushed the top of her hair with his lips.

"A little." A new thought assailed her. "I will have to meet the staff when we arrive at your house, won't I?"

"If you are fatigued, you needn't spend much time at it. They'll understand."

"No, I want to do what is right." She looked up with a small smile. "Honestly, I believe I am more overset than tired. I wish to make a good impression. It is, I think, most important to have the respect of one's employees."

"Don't worry so. They will love you. How can they help but do so?" He lifted her hand, turned it palm up, and kissed it lingeringly. "They will succumb to your charm as quickly and as thoroughly as I did."

"You are bamming me."

"Certainly not! The moment I saw you, I knew I must make you my wife." He looked briefly disconcerted, flushing slightly. "Didn't you know that?"

She shook her head. She had not. When *she* had first seen *him,* he had immediately become the central focus of her dreams. She hadn't known he shared the sentiment. The knowledge was quite disarming.

Adam laughed lightly. "You didn't notice my making a cake of myself, to the great amusement of the entire *ton?"*

"No." She giggled girlishly. "I was too occupied with dreaming of you."

"Both of us, from the very beginning," he mused. "We could have saved a great deal of time if we had known each other's feelings. We could have married straightaway and been spared the uncertainties of courtship."

Her heart felt as if it would burst. "I love you, Adam."

"I love you." He tilted her chin and sought her lips, parting them with his own and kissing her with a sweet passion that was rather unexpected, given the fact that anyone on the street could have glanced through the carriage window and witnessed the scene.

Davina sighed, melting into his embrace. It was very unfashionable for a married couple to appear to be in love, but she didn't care. At times like this, she and Adam had their own world. She didn't wonder if this was proper behavior for a countess. After all, her husband was an established earl from an old and distinguished family, and he had initiated this move. He should know what was right. Nor had she the power to resist. Adam had the uncanny ability to reduce her to shimmering jelly.

He finally lifted his head, grinning. "I think we had best desist in this activity. You know what it precipitates, and we must greet the staff before we go dashing upstairs."

She giggled again as warmth flooded her cheeks. She still wasn't accustomed to speaking of private activities. But he was, oh, so correct in his analysis.

Mention of the staff, however, reminded her of her duty. They couldn't be far from Trowbridge House, and she probably appeared most rumpled and travel worn.

"I must look a sight." She smoothed her hair and reached for her stylish blue bonnet on the seat opposite them. "No one will be much impressed by the appearance of the new Lady Trowbridge."

"Her husband is, and that is all that matters." He retrieved the hat and handed it to her.

"Yes, so it is."

Nevertheless, she wanted to look her best. Those of Adam's servants who had attended the nuptials had already seen her when she was prettily attired, but she didn't want them to think their fledgling countess was ordinarily devil-may-care in her grooming. Longing for a mirror, she tried to set the bonnet on her head at an elegant angle and tie a neat bow. She turned to Adam, brushing his face with the plume.

"How does it look?"

He sneezed.

"Oh, my dear, I am so sorry!" she cried.

He laughed, rubbing his nose. "You are exquisite, darling. Now cease primping. There is no need."

"Very well." She caught the side of her lower lip between her teeth.

He continued to grin. "How do *I* look?"

"Very handsome." She saw the mischief dancing in his eyes. "Oh, you! You are making sport of me!"

There was no time for further comment. The coach drew up in front of Trowbridge House. A footman leaped from his perch and came round to let down the steps and open the door.

"We're home, Davina." Adam teasingly chucked her under the chin with his fingers and stepped from the carriage, extending his hand to assist her down.

The bricks were solid under her feet, but she was shaky, nevertheless. The big, black-lacquered front door with its shining brass hardware was opening. Within was the blurred movement of the assembling household. Davina took a deep breath. How many were there? She should have asked Adam. If she'd known what to expect, it might not have been so intimidating.

"Come, my dear." Her husband protectively tucked her arm through his elbow and started up the steps.

Through the doorway, she could see a positive mob of people. They were all in position now and standing stiffly motionless, ready to judge her. They would compare her to Adam's lofty mother, who must never have set a foot wrong. Equaling her reign as countess seemed overwhelmingly impossible. She would be considered an upstart.

"I am terrified," she whispered, trembling.

"My goodness, Davina, they're only servants." He grinned.

Maybe to him. To her, unused to such a large staff, they were horribly menacing. But she couldn't confess that to Adam. He would surely laugh. Did it really take this many people to run Trowbridge House?

The butler, fastidiously dressed in decorous black, stepped onto the stoop and bowed deeply. "Welcome, my lord, my lady."

"Pinkham." Adam nodded. "It is nice to be home."

No, it wasn't! Davina wished with all her heart that they were back in Paris—anywhere but standing here in front of this rigid being.

"Welcome to Trowbridge House, love." Adam whisked her off her feet and carried her over the threshold.

Taken by surprise, Davina squealed in a very uncountesslike manner.

Her husband chuckled and swiftly kissed her lips. "See? This isn't so bad," he murmured, returning her to her feet.

Her cheeks burning, she gaped at a sea of faces. The older ones were proficiently schooled to sober expressions. The younger ones, though, exhibited stifled mirth. All were nerve-racking. Either they flatly didn't approve, or they were snickering at her.

"Hello," Adam addressed them. "I hope all of you are well. Lady Trowbridge and I are most happy to greet you. We had a fine trip, but it is good to be home."

There was quiet applause.

He led her forward to a reserved, middle-aged woman. "My dear, this is Mrs. Benning, our housekeeper. Mrs. Benning, won't you introduce the staff to my lady?"

"Of course, my lord." She gravely curtsied. "Ma'am?"

Nibbling her lip, Davina followed her through the interminable maze of humanity, mumbling salutations and witnessing countless bows and curtsies. Names and roles washed over her like so many foreign words. She wanted to explain that, in time, she would learn all their names and something about them, but she was too frightened to speak. And she was to be mistress of this complicated domicile? Oh my!

Mrs. Benning returned her to Adam, who was chatting with the butler. Anxiously, she sought his hand. Her nerves were somewhat eased by his firm clasp.

"Davina?" He caught her attention. "Which do you wish, my dear?"

"W-what?" she stammered.

"Mrs. Benning asked whether you would like to go to your room or partake in some light refreshment?"

"Oh." She gazed at him.

"Which?" he prompted.

"Um . . . um . . ."

"Let us have refreshment," he decided. "I do believe Lady Trowbridge would appreciate a glass of sherry. In the informal salon, I believe. Yes, Davina?"

"Yes." She stared dumbly. Her legs refused to move.

"Come, dear." Adam nearly dragged her down the hall, past the mob of servants.

"The salon is on the ground floor?" she asked curiously as they passed the bottom of the stairs.

"Yes. Rather unfashionable, isn't it? But it is a very big house and an old one. At the time it was built, London had plenty of space to build upon, so there was no need to conserve land, as is done today. I believe my ancestors intended to have a country house in the city."

Such wealth! Adam's ancestors had erected a veritable palace.

A footman opened the door to the designated room and closed it firmly behind them. From the hall came the muffled echo of hundreds of feet as the servants returned to their duties. Davina stared. Did Adam say this was the *informal* salon? If so, how grand must the formal one be? She stared openmouthed.

The color scheme of the huge room was green and gold, obviously taken from the immense Oriental carpet gracing the shining oak floor. The walls were pale jade; the woodwork a creamy white adorned with gold leaf. The deep jade satin draperies were fringed with gold and elaborately crowned with intricate festoons and jabots. Fabulous oil paintings graced the walls, and highly polished furniture marched stiffly around the perimeter of the room. Chinese porcelain occupied every available flat surface. It was magnificent, but it was hideous. And it wasn't informal, not by half.

"Wrong choice," Adam muttered, taking her arm. "Come, my dear, we'll go to the library. It is more intimate."

Davina stumbled after him. "We must tell someone where we will be."

"Don't worry about it."

Returning to the hall, she saw why he made that statement. A congregation of footmen stood ready to serve at a moment's notice. As if they knew whose turn it was—which no doubt they did—one followed them a few respectful paces behind. His presence made Davina even more self-conscious than she already was. How would she ever grow accustomed to Trowbridge House? Was there no privacy here?

Adam led her along the long, broad hall, then turned down a slightly smaller hall. Their trailing servant anticipated his next move and hastened to open a door. Entering, Davina found this room much more to her liking.

The library was paneled in mellow oak and boasted shelves bearing fine, leather-bound volumes. The red velvet draperies were as elaborate as the ones in the salon, but in this setting they exuded warmth. The hearth, with its cluster of two wing chairs, flanking tables, and a settee bespoke cheer and comfort for a cold winter's night. Davina smiled.

"This is pleasant, Adam."

"I thought you might like it better." He drew her close. "But you are beautiful, no matter what your surroundings."

She slipped her arms around his neck and gazed up into his clear, deep blue eyes. This room reflected Adam's character. It was one of his personal spaces, so of course she preferred it.

"I want you to remember, Davina, that you are now the mistress of Trowbridge House. Make any changes you wish, except . . ."

She laughed, finally beginning to relax now that they were alone again. "Except for your library."

"Well, I do rather like it as it is." He grinned.

"So do I."

He kissed her, not deeply but unhurriedly, then led her to a chair. "I am serious, darling, about the redecorating. Cost is not a concern. I want you to be happy here."

She thought of the so-called informal salon. It would be magnificent for a grand drawing room, but if its purpose was for the casual, it failed miserably. Still, she wouldn't make too many changes until she was sure of her role. Just a rearrangement of furniture would soften that room immensely. At first, she would do things like that.

Suddenly, she wondered how her bedroom would be. If it reflected the design of the informal salon, she would take Adam at his word and change it immediately. She must have some spaces at Trowbridge House where she could be herself.

After a dignified scratch at the door, Pinkham gravely entered, bearing a large silver tray. That was another thing that must be reversed. The staff must ease their stern attitudes and smile a bit. The stuffy livery should be simplified. The whole atmosphere at Trowbridge House had to lighten.

She smiled shyly as he drew up a tea table before her and deposited the refreshments upon it. "The cakes look delicious," she said unceremoniously, in an attempt to cause him to relax a bit.

He stiffly nodded. "Yes, my lady."

"Do you have a favorite variety?"

He started. "Uh . . . uh, no, my lady. Will that be all?"

"I suppose so. Thank you," she said sweetly.

Pinkham speedily exited.

"Trying to soften the old fellow?" Adam questioned, bending to pour her sherry from the decanter.

It was her turn to register surprise. "How did you know?"

"I am aware of your penchant for lightheartedness. It is one of the reasons I fell in love with you." He kissed her hand, then crossed the room to a cabinet from which he withdrew a glass and a bottle of brandy. "I expect Trowbridge House must seem terribly formal to you."

"Yes," she admitted cautiously, "but I realize a certain formality must be required in the house of a prominent peer."

"Good God." He turned, rolling his eyes heavenward. "In that, my mother would agree."

"I think she is very knowledgeable on what is proper."

"Yes. She is that. But you are the mistress of Trowbridge House now, and your husband is not all that prominent." He came to sit beside her on the sofa. "Mother's standards have been very rigid. Take Pinkham, for example."

She sighed. "He seems so stilted."

"Indeed." He nodded. "But you should be prepared to fail in divesting him of his starch. When a young man, he was trained by my mother. Oh, you may succeed in loosening him a bit, but do not be disappointed if he does not respond wholeheartedly."

"I won't."

"Besides," he said playfully, "aren't upper servants supposed to be haughty?"

She had never encountered servants so imposing as these, but she nodded in agreement. Beneath his jocular exterior, Adam must be trying to tell her to uphold the Trowbridge criteria of domestic dignity. In this, she perceived her first

lesson of being a countess. There was to be a great wall
between the family and the staff. Apparently, however, he
would allow some relaxation.

Davina thoughtfully took a sip of her sherry. "That
makes Pinkham's posture rather irreversible?"

"That makes it quite ingrained."

"But do you suppose it would be permissible for him to
smile now and then?" she asked in a small voice. "I do comprehend it is wrong for the servants to become too familiar,
but I think I shall go mad if I constantly see grim faces."

He laughed. "Do as you wish, my love. I certainly don't
want a madwoman as wife. If you persist, you may just
obtain a pleasant expression on Pinkham's countenance—
and on Mrs. Benning's, too, for that matter."

Another thought assailed her. "Oh, dear. What will they
think of Fifi?"

Fifi, a bright, loquacious Frenchwoman, had taken the
place of the dresser Adam's mother had hired for Davina.
Davina had suffered Draper's stolid presence all through
Italy. By the time they'd arrived in France, she could bear
her no more. She'd let Draper go and hired Fifi, a vivacious
lady's maid with a highly developed sense of style. Under
her ministrations, Davina became quite up to the mark in
fashion.

"No one must overset Fifi," she said fervently.

"I'm sure Fifi can hold her own." Adam's eyes sparkled.
"Trowbridge House is in for quite a change."

"Not too much," she assured him. "The house is very
beautiful, and I imagine it runs with well-oiled precision.
I don't want to disturb the balance. I only want it to be
somewhat . . . friendlier."

"Do as you please, my darling."

"Thank you, Adam."

Still, she could not take him at his word. There was too
much left unsaid. She could, however, make small changes
that should not affect the loftiness of the Trowbridge family.

Being a countess was going to require much adjustment on her part. Oh, how she wished Adam were not an earl! Marriage to a mister would have been so much easier.

But Adam was an earl, and being his countess was worth whatever adaptation she must make. Also, he did say he loved her lightheartedness. She should be able to strike a pleasing balance between gaiety and nobility. It might not be easy, but he was worth it. She solemnly finished her sherry.

"You look pensive." Adam slipped his arm across her shoulders. "And you've grown very quiet."

"Have I?" she said with a rush, then inhaled deeply. "I fear the excitement of returning has caught up with me."

"Perhaps you would like to nap before dinner."

"Yes. Yes, that might be a good idea. If Mrs. Benning will show me to my chamber . . ."

"I'll show you." He set aside his brandy and stood, drawing her to her feet. "Poor darling, it's been a wearying day."

"But a good one." She smiled. Every day with him was wonderful.

"If you are so very tired, I shall carry you up," he suggested.

Her smile turned wistful as she recalled how he had tenderly carried her to bed on their honeymoon. But this wasn't the rented villa in Italy. This was formidable Trowbridge House, and she was its countess and mistress.

"How shocking!" She laughed and pertly tapped his cheek. "Whatever would the servants think?"

"That their master and mistress were two lovebirds?"

"They will know that soon enough, without our being so appallingly obvious." She caught his hand. "Come. I am anxious to see my bedroom."

"One moment, Davina." He hesitated. "Though I am an earl, I am not a prominent man. You aren't daunted by it, are you?"

"Not of you," she said softly.

"Good, that's the way I want it to be. Now, shall we?" He tucked her hand through his arm and started toward the door.

Leaving her to her nap, Adam kissed Davina's cheek and drew the covers over her shoulder, then slipped from the bed. Something had gone awry today, and he wasn't quite sure what it was. Probably Trowbridge House in general.

As he dressed, he tried to look at it through Davina's eyes. It was exceedingly grand. She must have found it heavy, somber, and rather intimidating. She was right. His mother and the countesses before her had never established what one might call a comfortable home. Every element of decor was chosen to impress onlookers with the stateliness of the Trowbridge family. As a result, the atmosphere was stuffy and artificial.

Adam had learned that surroundings could be different in the homes of friends and certainly in Davina's aunt's home where, though everything was in good taste, an air of comfort prevailed. He wanted Davina to create that sort of atmosphere in their house.

Looking back on what he had told her, he doubted he had encouraged her sufficiently. Maybe that was what was wrong. That, or she really was exhausted. It had taken him slightly longer to warm her to their lovemaking. Probably he shouldn't have placed that additional demand on her, but when Davina and a bed were in close proximity, he was lost. Wasn't that part of being a newlywed?

Silently leaving her room, he strode down the short adjoining passage to his own chamber. Turnbull, his valet, was in the dressing room, unpacking his trunk, frowning over the wrinkles in a batch of neckcloths. He looked up and sprang to attention.

"My lord?"

"Fetch a bath, won't you? I'll freshen up now for dinner."

"Certainly, my lord."

As the servant departed, Adam strode to the window. The square below was quiet. Most residents were either secure in their homes or had gone to the park for promenade during the fashionable hour. Later, there would be a light flurry of traffic, but the significant movement would occur late, after dinner, when the *ton* embarked upon the night's social activities.

He was glad he would not be a part of it. Again, like any newlywed, he preferred to be alone with his bride. Her company was all he needed at present. There was plenty of time for them to enter the social scene. But not now.

He might have avoided London and its social commotion and taken her to his country seat, but he hadn't wanted to do that just yet. His mother was there in the dower house, and he wasn't quite up to facing her. And from Davina's earlier attack of nerves, he knew his wife wasn't ready to experience the dowager's scrutiny. No, coming to London was best. With more encouragement, Davina should soon gain enough confidence to withstand even his mother's ruthless inspection.

Behind him, he heard the stir of Turnbull's return. "Your bath will arrive shortly, my lord."

"Very well." He turned. "Tell me, Turnbull, do you find Trowbridge House formidable?"

The valet stared uncomprehendingly.

"Intimidating?" Adam offered.

"I wouldn't know, my lord," he finally replied carefully.

He frowned. "You must have some impression."

The servant obviously noticed his master's slight scowl and sought an answer. "Well, my lord, I consider it to be the proper home of a distinguished peer."

"I see."

That was the only answer he could hope to receive. Distinguished peer! That designation made him feel positively ancient.

He strolled to his dressing room and peered at himself in the pier glass mirror: blond hair styled conservatively, unusually dark blue eyes with not the faintest signs of laugh lines. His mouth was the same—no clue of laughter there, and his disgusting nose was too aristocratic by half. What had the lively Miss Davina Halderton ever seen in him?

He shook his head. They'd been poles apart, but they'd fallen in love, and he had no regrets. The chilly, sophisticated Lord Trowbridge had begun changing as soon as he grew to know her. He actually laughed, and not just by polite pretense. She daily showed him how amusing the world could be. He truly had never been happy before Davina. And Trowbridge House *was* stodgy. He'd make a definite point to encourage her to change it thoroughly.

"Turnbull?" He glanced over his shoulder. "Could you arrange my hair in a more careless style?"

The valet gaped.

Adam looked back at the mirror. "I look like a fussy old man."

He looked at Turnbull's reflection in the glass. His personal servant's mouth was ajar. Adam grinned.

"Yes, I'll turn up for dinner with my casual hair and see how Lady Trowbridge likes it."

The valet managed a croaking "Yes, m'lord," before he was startled from his immobilization by the footmen arriving with the master's bath.

Two

Davina awoke from her nap with her nerves on edge. A glance at the hideously ornate clock on the mantel told her she hadn't much time to prepare for dinner.

That was not all that distressed her. This bed had probably belonged to Adam's mother. She could not be herself there. Feeling unrested, rumpled, and tense, she donned her dressing gown and swung from bed, glad to hear Fifi moving about her dressing room.

"Oh, Fifi!" she called. "It is so late! Do send for a bath as quickly as possible."

The Frenchwoman poked her head into the chamber. "I already did that, my lady. It should be soon here."

A scratch at the door underlined her words.

"Thank heavens," murmured Davina, as footmen entered bearing the tub and ewers of water. What a treasure Fifi was! Draper probably would have stuck to strict conduct and taken no initiative without her mistress's direction.

When the menservants left, Davina padded into the dressing room. "Thank you so much for anticipating my need."

"I want you should look beautiful at all times," Fifi said pertly.

"Well, I don't feel very beautiful now," Davina admitted, climbing into the tub and modestly removing her robe.

The abigail hastened to catch her hair. "We must pin it up! Not enough time to dry."

"I'm sorry. I didn't think."

"No matter, my lady."

Settling into the warm, perfumed water, Davina held up her long blond tresses while the girl went for pins. Bathing in front of a servant was a difficulty she was only beginning to conquer. At Halderton Manor and at her aunt's residence, she had bathed herself in privacy. The new Lady Trowbridge, however, was to be coddled by servants, and there was nothing she could do about it.

Fifi pinned up Davina's hair and began to wash her back. "Is different at this place."

"At Trowbridge House? What do you mean?" Davina asked, interested.

"Is—how you say?—dead persons' faces. Everyone *blah.*"

"Yes, everyone seems very solemn here, but I hope you can bear it, Fifi," she said worriedly. "I don't know what I would do without you."

"No matter. I like serving *madame.*" She shrugged flippantly. "I soon cheer them up."

Davina took the sponge as Fifi began to cleanse her arm. "I'll do that."

"You do not let me spoil!" the maid protested.

"I must not become too lazy." She laughed lightly, then sobered. "I wish I knew what to wear tonight. I am not aware of the customs of this house."

"*Madame* sets the style. You are the mistress." The Frenchwoman scurried across the room to hold up a gown. "But I thought this might be nice."

Davina eyed the deep blue confection. It was another of the fashions Adam had insisted on buying in Paris. Always, whenever Fifi had the choice, she unerringly chose the French dresses from amidst the English ones. She was correct in doing so. The Parisian styles were highly sophisticated and just right for Davina's figure.

Davina nodded. "That will be fine."

"But only pearls to go with it," the maid lamented. "This important family must have jewelry."

"My mother-in-law probably has it all," Davina reasoned.

"If so, is wrong. *Madame* is *the* Lady Trowbridge."

Again, Fifi was right, but Davina couldn't admit it. "My lord may have forgotten," she offered.

"Then tell him."

"I cannot do that." She solemnly shook her head. "It would be too forward."

"But *you* are the countess, not his mama!"

"Nevertheless, no, I shall not do that."

The Frenchwoman shrugged and sighed eloquently.

Davina finished her bath and dressed. She instinctively knew she could not engage in anything that might affect Adam's mother. The woman was so very cold to her. If she asked for the jewels or made significant household changes, she would court severe disapproval. Where her mother-in-law was concerned, she must bide her time and move very cautiously.

"Only pearls," Fifi muttered as Davina eyed herself in the full-length mirror.

"They look very fine to me." Davina changed the subject. "How is your room, Fifi? Is it comfortable?"

"Look at it. It is there." The girl nodded toward a door Davina hadn't opened.

"There?" It opened right off her chamber. Housed there, the abigail could eavesdrop on whatever went on between her and Adam.

"Mrs. Benning told me that is my room."

Davina took time to investigate. Throwing open the door, she saw a small chamber, spartanly furnished with bed, chair, and low chest of drawers.

"Fifi, this will not do."

The maid simpered knowingly.

Davina flushed. "You will be more comfortable in other quarters. I shall arrange it as soon as possible."

Hurrying from her bedroom, she descended the stairs, wondering where she was to meet Adam before the meal. She felt foolish for not asking him in advance. There were so many mundane details about Trowbridge House that she didn't know.

Happily, a footman met her at the bottom of the steps. "If my lady will come with me?"

"Thank you so much." Her smile did not influence his sober, unflinching countenance.

He led her to the library, scratched lightly on the door, and opened it.

Adam came forward to take her hands. "I wasn't certain you'd know where to find me."

"I was well escorted." She turned to acknowledge the footman, but he was already gone. Turning back, she studied her husband, immediately noticing the careless arrangement of his hair.

"Do you like it?" he asked anxiously.

"I do." She reached up to smooth one lock that was too much astray. The style was boyish, casual, and simply begged to be touched. If possible, the look made him even more irresistible than he already was.

"It's different," he said.

"Yes. It will require me to chase away vast numbers of swooning ladies."

Laughing, he guided her to the sofa. "I only wish the regard of one lady. Shall we have a preprandial drink?"

"If there is time." Her humor fading, she bit her lip. "I fear I slept overly long."

"If you wish for sherry, then you shall have it. The servants will delay the meal." He grinned. "It is the policy that Lord and Lady Trowbridge are never tardy."

She lowered her eyes. "Was your mother ever late?"

"Probably not." He laughed ruefully, fetching her drink. "As long as I can remember, she was the model of punctuality. But if she'd the notion to be deterred, I doubt she'd have given it a second thought."

"I want to be as stellar a countess as she," she asserted.

He sat down beside her and lifted her hand to be kissed. "Just be my wife, darling. The countess part of it will fall in line. You must play the role in your own way."

She thought of her maid's room. "There is one immediate change I wish to make." She told him of the arrangement. "Adam, I will feel quite beleaguered by the proximity."

"I agree. We'll ring at once for Mrs. Benning."

When the housekeeper arrived, looking rather askance at being summoned at such a time of day, Davina looked to Adam to give the instructions. When he didn't, she said hesitantly. "My personal maid must have another room."

Mrs. Benning raised a surprised eyebrow. "Surely she did not complain, my lady?"

"No, it is that I . . . we . . ." She cast an appealing glance at Adam, but received no assistance. "It is impossible for her to be housed in our apartment."

The housekeeper, too, chanced a peek at Adam as if for confirmation. When none was forthcoming, she slowly bobbed her head. "As you desire, my lady. However, might I point out that you might find it helpful to have the girl nearby, as her ladyship did?"

"No." Davina smiled shyly. "If a room is available, she shall lodge elsewhere. I do assume the servants' area is large enough to accommodate her?"

"It is. I shall attend to it. Will that be all, my lady?"

"I believe I should like a tour of the house tomorrow morning," she added. "Say, ten o'clock?"

"As madam wishes."

"And . . ." She nibbled her lip. "Would it be possible for the servants to relax a bit?"

Mrs. Benning gaped.

"I would like to see some smiles," Davina almost whispered.

"Yes, my lady." Mrs. Benning curtsied her way out.

"Very good," Adam applauded when the door had closed.

"I thought you might lend me support," she murmured.

"It isn't necessary. Mrs. Benning understands you are the mistress here."

Did she? Davina was not so sure. Hadn't Adam noticed the telltale glance the housekeeper had sent his way? But perhaps it was only normal. Transitions must take time. Tomorrow, all things might be different. Mrs. Benning had probably spent most of her life in the service of Adam's mother. Adjusting to a young mistress would be strange to her.

Pinkham entered shortly thereafter to announce dinner.

"You are ready, my dear?" Adam inquired.

"Yes." She finished her sherry and rose to take his arm.

"By the way, you look most delicious," confided her husband as they followed Pinkham's stiff back down the hall.

Giggling, she smiled up at him. The gown Fifi had chosen must be correct. The Trowbridges dressed somewhat formally for the evening meal. But how could she doubt it? Most everything else was so formal here.

She inwardly groaned. Tomorrow, while she toured the mansion with Mrs. Benning, she would begin to institute small changes. For the most part, they would be nothing big, of course, but enough to begin to endow her home with her stamp.

The greatest change would occur with her stilted bedroom. It must be totally refurbished. She almost cringed as she pictured the opulent, stuffy furnishings. She could never be comfortable in such a majestic place. She must redecorate it . . . and eliminate the subtle presence of Adam's mother.

* * *

With his lordship off to dine with his new windswept hairstyle, Turnbull entered the hall through the dressing room door to descend to the upper staff dining room for his own meal. Horribly, just as he set out, he heard the door of her ladyship's suite. He quickened his pace.

That Frenchwoman! Fifi had been the bane of his existence almost from the moment she had been hired. She chased him, ordered him about as if he were *her* servant, and put on airs as if she were better than he was. As they were both upper servants, he was forced to dine with her, but Fifi wasn't quite so bad in front of others. If only he could escape now . . .

"You!" Fifi shrilled.

Turnbull groaned. He couldn't run; that would hurt his vanity. He halted.

"I have business with you," she informed him.

"What is it now?"

"Madame has no jewels," she said grandly.

"So? What d'you want me to do? Go out and buy some?" He laughed nastily. "I can see what a fine caper I'd cut at Rundell and Bridges."

"Who is that?"

"Jewelers, ninny! Don't you know anything?"

"I am French lady." She lifted her nose. "How can I know England?"

"You are a French *woman,* not a lady, and I wish you had stayed in your own country, instead of seeking to wreak havoc in mine."

She kissed her fingers and flicked them eloquently. "You are nothing!"

He pursed his lips in a magnificent pout. "I am an aristocrat of the chamber."

"Fah! You are his lordship's lackey!"

"A pox on you!" He walked toward the backstairs.

Fifi caught up. "I am not finished! We talk jewels. Is not this family rich? There must be jewels."

"A regular treasure chest full," Turnbull avowed.

"Then you must tell my lord to give them to *madame*. She needs jewels to be in looks."

"Me?" cried the valet. "Are you mad?"

She nodded sharply. "Is your job."

"It is not! I won't do anything of the sort." He scowled at her. "I'd be fired for such impertinence."

"You will think of a way." She darted in front of him, blocking his way and shaking a perfectly manicured finger under his nose. "You will! Else I make life hard."

"Miss Bertrand, you don't understand. You cannot advise an English lord on something like that. He'd be furious!"

"You will think of a way," she screeched.

"Shh," Turnbull pleaded. "Your voice is enough to wake the dead."

"Tomorrow I will see jewels, or I make life hard." She stingingly patted his cheek and started down the stairs. The *front* stairs.

"Miss Bertrand!" he gasped. "Not that way! The servants' stairs are this way!"

"Ooh, la." She waved negligently and went on her way.

With a moan, Turnbull retraced his steps to Lord Trowbridge's chamber. Fifi had taken his appetite, but a nip of his lordship's brandy should restore it. Hungry or not, however, he didn't want to miss the meal. If Fifi were seen making free with the grand staircase, she might get her comeuppance from Pinkham or Mrs. Benning. He certainly didn't want to miss the opportunity to see that.

The pesty minx! Turnbull filled a silver chalice with the fine French brandy and settled into his lordship's cozy chair by the hearth. With Fifi's luck, the butler or housekeeper wouldn't see her. He could tattle, of course, but that wasn't good enough. There must be a way to place Fifi's audaciousness on parade. Chuckling, he rolled the superb liquor across his tongue and began to plot the wench's demise.

* * *

Adam settled Davina in the mistress's chair at the foot of the table and took his position at its head. Immediately, he saw it wouldn't do. She was so far away he'd literally have to raise his voice to converse with her. The Trowbridge House banquet room was made for large numbers of people, not for intimate suppers, and the house did not boast a breakfast or family dining room. He'd have to make other arrangements.

He leaned sideways and peeked past elaborate candelabra and a majestic silver saltcellar shaped like a ship in full sail. "Davina, this is impossible."

"Indeed," she said in a tone that sounded like a whisper.

"I did not notice what a distance there was when Mother and I dined here." He grinned crookedly. Was there significance in that?

Davina did not wait for further exchange. She rose, picking up her charger and soup bowl.

"My lady!" Horrified, Pinkham took the china from her hands and followed her to Adam. Scurrying footmen brought the rest of her service.

Adam chuckled at the astonishment on the servants' faces. Standing, he pulled out the chair beside him and seated his wife. "Ingenious, my love."

"The perspective was rather ridiculous." She folded her hands in her lap while the servants reset her place.

"We have no family dining room," he explained.

She sipped her wine. "Somehow, I am not surprised."

"You are not." Feeling slightly defensive, he made it a statement instead of a question.

Her cornflower blue eyes widened apprehensively. "I did not intend to criticize. I merely meant to acknowledge the house's formality. It stands to reason the home of an important peer must be grand."

He laughed, covering her hands with his. "Do not start up again! I am not important."

Her eyes softened with love. "You are to me," she said softly.

He lost all thoughts of defensiveness. "Trowbridge House is pretentious, isn't it?"

"I did not say that," she stressed.

"No, but it has been on your mind since you entered it. Don't fib to me, darling. I've begun to see it through your eyes, and it's deuced uncomfortable. There are few places in it where we may be nonchalant."

She bowed her head, sampling her soup.

"I want you to make changes," he vowed. "I want you to imprint it with your warmth. Please do not hesitate to do whatever you will. I can afford it."

She looked up. "It is a princely house, full of marvelous treasures."

"But it is cold." He thought of the glow that had attracted him to her in the first place. She exuded warm-hearted charm and sparkle. She had none of the brittle edges that characterized such lofty *haute ton* ladies as his mother. Trowbridge House should reflect her unfeigned sincerity.

"I have an idea," she said suddenly.

"What is that?"

"The lady's maid's room. We could turn it into our own private breakfast room."

The plan had merit. "For that matter, we could take all our meals there," he suggested.

"Yes, but," she demurred, "I would abhor asking the servants to carry all these dinner courses up there. We could start the day, though, in comfort and relaxation. For our other meals, we can do just as we are."

"Very well. We shall make the change tomorrow."

"Do you suppose there might be a table and chairs in the attic?"

"We'll buy new. In fact, we could make the room a combination sitting/dining room," he mused. "We'll use it when we are tired of the library."

She nodded eagerly. "Though I don't know if I'll ever tire of the library. It is a wonderful room!"

He grinned, pleased. It and his bedchamber were the only rooms he'd had a hand in decorating. The rest were products of a renovation his mother had commenced upon his father's death, when he was so young and inexperienced he'd given her *carte blanche,* not caring what she did with the place. Now he was opening his purse to another lady. This one, he knew, had less grandiose ideas. Hopefully, Davina could turn the entire mansion into a home. It was absurd that they felt comfortable in so few rooms.

"Remember," he added, "the whole house will be awaiting your touch."

"Oh, my." She rolled her eyes. "That is a challenge. First, however—after our private breakfast room—I'd like to redo my chamber. It's . . ." She burst into laughter.

"Yes?"

Eyes dancing, she glanced at the hovering Pinkham and his minions. "I shall tell you later."

"Now," he appealed. "You've pricked my curiosity."

"I cannot." She giggled girlishly and lowered her voice. "It is naughty."

"Then we had best hasten the meal," he warned, "for not only is my curiosity aroused."

"Adam," she chided, flushing beautifully.

He held her to her word. As soon as they had finished the delicious repast, he stood and offered her his arm. "I'm sure you will not hold me to remaining alone in the dining room for port."

"Certainly not. I would miss you far too desperately," she said pertly. "My heart would break."

"Witch." Despite the presence of Pinkham, he kissed her swiftly on the cheek. "You have me in your spell."

Their spirits high, they proceeded to the library. Adam's

fascination was so acute he could scarcely wait for the cere-
monious butler to serve his port and Davina's coffee. Her
bedroom, naughtiness—the combination was irresistible.

"Now, minx, you will disclose your roguish secret," he
ordered.

Her lovely eyes twinkled. "When I arose from my nap,
I felt . . . I felt guilty."

That was naughty? Somewhat disappointed, he lifted an
eyebrow. "Whatever for? You can get up whenever you
please."

"It's not that. That is your mother's bed, isn't it?"

"I suppose so." He shrugged. "When my father died, she
insisted I move into the master suite. She herself took a
room elsewhere, but I don't think she moved any furniture.
I believe she bought new."

She began again, growing surprisingly serious. "When I
arose, I felt like a . . . a . . ."

"Like a sloth?" he guessed.

"No. Like a . . ." Her cheeks burned red. "You must
know, Adam, after what we had done *before* my nap."

He was lost. They had made love quite rewardingly before
she slept, but he didn't know what that had to do with her
getting up—or with redecorating her chamber, for that matter. "I'm afraid I don't understand. You'll have to tell me."

"Adam!" she wailed. "You know! Like a woman who . . .
who . . ."

"Who neglects her duties as mistress?" he deduced, deciding that provided the connection with his mother. "You
were not disregarding your duties."

"Not that," she lamented.

"Then for goodness sake, love, tell me, instead of playing
this guessing game. Moreover, I cannot imagine why that
bed should make you feel any way in particular."

"Well, it does," she declared, flushing even more deeply.
In the midst of the garbled revelation, she had lost her

humor. Observing her unhappy perplexity, Adam decreed, "I demand to know what is disturbing you."

"Your mother's bed and her untouched chamber make me feel like a . . ." She lowered her voice and leaned close to his ear. "A strumpet."

Adam began to laugh. "Why are you whispering?"

"Because a lady is not supposed to know about women like that," she said archly, smoothing her skirts as if to proclaim her virtue.

"So whispering makes you innocent?" he teased. "Really, darling, I am appalled to learn my sweet wife knows of such women."

"Oh, Adam." She buried her face in his shoulder. "Do not mock me. I am very serious."

"That you feel like a strumpet? To be sure, I regard that quite profoundly. We'll add bedroom furnishings to our shopping list. However, though, I might add that while I do not wish you to feel like a tart, I rather enjoy you acting like one."

"Adam!" she shrilled, straightening to regard him with horror. "Do not tell me that I behave as—"

"As I said, it is wonderfully enjoyable. You are a passionate woman, my love," he said frankly. "If all men had wives such as you, they would have no need to seek pleasure elsewhere."

He meant it as a compliment, but it almost embarrassed him and it definitely was too warm for his youthful bride. She clapped her hands to her cheeks.

"I shall never show my face again," she moaned.

"Yes, you will." He gently peeled away her fingers, exposing her comely countenance. "Let us always say whatever we wish to each other, leaving nothing between us."

"Can we?" she asked meekly.

"Why not? There is no sense pretending certain things or people do not exist."

She thoughtfully wet her lips. "I suppose you are right."

"Indeed."

She instantly brightened. "Oh, my! What conversations we can have! There are many matters I have longed ever so much to know."

Adam was abruptly not so sure he should have opened the dialogue to any and all subjects. His sweet wife might ask him things he'd rather not discuss . . . or admit to. But he had instigated this course, and he couldn't go back on his word.

"My," she said again in wonderment. "What I shall learn."

Unnerved, Adam reached for his wineglass and took a long drink. "Yes, but at present, I think we should talk of our shopping venture. Before going, we want to be sure of our needs."

"I suppose we must," she said, chagrined, then cheered. "After all, we have a lifetime to speak of more interesting matters."

Three

The next morning when Davina and Adam descended the stairs to breakfast in the huge dining room, they did so with the buoyant feeling that soon they would be arising to a more informal start to the day.

They had already decided that their private breakfast room would be painted yellow with ivory woodwork. Such cheery, warm colors would lift the spirits and set the tone for a happy beginning. The furnishings would be light, too, with airy draperies and graceful French furniture. The china would be a sunny floral, and Davina planned to maintain casual, country-style flower arrangements. Pastoral watercolors would trim the walls.

Davina was glad Adam took an interest in the details of the decor. Spending money and making changes rather intimidated her. With his active participation, she felt much easier in executing the task.

"Unless we are extremely lucky, I doubt one shopping trip will accomplish all," she mused, helping herself from the ample selection on the sideboard.

"You're right." He followed behind her, filling his plate. "There is still your chamber to redecorate. Have you any thoughts on that?"

"Not many. I've been concentrating on the other." She seated herself next to his place at the head of the table, as she'd done last evening.

To alleviate her discomfort in the mistress's bed, they had spent the night in his room.

"Spare no expense," he reminded her, sitting down. "I want you to be perfectly suited, especially in your own bedroom."

She giggled girlishly and leaned toward him, lowering her voice so the attending footman would not hear. "It's almost ridiculous for us to have two beds, but I suppose we must, for appearance's sake."

"Shameless, aren't we, to have such thoughts?" he grinned.

"Indeed," she whispered. "I want my room to be bright and artless, in the same ambience we are planning for our breakfast room. French styling would probably be best, although it will provide a somewhat sharp contrast to your chamber."

"My room is rather fusty, isn't it?" he admitted.

"No, it is magnificent! And comfy, too," she added. "I wouldn't change a thing."

"Are you sure?"

"Definitely."

Adam's room was the ideal setting for a lofty, sophisticated nobleman. Done up in blue and gold, its massive furniture was totally masculine in scale, but Davina felt contented there. It somehow expressed him and his elegance.

She smiled to herself, sampling her creamy scrambled eggs. Her husband might admire her carefree, genial ways, but she cherished his polish and social grace. No situation ruffled Adam. She envied him that. And she intended to learn to be as poised and refined as he was. Her upbringing had not endowed her with finesse. The Haldertons were anything but suave. Again, she marveled at her good fortune. To possess the love of a gentleman like Adam was almost beyond belief.

"I know one thing I never would alter," she said, biting

into a buttery croissant. "The chef! The food of last night and this morning is outstanding."

"Jacques has been with us a long time," he told her.

"I might have known he was French. French chefs are all the crack." She lifted a shoulder. "As you might guess, the Halderton cook is English. I fear Papa's palate is rather uneducated."

"I like good English cooking," Adam protested. "As you will find, our cook in the country is an Englishwoman."

"Jacques does not accompany you to Trowbridge Hall?"

He shook his head. "A condition of his employment. He despises the country. Of course, you may succeed in wheedling him into it, if you prefer. The sweet words of a lady have been known to modify the views of many a man."

She laughed. "No, let us continue as you are accustomed. I'm certain your country chef is superb."

He raised an eyebrow in a mock warning. "She prepares plain English fare."

"If she pleases you and your mother, I'm positive she will delight me."

Privately, Davina acknowledged she knew little of cuisine. In some homes where she had dined, she hadn't liked some of the rich, elaborate French dishes, even though they were the height of fashion. But she was not concerned about Jacques. She had control of the menu. She needn't include those receipts unless Adam desired them. She sighed. There was much to discover about her husband and his preferences.

"I believe you have an appointment with Mrs. Benning to tour the house," he was saying. "I'll make the arrangements for the painting of our future breakfast room while you are occupied with her."

"Good! That will hasten matters," she agreed.

"Then after luncheon, we can shop."

"Very well." She suddenly wondered if he had important

matters of business he was putting off. After all, they had been out of the country for a lengthy time.

"Adam, do not allow me to prevent you from attending to your endeavors."

He laid down his fork and took her hand. "I have nothing more important to do than to be with you, darling. Think no more of it."

"All right." She smiled. "But do not allow my presence to overset your routine."

He grinned and kissed her fingers. "You have overturned my routine from the first moment I saw you, and I have loved every minute of it."

She wanted to throw herself into his arms, but she couldn't, given the hovering footman. How was it possible to be so much in love? She could verily feel her eyes shining with the emotion.

"Oh, Adam," she whispered, "I am so happy."

"So am I. I never imagined such a perfect life. Davina, you have made me the luckiest man in the world."

She looked deep into his dark blue eyes. "I am the most fortunate woman."

She remembered the servant and glanced swiftly at him. He stood stiffly, staring up at the ceiling. "Whatever will he think of us?"

"That we are ecstatically in love," Adam said, color tingeing his cheekbones.

Davina's heart fluttered as it always did when he expressed his devotion with that charming tint of pink. Her self-composed earl had come a long way from his outright, profound blushes of the earlier days of their match, but she hoped he would never completely overcome them. It was *him*.

Minxlike, she brought his fingers to her lips, thoroughly catching him by surprise. "I love you," she mouthed.

Adam caught his breath, flushing in earnest. He bent

close to her ear. "Witch! If you didn't have that appointment with Mrs. Benning . . ."

She batted her lashes. "What?"

The footman coughed violently.

One morning was insufficient time to explore the whole of Trowbridge House, but Davina became acquainted with the important rooms. Like the so-called informal drawing room, the other main rooms all bore the stamp of grandeur and ceremony. They were beautiful, but Davina could not imagine she could ever be comfortable in them.

Though she did not want to live in a version of her ramshackle childhood home, neither did she want to dwell in a place where she was afraid to sit on the upholstery. She felt as if she should examine her shoes before entering the main drawing room.

This wouldn't do, but she was too daunted by her role to make sweeping alterations. Little changes required enough nerve. Armed with pages of notes she had made, she and Mrs. Benning, accompanied by several footmen, began with the opulent salon.

"First," she told them, "there is too much bric-a-brac everywhere. The *objets d'art* are splendid, but they are too cluttered to make a favorable impression. We shall put some of them into storage and change them at intervals."

Mrs. Benning frowned slightly.

"Is something wrong?" Davina asked, quaking inwardly and fearing she had committed some awful transgression.

The housekeeper quickly cleared her brow. "No, my lady. It is nothing. For a moment, I just recalled how Lady Trowbridge . . . er, the dowager Lady Trowbridge took such pains to assemble the things."

"I'm sure she did." Davina wished she could take the upper hand and severely declare that she was the mistress now, but she couldn't be so bold. Leaving her protest unfinished, she started around the room, gathering up items to be packed away. In the end, she did not remove nearly so many items as she originally had planned. Mrs. Benning's disapproval was all too evident.

Awaiting the footmen to carry away the objects on several trays, she gingerly sat down on a little gold chair by the door. "There is also too much furniture."

Mrs. Benning blanched. "My lady, if I may make a suggestion?"

Davina nodded.

"What might appear as too much may be quite necessary when you and his lordship entertain."

"We have no plans to entertain for quite a while," Davina informed her. In fact, Adam had stated that he did not wish to leap immediately into the social realm. For that, Davina was greatly relieved. She could ease into her new role without being faced with the entire *haute ton,* who would certainly be ready to criticize.

The housekeeper merely bowed her head.

When the footmen returned, Davina selected pieces of furniture to be stored. When that was accomplished, she began to direct the rearrangement until the stiff lines of chairs and settees lining the walls were drawn to the middle of the room and placed in conversational groups. When she was finished, the drawing room was much more inviting, though not truly comfortable.

Adam, who had been overseeing the upstairs work, appeared as they were finishing. "My God, what a change!"

Surreptitiously, Davina glanced at Mrs. Benning, who was looking rather smug, as if she were expecting the earl to complain. She swallowed and caught her breath.

"Much better," he approved. "I like it. It was vastly muddled before, wasn't it?"

Davina breathed.

"I didn't realize how much litter there was." He caught her hand and kissed her fingers. "Very nice, my dear."

She beamed. "Thank you. It will be even better with flowers."

"I hope you apply your touch to all the rooms here, and at Trowbridge Hall, as well. Now come see your breakfast room. It is ready for your inspection."

Mrs. Benning slowly shook her head as the earl and his countess clattered up the stairway. "To think I'd see the day."

"Nice, ain't it?" piped a young footman.

"Button your lip! What do you know?" she retorted.

"I know things're going to be better than with the old countess," he rejoined. "This one'll be easy to do for."

"Yes, that's all you would think! To Hades with the family name!"

"I don't know what that's got to do with it," he voiced.

"A great deal." Pinkham joined them and overheard. He looked around the room, his face frozen with censure.

"So many of the pretty things are put away," Mrs. Benning lamented. "What will people think? They're used to seeing the countess's treasures."

"Dust catchers," muttered the footman.

"That will be enough, young man," warned the butler. "One more word, and you'll be out in the street!"

"What will Lady Trowbridge say when she sees this?" Mrs. Benning went on, seeing no need to define which Lady Trowbridge she meant. "She was so particular about this room."

"She'll cut up something fierce," Pinkham replied. "I hope I'm not around when she does. She could up and fire everyone in sight."

They gazed at each other.

"Well, I don't suppose she can." Mrs. Benning shrugged lightly. "She isn't our mistress anymore."

" 'N' I'm glad," the footman chanced.

"What did I tell you?" Pinkham demanded.

He hung his head. "I like our young countess. She's natural and not stuffy like . . ."

"Enough!" Pinkham clapped his hands. "Get out of my sight!"

The footman fled, meeting up in the hall with his colleagues, who had been eavesdropping.

"You've got the nerve!" one of them stated. "But I agree. I like our new ladyship. She actually smiles at us, and doesn't go 'round with that high-nosed, sour face like the old countess."

"And they're in love," another added. "His lordship's so besotted with her that he don't know night from day!"

"Aw, he knows night all right!"

They all chortled.

Pinkham strode into the hall. "What's all this yammering? There is silver to be polished!"

They scurried to their chores.

The creation of the breakfast room and the redecorating of her chamber remained the most extensive alterations Davina made to Trowbridge House. In the other rooms, she quickly accomplished the removal of clutter, the rearrangement of furniture, and the addition of flowers.

Of her plan to make the home more pleasing, the servants' demeanor was the most difficult to modify. Of course, it was easier to succeed with the younger ones. Even though Mrs. Benning had evidently told them of Davina's desires, the staff was reticent when the housekeeper or butler were present. When neither of those two dragons were about, however, they offered subdued smiles in response to her friendliness. Once, Davina was gratified to hear a housemaid actually humming. Adjustment was slow, but the big mansion did seem to be easing its stiffness.

Society represented the next hurdle. As soon as it was

known that the newlyweds had returned to town, they were besieged by flocks of callers and innumerable invitations. Davina had never experienced so many demands for her company. It was very flattering, but aggravating in that she wished to spend all her hours alone with Adam. If being at hand for each visitor and accepting every invitation was what it meant to be a countess, she didn't like it one bit.

Adam appeared to agree from the very beginning. Though he was accustomed to all the clamoring for his presence, he wasn't prepared to give up one single moment with his wonderful new wife. Moreover, he had never cared much for socializing in the first place. He had participated because of duty, and, of late, because of his surreptitious search for a wife. Now that he had found his perfect lady, he saw little reason to go out, unless the invitation was of such stature that they couldn't escape.

"The columnist calls our presence at the Fenwick ball 'a rare appearance'," he mused one morning, glancing at her over his newspaper, as they lounged about in their breakfast room. "I suppose people think we're very reclusive."

She was quick to study his expression. "Do you dislike it?"

"Lord, no! Society holds no charm for me." He nodded toward the stack of envelopes beside her plate. "Are those invitations?"

"Yes." She sighed, lifting them up, then dropping them in place. "I wish I knew what to do with them. I must send replies. They cannot wait another day."

He tossed his paper aside. "Let me see them, darling."

She pushed them toward him and smiled ruefully. "Not so long ago, I would have been thrilled to receive so many requests. Now they hang over my head like a lead weight."

He grinned. "Surely not that bad, my dear."

"No, much worse." She cut a bite of rosy ham. "Everyone seems to beg our attendance. I do believe London consists of nothing but one movable, never-ending party."

"We could remove to the country," he considered.

The country and Trowbridge Hall were synonymous, as far as Davina was concerned. Both meant an encounter with her husband's frightening, high-stickler mother.

"No," she said. "We would lose our privacy there, as well."

He arched a knowing eyebrow and laughed. "That is certain! After all, aren't we still on our honeymoon?"

"I want our whole life to be one long honeymoon," she murmured dreamily. "Hopefully, we will grow very old, still delighting in each other."

"A pretty sentiment." He peered at one or two of the invitations, then shoved the batch aside. "I shall request my secretary to answer them. There is no point in spending your time doing it, especially when I covet each moment of your attention. I am a jealous husband, pet."

"I, too, adore every moment with you." She blew him a kiss, then popped the morsel of ham into her mouth, chewing thoughtfully. "I do, however, recall that you've a matter of business to tend to this afternoon."

"Yes, more's the pity. I can't avoid it."

"And," she went on, "we've a ball to attend tonight at the Montclair residence."

"Damn. Let us escape it."

"We did accept the invitation," she reminded him. "Shall I invent an excuse and send our regrets?"

"That, or we'll simply ignore it. The Montclair entertainments are tremendously popular. There will be such a crush that no one will miss us. Or we could go and leave early, as we have done in the past."

"Let us do that," Davina suggested, "since we have already accepted."

"Very well, but we shall leave *very* early." He picked up the rose-covered china tea pot and replenished their cups of tea. "Now let us enjoy our breakfast and not worry over social events. Dining like this is so very comfortable, darling. I'm glad you thought of it."

"Thank you, my lord. I highly approve of it, too."

Davina glanced around the little room. It was such a cozy place. She and Adam could arise in the morning, throw on their dressing gowns, and dine in delightful seclusion and comfort. Lolling about without getting dressed was a good way to start the day, especially for a man and woman who sometimes returned to bed.

Once again, she marveled at her good fortune. She had come a long way from Halderton Manor. Her beautiful, well-run home, even with all of its stuffiness, was far above that shabby domicile. Hadn't her mother ever tried to improve that eyesore? Perhaps she had, and had been forced to give up.

Adam broke her reverie. "You're very deep in thought, my dear."

"Yes." She laughed lightly. "I was thinking of Halderton Manor."

"Perhaps you'd like to visit your family. We could go there if you want."

"Heavens no!" The very thought filled her with panic. It was the last place she wished to show him. The awful house would drive her sophisticated husband to insanity. No, she would *never* take him to her childhood home.

"I am satisfied right where I am," she assured him. "My only other desire would be to have a cottage by the sea. The ocean air would be so invigorating, and the beach would be marvelous for long walks."

"I'll inform my man of business. Perhaps he can find something," he promised.

"You would? How wonderful!" she marveled, then had second thoughts. "A place on the shore might be awfully expensive."

"That doesn't matter."

"It doesn't?" She eyed him in awe.

"No. I have the funds, and I wish to give you everything you ever wanted." He beckoned to her.

Davina hurriedly rose and came 'round the small table to drape herself across his lap, her arms around his neck. She eyed him lovingly.

"Oh, Adam, you are everything I've ever wanted. All else is superfluous."

"Nevertheless, whenever I discover something you want, I shall go to all lengths to obtain it." He kissed her nose. "I want to spoil you shamelessly."

"You are succeeding. I want to spoil you, too." She lay her head against the hollow of his shoulder. "I want to be all things to you."

"You are." He brought his mouth down upon hers in a soulful, satisfying kiss that left her lips tingling.

She sighed. "When you kiss me like that . . ."

"Yes?" he prompted.

"When you kiss me like that, I feel as if I am the only woman in the world."

"For me, you are." He playfully nuzzled the top of her head. "Talk of leaving London has whet my appetite. Let us prepare to leave for Brighton in several days. I would like to walk along the shore with you."

She bounced excitedly. "Oh, can we really do that?"

"Certainly. Aren't we still on our lifelong honeymoon? And maybe we'll find a house of our own."

"Just a little common cottage would be agreeable," she suggested.

"I think you'd want something a bit bigger than that, my love." He grinned. "We do need room for servants."

She giggled girlishly. "We do not. I can take care of you all by myself! We can have a milch cow and chickens . . ."

His smile became a laugh. "I did not realize you knew how to milk a cow."

"Well, I saw it done once. It shouldn't be difficult."

"Such a practical wife! And I assume you will also kill the chickens for dinner?"

Davina grimaced. "On second thought, I suppose we do need servants—but not many. I want to feel we are alone."

"We are alone now, even in a houseful of servants." He gazed into her eyes. "Davina?"

Without waiting for a reply to his unvoiced question, he lifted her up and carried her into the bedroom.

Four

The morning sun shone steadily through the leaves of plane trees, creating a dappled pattern on the flagstone terrace of the bower House at Trowbridge Hall. It was early yet, the air still heavy with the scent of roses and dark, rich earth, but two elderly women were already seated in wrought-iron chairs, partaking in tea, nut bread, and poppy-seed cake.

It was easy to see they were sisters. Both were nearly identical in features and figure, but one was obviously older. While the younger sibling seemed cheery, bright, and friendly, the elder possessed a stiff and formal bearing and bore the hawkish countenance of cold command.

Everyone on the estate was afraid of the dowager Countess Trowbridge, except her little sister. Though frail and delicate, she refused to be intimidated. The ladies made a strange pair, but each, in her own way, was totally devoted to the other. Even so, they were at cross-purposes at the moment.

"As you see, I shall be doing no entertaining ever again," the countess announced in her stately nasal voice. "My *quarters* are much too small."

"Fustian," scoffed Mrs. Wainwright. "I'll wager you have fifteen rooms here. That is space enough for any party you may hold. By rights, the populous grand assemblies will be held by Adam and Davina."

"Ha!" The dowager threw back her head and rolled her eyes. "That little chit is perfectly unsuited for planning such significant fetes. Mark my words, this will be the end of Trowbridge hospitality. I can feel it in my bones."

Her sister tittered. "Now, now, Eleanor. Give the gel a chance."

"Have I any choice?" She groaned. "I cannot imagine why Adam did such a thing. Don't get me started, Daphne. I could go on for hours about that girl and her awful family!"

"Well, I don't want to hear it."

But the dowager was already launched. "According to all the *on dits,* Adam fell head over heels for that gel the very first time he saw her. Ridiculous! Has my son no brains? I had lectured and lectured him on his family responsibility. He *knew* he was to choose a bride on the basis of pedigree, wealth, and reputation. So what does he do? He ignores his lessons and marries Davina Halderton! How can such a thing have happened? Perhaps she is a witch and has cast a love spell on him."

"Oh, that cannot be." Daphne laughed, her eyes twinkling merrily. "I think it's terribly romantical. More and more young people are wedding for love, you know. Arranged marriages are old-fashioned. Good riddance, I say! Let our young ladies and gentlemen select their own mates. That is the natural thing to do."

"Natural!" Lady Trowbridge snapped. "Would you turn us all into animals?"

Her sister had no opportunity to reply. The dowager's dignified butler stepped out on the terrace, bearing a silver tray upon which rested a single, cream-colored envelope. He bowed deeply to his employer.

"Madam."

The lady picked up the missive, fixating on its frank. "Hmm, correspondence from my dear friend, Adeline."

She opened the note, read silently, then let the paper slip

through her fingers and float down to the flagstones. "Merciful heavens, I have never been so overset."

"What is it?" Mrs. Wainwright asked excitedly.

"It's Adam and that wife of his." The dowager closed her eyes and lifted a limp hand to her forehead. "Their behavior is outside of enough! I just don't know what to do."

"What are they doing?" her sister urged.

Lady Trowbridge took a deep breath. "I scarcely know where to start. Perhaps you'd best read the message yourself."

Daphne practically dived on the fallen scrap. She smiled as she read. "Is this all? What a ninnyhammer Adeline has become."

"All?" shrilled the countess. *"All?* I will have you know Adeline most certainly is not a ninnyhammer. She is a very important hostess and a veritable arbiter of proper etiquette. Why, on occasion, even the patronesses of Almack's consult her!"

"Fiddlesticks." Her sister laid the letter on the table between them. "Actually, I think it's rather sweet."

"Ooh." Lady Trowbridge shuddered. "You think it's sweet, and I think I've never been so humiliated. Apparently, you did not comprehend what Adeline was telling me. Otherwise, you would know I am rightfully shocked and concerned."

"Do remember it is a love match, Eleanor."

"Love or hate, what matter?" She airily waved a hand of dismissal. "Whatever the emotion, proper social manners must prevail. Can you not fathom my point of view . . . and the opinion of the *ton,* as well?"

When her sister did not reply, the dowager went on. She retrieved the letter. "Just listen to this: *The earl and his new countess decline most invitations. Rumor claims they prefer to be alone. When they do accept a bid, they barely put in a cursory appearance before they leave, and usually they are not at home to callers.* Daphne, you know this will not do. They are compromising the family duty and reputation."

Mrs. Wainwright refilled their delicate Haviland cups with tea. "You and the others are probably overreacting. Our newlyweds are merely extending their honeymoon. In time, they'll come 'round in their actions."

"Nonsense! There isn't time. The family name is in jeopardy!"

"Oh, Eleanor, can you not leave well enough alone?"

"Adam knows better than this," the dowager railed on, as if her companion had not spoken. "When he was just a lad, I painstakingly instructed him in responsible etiquette and family honor. He learned his lessons well and never disappointed me until he married that chit. Dear Lord in heaven, if a great hole suddenly appeared in the floor, I would leap into it and never be seen again."

The younger lady smiled perceptively. "You must be patient. I have full confidence all will be resolved in the end. Moreover, I've always thought the Trowbridge family was a trifle stuffy. Perhaps it is time for a change."

Lady Trowbridge gasped. "How can you say that? You are obviously in the minority, or Adeline would not have written to me to express the *ton's* point of view. My word, Daphne, are you attempting to pacify me? You cannot be serious."

"Dear Eleanor, give the children a chance."

"I must intervene." The dowager countess rose and began to pace, her heels clicking busily on the flagstones. "I knew no good would come of this match, but would Adam listen to me? No! He had to have that gel, despite her awful family. I knew he would pay, but I didn't expect social retribution to come so swiftly. I must go to London."

Mrs. Wainwright gasped. "You cannot!"

"I most certainly can. If I do not straighten out this predicament, who will?" Her heels clacked louder, setting her sister's teeth on edge. "Ever since I married into the Trowbridge family, I have striven to uphold their honor. Indeed, I have even tried to advance their social excellence."

"Yes, Eleanor," Daphne said dryly. "You've always had the knack to do whatever is proper, even in the gray areas of etiquette. I have often envied your special skill."

"Thank you." The dowagers nose rose a bit higher.

"But you are wrong to meddle in this."

Lady Trowbridge halted. "Your brain is muddled, dear sister. You compliment me on my knowledge of good form, yet you advise me to ignore those very conventions. Well, I will not listen to your advice. I will go to London and speak severely with Adam. Goodness gracious, he knows better than this! Then I will instruct that gel in the art of being a countess. Obviously, she hasn't the slightest idea what she should do."

"Isn't that Adam's responsibility?"

"Evidently, he is shirking it. I only hope I arrive in time to prevent complete social estrangement. I knew I should have remained in Town! But at the moment, it seemed proper to bury myself on this dreary estate and allow the newlyweds to live alone. I shall never make that mistake again, not until the gel's transformation and not until Adam comes to his senses. Besides, when I married the earl, my mother-in-law counseled me on family expectations. I was very grateful."

Her sister sighed. "Very well, Eleanor, but I still feel you shouldn't meddle."

"I am not meddling! I will be *instructing*. Coming from that awful family, the gel cannot have developed a sense of propriety."

"When I met them at the wedding, I found her family to be quite pleasant."

The dowager countess gritted her teeth. "They were on their best behavior. Beneath that counterfeit *façade* lurked their traits of irresponsibility, devilry, and disrespect. Oh, why did my Adam marry into such a batch of buffoons?"

The statement apparently did not require an answer. Daphne Wainwright returned her attention to their repast. Carefully, she buttered a slice of nut bread.

"How can you eat at a time such as this?" cried her sister.

"Easily," Daphne said flatly. "I'm hungry."

"Ooooh!" The dowager's pace became more frantic. "The Trowbridge reputation is in danger of flying right out the window, and you eat! You may be related to the Trowbridges only through marriage, but you could exhibit some pity for me and show me some support."

Mrs. Wainwright rolled her eyes. "Eleanor, I have tried to offer solace and advice. You refuse to heed me; therefore, what can I say? I am mightily sorry you are disturbed, but you should not tamper with Adam's marriage."

The dowager countess paused. "Why can you not understand my duty to the Trowbridges?"

"Fiddlesticks! The Trowbridges are not so sacrosanct that we mere mortals must fall to our knees and worship them. Goodness, Eleanor, you may idolize them, but don't expect the rest of the world to agree." She defiantly popped the last bite into her mouth.

Lady Trowbridge made a sound like that of a dog growling. "Just answer one more question, Daphne, and then you may wallow in that swill as long as you wish. Do you intend to accompany me to London?"

"No," her sister said succinctly, and daintily wiped a drop of butter from her forefinger. "I won't be a party to such nonsense, and nonsense it is. You should be rejoicing in the fact your son has made a love match. That's a far cry from your own nuptials, that cold arrangement which you continually deplored throughout your husband's lifetime. Think on that, Eleanor, and leave those children alone."

"No! My circumstance does not apply!" The countess

paused at the stone railing and wrung her hands. "People may love each other, but they still have an obligation to uphold their station in Society. You will not accompany me to London? Very well. I shall go alone. I *will* see this situation remedied."

"I pity our newlyweds," Mrs. Wainwright softly intoned. "I pray their love is strong enough to withstand the assault of this virago I call sister."

"What is that, Daphne?" Lady Trowbridge quizzed. "Must you mutter?"

"Nothing," she replied. "Since you will be leaving here, I suppose I may as well go home to that horrid drinking, gambling creature I was forced to marry. I wish I'd had the opportunity to wed someone I loved. But I doubt that makes any difference to you, does it, Eleanor?"

"No, it does not," declared the dowager countess.

Her head throbbing, Davina entered the breakfast room and sank down into her chair. Sleep had not eased the headache she'd suffered at the Montclair ball. She leaned toward the open window and breathed in the stale, hot city air. Now that they had decided to go to Brighton, oh, how she longed for fresh air! If only Adam did not have these matters of business to attend before they left.

He put down his paper. "You are no better, are you?"

It was a great effort to shake her head. She looked at him through bleary eyes. "My whole face hurts. I feel as if my brains were going to burst through my nose."

"My, darling, what a picturesque description," he said, trying to cheer her. "That would not be a pleasant experience."

She managed a smile.

He sobered. "I should send for a physician."

"Please, Adam, no," she protested. "I have had headaches like this before, and they do not occur frequently. I shall be fine. Besides, he would only prescribe powders, and I have already taken those."

"If you are certain." He filled her cup. "I ordered coffee for you this morning, hoping it might help. And this, too." He added a portion of brandy.

"My goodness, I shall be flying high!"

He grinned. "It might help."

"I've never had brandy." She took a small sip of the blend. "That has a kick to it. Maybe it will help."

"Poor darling. I imagine leaving the city would help far more." He closed his hand over hers and squeezed. "Why don't you go on to Brighton today? I'll follow tomorrow."

She eyed him with horror. "Leave you? Never!"

"If it would help—"

"Never, never, never. You are wasting your breath. I will not do it, Adam. I will never be separated from you. We will travel together."

He grinned. "Good. I didn't really want you to go off without me. Now, Davina, you must try to eat something."

She made a face of distaste. "Let me finish this first."

The coffee and brandy did seem to be helping. One or both of the components did seem to dull the pain. She drained the cup and partially refilled it with coffee.

"May I have more brandy?"

He gave her the flask. "Be cautious, my love. You are unaccustomed to drinking such potent spirits."

Davina giggled, pouring herself a generous amount. "It might serve me well to become foxed. It would definitely be a novel adventure. What is it like to be cup-shot, Adam?"

He lifted an eyebrow. "How should I know?"

"Come now," she scolded, feeling better and better as she drank. "At some time you must have become disguised."

His eyes twinkled. "That is not a subject for polite company."

"Remember," she reminded him primly. "you said we could talk of anything."

"I was afraid you wouldn't forget that." He pondered, slowly chewing a slice of crisp bacon. "You must eat, Davina, or you will learn firsthand what it is to be top heavy."

"Very well." The headache was nearly gone, and her stomach was rumbling with hunger. She helped herself to bacon, scrambled eggs, and a muffin.

"Do continue, Adam." To fully satisfy him, she ate a forkful of eggs.

"If one is in his altitudes, one is happy, dizzy—it depends upon how much one has drunk, and it affects different men in different ways. But there is one thing certain: If one drinks too much, there is hell to pay later. Headache, nausea . . ."

"That doesn't sound pleasing."

"Absolutely not," he said firmly. "That is why you *will* be prudent, my darling, or you will be far more ill than you were in the first place."

"I shall," she promised. "How many times have you been foxed, Adam?"

"Davina!"

"You said—"

"I know what I said, but this is outside of enough," he appealed. "Please cease your inquisition on liquor."

"All right, let us chat about bits o' muslin."

"Come now!" Heedless of the scratch at the door, Adam threw a muffin at her.

Davina ducked, bursting into laughter. Picking up her roll, she took aim and hurled it, striking Pinkham in the forehead as he quietly entered the room. Her lips formed an O, but she was speechless.

It seemed to take Pinkham minutes to lower his head to stare at the projectile on the floor. His whole body appeared to puff up. He took a long breath.

Adam stiffened. "I gave orders we are not to be disturbed after the meal has been served."

Davina felt like crying. Pinkham would surely tattle to all the staff. They'd think her a genuine hoyden.

"What is it?" her husband said so chillingly that it gave her the shivers.

Pinkham bowed solemnly. "My lord, I believe my message surmounts the command, or I would not have interrupted, and I did hear you bid me to enter."

"What?" Adam said shortly. "Oh, never mind. Continue."

"You have a caller, my lord—or rather, a house guest," he announced, glancing at Davina. "Your lady mother has arrived, sir."

"What?" Adam exclaimed.

"The dowager countess has arrived with trunks, my lord. I presume she means to stay."

"Hell and damnation!" He exhaled. "You'd best send my valet and my lady's abigail, Pinkham."

"As you wish, sir." With a slight frown, the butler departed.

"Damnation!" Adam said again. "If this isn't all we need."

"We can't go to Brighton," Davina pronounced.

Her husband spontaneously murmured an awful expletive, giving her cause to wonder if he were as polished as one might assume. He swiftly apologized.

Davina felt like cursing, too, but she wasn't *that* much of a hoyden. Besides, it was his mother. He wouldn't appreciate her expressing her opinion of the old virago. Oh, Lord, the day she had dreaded had come. She was to be thrown in close company with the frightening Lady Trowbridge.

"Darling, your headache . . ."

"It's nothing." She waved her hand dismissively.

"Then if you do not wish to return to bed, we'd best dress."

"Yes." Davina rose. "I wish she had given us notice. The house, the food—nothing is ready for her visit! Oh, what shall I do?"

"There is nothing wrong with anything," he assured her. "This house is our home. We are its master and mistress. My mother is not. If our way of life suits us, we need answer to no one. Besides, she is merely family, so do not worry your pretty head. There is no need."

Yes there is, Davina thought as she kissed Adam and proceeded to her dressing room. Men just did not understand. Her mettle as hostess and daughter-in-law would be sorely tested by this visit. She had best not come up wanting, or Adam's mother would make life very difficult for her. She shuddered.

She was decidedly afraid of the dowager. The lady had a dreadful way of looking down her slender nose, totally intimidating the subject of her interest. Davina had spent little time with her, but already she had been exposed to this treatment more than once. Oh, why had she come? Life had been so happy.

Entering her dressing room, she feverishly began sorting through gowns in a frantic effort to find the one best suited to the occasion. Even the finest ones, the gowns Adam had bought her in Paris, suddenly seemed to have something objectionable about them. She finally chose a low-key apple green one and placed herself in the hands of her capable maid. Already, she'd probably roughed up the dowager's hackles by being caught lounging about instead of tending to the running of the household. Even though Adam had wanted it this way, too, she would be condemned for indolence.

Her stomach was tied in knots as she glanced in the mirror one final time. She looked well, but she guessed her mother-in-law would not set as great a store by her appearance as by her tardiness. "Oh, Fifi, do I look as awful as I feel?"

"Still the headache?" the maid inquired.

"No! I am . . ." She could hardly admit she was afraid of Lady Trowbridge. "My mother-in-law is . . . formidable."

"Ooh, la! She is not to fear. She is nothing now." Fifi shrugged lightly. "You are the great countess."

"I doubt it works that way with Lady Trowbridge." Davina poked at a wispy curl that usually looked becoming, but abruptly seemed simply unkempt.

Fifi fluffed it back the way it was. "Not to worry. You are beautiful."

"I hope so," Davina said with longing. "Well, I'd best go."

"Shall I keep packing for the seashore?" the girl asked.

She smiled sadly. "No, we won't be able to go."

"But you looked forward so! *Madame,* do not allow this woman to stop you."

"No, it can't be helped." She turned from the mirror. "We must postpone the trip until after her visit."

Fifi gazed mournfully at her, then overtly compelled herself to smile. "She maybe leave soon."

"Perhaps."

But Davina doubted it. She had a hideous premonition the dowager countess would not hasten her departure. There was nothing she could do about it, though. Adam's mother was in control. They'd probably been lucky to have this stretch of time alone together. Setting her jaw and catching her breath, she reluctantly left the room and trod toward the ominous meeting.

Five

Adam quickly descended the stairs. He had dressed so hurriedly and haphazardly that his valet had gaped in disbelief. But he hardly had to explain. Turnbull knew full well the dowager's dislike of waiting. Also, Adam wanted to be sure of making an appearance before his wife. His mother was not pleased with his choice of brides. If she was angered by the delay in being greeted, he did not want Davina to bear the brunt of it.

The entrance hall was littered with trunks, bandboxes, and portmanteaus of varying sizes. The dowager apparently meant to spend a lengthy time. Adam frowned in dismay. Just his luck! When he was the happiest he'd ever been in his entire life, she had to come along and interfere. What would happen to the trip to Brighton? He so wanted to take Davina to the shore, especially if the city air was making her suffer. If headaches continued to plague her, they would leave in spite of his mother. Disliking the seashore, his mother would be angry, but that was just too bad.

He approached the formal drawing room with such speed that a waiting footman scarcely had time to open the door for him. Entering, he stiffened his shoulders and bowed to the slender yet domineering female who stood by the mantel, tapping her foot impatiently.

"Good morning, Mother."

"Good morning." Her penetrating gaze sliced him up and

down. "Though why I should call it good, I shall never know. Due to the breakage of an integral piece of harness, I was forced to spend a disagreeable night at the most noxious inn I have ever chanced to encounter. Had that not taken place, I would have arrived late last night."

Thank God for the troublesome strap. It had provided him with several pleasant hours of respite. Careful to keep his expression reserved, he escorted her to a chair.

"What a pity, Mother. Such things will happen at the worst of times." He seated her and took the chair opposite. "Have you breakfasted? Perhaps you would like a tray."

"Tea only," she requested.

Adam nodded to Pinkham, who had positioned himself inside the door in anticipation of attending to just such a wish. He turned back toward his mother. As he did so, his ruby cravat pin fell to the floor.

"My goodness, Adam, what is that?" She lifted her lorgnette to peer at the hapless jewelry.

He felt a flush rise to his cheeks. "Pardon me, Mother. I dressed with great speed."

"You weren't even *dressed?* It's remarkably late in the morning."

Adam felt like cursing. Why did he allow her to make him feel so small? He should simply ignore her cutting observations, but he couldn't. Why? Force of habit, he supposed. The intimidation must end. He was a grown man with a wife and perhaps soon children. He didn't need to be bullied.

He picked up the pin and tried to insert it into his neckcloth. It ended up crooked—he could tell by the disapproving glare on the dowager countess's face.

Lowering the lorgnette, she crossly shook her head. "My dear Adam, I have never known you to be so . . . so . . . jumbled. Not only is the pin awry, but your entire cravat is askew. You used to be so elegant! What have you become? I am more than appalled."

"Don't set such a high price on it, madam. I was hurried, that's all." He frowned slightly and muttered, "Good God, a bit of dishevelment is not a capital crime."

"Maybe not," she replied with alacrity, "but it certainly is an offense to the onlooker. I have taught you better than this. Please do not tell me you've forgotten your painstaking lessons on refinement."

He sighed, feeling like a lad. "No, Mother."

"Excellent!" She actually applauded. "I have also noted your hair is a bit carelessly combed. Perhaps you had best return to your room and make yourself properly presentable."

He'd half risen before he caught himself. "Mother, I like to wear my hair this way. Additionally, this is a family setting. I don't believe I'll be overly concerned with every foible of my appearance at the moment."

"Callers might arrive."

"This early? Then we won't be at home to them. Must we always stand on such ceremony?"

She eyed him with unmistakable aggravation. "One should be prepared for any eventuality. That includes being appropriately attired."

Adam longingly thought of the array of spirits located in the liquor cabinet across the room, but he banished the notion from his mind. If he imbibed every time his mother was difficult, he would become a regular sot. He shook his head.

"If it will set you at ease, Mother, I shall advise Pinkham to turn away any caller who might venture forth so early in the morning."

"Hmmph! It isn't early. I daresay everyone is about by now."

He sighed and rose. "Then I shall return to my room and repeat my toilette."

"No!" she objected. "Sit down, Adam. In the interest of

brevity, I shall endeavor to overlook your slovenliness. But where is Davina? Why has she not come to welcome me?"

"She is dressing, Mother."

"She, too?" She made a great show of peering at the ormolu clock on the mantle. "At this hour? What can you both be thinking?"

"We were breakfasting in our private salon, wearing our dressing robes," he explained.

"What?" she gasped.

Adam did not further enlighten her. Luckily, at that moment, Davina dashed into the room, followed by Pinkham with the tea tray. He rose. "Hello, my dear. How lovely you look."

"Thank you, Adam." She smiled rather nervously and curtsied to the dowager. "How do you do, ma'am? It is kind of you to visit."

"I doubt you believe that, but I am well, thank you, Davina. And you were not required to burst into the salon like a hoyden." Her nose twitching, his mother briefly surveyed her, then returned her attention to him. "What were you saying, Adam, about the private salon?"

Poised to defend his wife's haste, Adam desisted, thinking it best to avoid certain argument. "Davina has turned the lady's maid's room into a private room for the two of us," he said instead. "We breakfast informally there."

"But that is supposed to be an abigail's room."

"Not anymore."

The dowager gave a small gasp. "What of Davina's maid?"

"She has a room in the servants' quarters." From the corner of his eye, Adam watched his wife pour the tea. Her hands were trembling mightily.

"That will not do. Davina must have her servant close at hand." His mother sniffed. "Do I detect the scent of brandy?"

Adam held his breath. If his mother discovered the liquor

on his wife's breath, there would be no end to the hell she'd impart. He prayed Davina would not admit to her headache cure.

The dowager glared at them. "It *is* brandy. So early in the day!"

"Ma'am, I—" began Davina.

"I know what happened," Adam interrupted loudly. "Last night, Davina poured me a glass of the stuff. She must have left the stopper out."

He made a great issue of crossing the room and opening the liquor cabinet. "Yes, that is it. You were saying, Mother?"

"I don't remember," she said suspiciously.

"Oh, well, it will surely come to you. Have your tea." He laid his hand on the nape of his wife's neck and pinched. "Do continue serving, my dear. Do not allow me to interfere."

Flinching, Davina extended a cup and saucer to the dowager. China rattled. Several drops of tea sloshed over the rim.

"Goodness, child!" Adam's mother cried. "Has no one taught you to serve gracefully?"

"I . . . I am a bit tense, ma'am," Davina managed, turning scarlet.

"Whatever for? If serving tea to your family so greatly oversets you, I would hate to see how you would pour it for guests."

"Mother," Adam said in an undertone.

"Be still, Adam," she snapped. "Davina, I will help you with the social graces. No member of this family must lack a thorough knowledge of the highest etiquette. We shall begin with the fundamentals as soon as possible."

Again, the earl wished he could trade his cup of tea for a large glass of brandy. How long would they be subjected to this tyranny? Even a short time seemed like an eternity, and he was accustomed to his mother's barbs. How much more difficult it must be for Davina.

His wife clutched her saucer as if it were a lifeline. Pinching the handle of the cup, she attempted to take a sip. A tiny drop fell to the bodice of her gown.

The dowager saw it. "Goodness gracious, Davina, if you are beset by such anxiety, you should never chance taking a drink."

"Yes, ma'am." Davina flushed deeply and set her cup and saucer on the tea table.

"Just between the three of us, we must admit Davina's social education has been sorely neglected," his mother continued.

Adam saw his wife's knuckles become a stark white, she'd folded them so tautly. He couldn't see the expression in her eyes, for her head was bowed low. His temper flared.

"Mother, Davina's demeanor is perfect. If she has made nervous errors this morning, it is because of you. When you practice this awful beleaguering, you possess the capability to make *me* uncomfortable, let alone someone who is unaccustomed to it. You are belligerent and intimidating. It is no wonder my wife spills a few drops of tea. By your manner, you are effectively tormenting her."

Both women stared at him in shock. Davina's beautiful cornflower eyes were enormous. The dowager's gray ones were narrow and chilly; her bosom was heaving.

"If you imagine I am such a tyrant, then I apologize," she pouted. "I consider my comments to be for the gel's own good."

Davina smiled tremulously. "It's all right, ma'am."

"No, it isn't," Adam snapped.

"Davina is a premier representative of this family," the dowager stressed, ignoring him. "I am certain she wishes to carry on suitably. Don't you, my dear?"

His wife nodded almost forlornly.

Adam gritted his teeth. His mother was insincere in her

concern. He'd trust a brigand further than he would trust her. She could match any member of the *ton* in the ability to commit verbal murder. He must severely warn her not to trample Davina's tender feelings.

The dowager glanced smugly at him. "Perhaps it would be politic to change the subject. Do tell me about your honeymoon."

"It was wonderful, ma'am." Davina was so obviously relieved at this turn that she almost gushed. "I was so thrilled by the Roman ruins that I vow I could spend an entire year just looking at them! And Paris . . . it was all I thought it would be. Adam bought me any number of designer originals and accessories for them as well. My wardrobe is simply overflowing with beautiful apparel."

"Where do you wear them?" his mother asked.

Davina quizzically cocked her head sideways. "I beg your pardon?"

"Where have you worn these fine gowns? To balls? Soirees? The opera? I have several friends with whom I correspond. They've declared they seldom see the two of you in public."

Davina laughed and smiled fondly at her husband. "Adam and I feel as if we are still on our honeymoon."

The dowager's laugh sounded patently false to Adam. "I suppose my visit will cause that to cease. Ah, well, such pleasant interludes must end sometime. Now, however, you must assume the role of a proper countess and set aside this somewhat *bourgeoise* behavior."

Davina lost the merry air that talking of their honeymoon had caused. She grew solemn. "I suppose I shall."

Adam stepped in. "Mother, she is already a *proper countess.*"

The dowager waved airily. "Do not heed him, Davina. Men know nothing of these things. But never fear! I shall guide you in what is expected of you. I am positive you will absolutely shine in the endeavor."

"I hope so," Davina murmured, again bowing her head. "I want to be an exemplary countess."

"Bravo, my gel! There, I have set the stage for future success. Davina, I know we will become the very best of friends." She rose. "Now I shall seek my room in order to rest up from the trip and my stay in that horrible inn."

Adam and Davina stood.

"I'll see you at luncheon, children." She wiggled her fingers and left the room.

Davina turned worriedly to him. "I want her approval so very badly, but she frightens me out of my wits!"

He enfolded her in his arms. "She is formidable, I know. I wish she had not come."

"I suppose I must become comfortable with her sometime. It may as well be now," she said ruefully. "She is right. Our honeymoon has ended."

He drew her closer, relishing the feel of the soft curves of her body against his. "Hadn't we planned for it to last all our lives?"

She smiled up at him doubtfully. "At times like these, I wonder if such a thing is possible."

"What do you think?" He bent his head and kissed her, lingering on her mouth, then along her jawbone to her ear.

"Um," she murmured, slipping her arms around his waist. "My wonderful husband, I again believe it is."

When Davina and Adam left the drawing room, they returned to their chambers to repair the errors in their appearances that hasty dressing had caused. As Fifi heated tongs to better curl the wisps of hair framing her face, Davina gazed into the mirror and considered the new arrival. Her thoughts were not particularly pleasant ones.

Adam's mother had always frightened her. She sensed the dowager did not like her and had been very unhappy when Adam had made her his bride. When they had first met, Lady Trowbridge had looked down her nose and peered rudely at Davina through her lorgnette. Davina had felt inferior and unworthy of becoming Adam's wife.

At the wedding breakfast Davina's parents and aunt had hosted, Lady Trowbridge had remained aloof from the Haldertons, sneering down her haughty nose at them from across the room. She had encouraged her relatives to follow suit, causing an uncomfortable line of demarcation to be drawn between the two families. On the one hand, Davina had been glad, for she had been frightfully worried that her family, with their outrageous sense of humor, would embarrass her. On the other, she had been miffed, for though the Trowbridges greatly outranked her relatives, her family was an old one and just as good as any branch on Adam's ancestral tree.

But those scenes were past, and she was a Trowbridge now. Still, however, it seemed the dowager was going to be difficult, even if she did profess to be helpful. She winced and groaned softly.

"My lady!" Fifi hurriedly removed the tongs from her hair. "Have I burned you?"

"No," Davina assured her. "I am plagued by a hurdle for which there seems to be no solution."

"May I help?"

She shook her head. "No one can help, but I thank you for asking. No, I must face this alone."

"Is that old woman, no?" The servant briefly laid a consoling hand on Davina's shoulder, then continued her work.

Davina sighed. "I suppose one cannot expect to live always in such perfect happiness, but having known this bliss, I am reluctant to let it go."

"Why must you?" Fifi asked. "You have everything—youth, beauty, a wealthy handsome lord who is devoted to you. Why can you not live in such absolute joy?"

"I do not know." Davina shrugged unhappily. "But I have a feeling life is soon to become very difficult."

"Ooh, la, not to fear! All will be well."

"You are a treasure." She reached back and squeezed the girl's arm. "Thank you for your confidence and encouragement."

But Davina knew change would come. The dowager Lady Trowbridge would insist upon her learning to be the ideal countess. But wasn't that what she wanted to be? Adam deserved perfection. Who better to learn from than his socially flawless mother?

After washing away her travel soil, changing clothes, and having her coiffure redone, Eleanor Trowbridge chose not to nap. Instead, she wandered through Trowbridge House, looking for changes that might indicate Halderton bad taste. She was not surprised when she found many of her beautiful bibelots had disappeared. That girl would have no idea of the value of such *objets d'art* or the impression they created. Adam should have intervened.

The furniture was also askew. She'd have to have that returned to orderly fashion. But nothing else seemed to have been adversely affected. Of course, she hadn't seen that private room Adam had mentioned. She wasn't overly concerned, though. It wouldn't take long to convince Davina of the necessity of having her personal maid within calling distance.

Despite believing she could educate Davina, the dowager felt her spirits sink very low as she left the billiard room. Her son's marriage was such a tragedy. Why, oh, why couldn't he have made a conventional match with a young lady of similar station in life? How different things would have been.

As she strolled into the entrance hall, she spied Mrs. Benning coming down the stairs with a sheet of paper and a number of envelopes in her hand. She hailed her.

"Come with me, Benning." Without waiting for a sign

of assent, she turned on her heel and marched toward the morning room.

The morning room, with its lovely view of the rear garden, was the chamber in which the dowager had spent most of her time when she was the mistress of the house. In those still recent days, she had gone, first thing after breakfast, to her dainty desk to confer about the day's activities with the housekeeper. Now she took her old position by force of habit.

"Good morning, Benning," she said cheerfully, as if she were greeting the housekeeper for the first time that day. "How are you this morning?"

The servant curtsied. "I am well, madam."

The countess nodded to the paper in the woman's hand. "What is that? Surely this cannot be today's menu?"

"Yes, my lady."

"So late in the morning?" she barked. "Such a matter should be attended to immediately after breakfast!"

The housekeeper quailed. "Yes, my lady."

"The chef must receive adequate notice." She snatched the missive from her. "Be seated. I'll tend to this."

Mrs. Benning looked slightly daunted, but obeyed.

The dowager glanced over it. "Scalloped oysters? I think not. Does Chef not remember that I abhor them?" She read on. "Ham? In London? What is its source? If it had come from Trowbridge Hall, I would know of it. No, we will not serve this questionable meat. Let us have a beef rib instead." She drew through the items and added her own corrections.

"But, madam," the housekeeper nervously managed, "Lady Trowbridge wanted . . ."

The lady lifted her nose and stared down it with a look that never failed to intimidate. "The new Lady Trowbridge is unfamiliar with administering a household of this size and quality. She is to be instructed by me. I plan to begin with items other than menus. For the time being, I shall approve the meals so she may concentrate fully on other matters."

"Yes, ma'am," said Mrs. Benning.

The dowager countess allowed herself a rare smile. "I'm sure you are thankful I have returned. The new mistress cannot possibly know what to do, can she?"

The housekeeper bowed her head.

"Can she?" the dowager shrilled. *"Can she?"*

"She . . . has her own way, my lady."

"Oh?" she sniffed. "And what is that?"

Mrs. Benning swallowed with difficulty. "The young Lady Trowbridge is very . . . informal."

"What do you mean by that, Benning?" she demanded. "Give me specifics."

"Well . . . she does not command absolute solemnity on the part of the servants. She wants them to smile in greeting. And they may chat or sing or hum while going about their duties. Of course, *I* cannot bring myself to such familiarity." She shifted from foot to foot. "Also, she allows me to make most of the decisions regarding the schedules. In addition, she has increased everyone's weekly free time by one half day."

"Ridiculous!" cried the dowager. "You shall cancel that order at once. What complications such a policy would cause! I do not see how you can maintain a proper agenda. Furthermore, I must insist upon orderly decorum. The young lady cannot imagine what a madhouse such casualness could promote. Oh, what great a need has she for a mentor!"

"Yes, ma'am," murmured the upper servant.

"Ah, there is much to be accomplished. I am pleased to depend upon you, Benning, for assistance."

"Thank you, my lady."

"Now what are those?" She pointed to the envelopes in the housekeeper's hand.

"I think they are invitations, ma'am."

"Let me see." She took the envelopes which had been bundled together with a ribbon and topped with the direction that they be given to Adam's secretary to be declined. "This is absurd! What will people think? Ah, I already know the answer to that, do I not?"

"Yes, my lady," Mrs. Benning guessed restlessly.

"I will take care of these. Never you mind. And, Benning, do not fear. It will not be long before this house is returned to its former organization." She nodded curtly. "That will be all at present."

The housekeeper curtsied again and left the room.

Sadly shaking her head and sighing, the dowager began opening each invitation and entering the dates on a blank calendar, then setting them aside to pen affirmative replies. Adam and Davina would have a suitably frantic social schedule, and when the hostesses learned of the dowager's presence in town, they would extend invitations to her, as well. There would be no more of her son and his wife arriving at parties only to leave shortly afterward. She herself would be there to see that they minded their manners. Finishing the task, she rang for the butler.

"Pinkham," she announced as he entered, bowing, "you shall present these to his lordship's secretary immediately and beg him to answer them at once."

"Yes, madam," he replied willingly, but a slight frown creased his forehead.

She glanced at the carved marble clock on the mantel. "Ah, I see it is the calling hour. Have visitors appeared yet?"

"No, my lady." He glanced wistfully at the door.

"In my day, the drawing room would have been crowded by now," she observed. "Tell me, Pinkham, what could be wrong? New brides are always novel and popular."

He grimaced.

"Well, what is it?" she demanded. "What is going on in this house? You look as if you are concealing something."

"No, my lady! Never!" he gasped. "I would not hide a thing from you! Why, you yourself oversaw my training and elevated me to this position."

"Then if you are so grateful, you will answer my question. Why are there no morning callers?"

"Well," he said, shifting from foot to foot as Mrs. Benning had done, "my lord and lady discourage the practice."

"What?" she screeched.

Pinkham literally jumped.

"What did you say?" she shrieked.

"My lord and lady are never home to callers."

"Goodness!" The dowager was so overset she trembled. "Some sherry, Pinkham."

When he returned with the drink, she was somewhat recovered, but her fingers still quivered on the glass. She took a great sip, closing her eyes as if to ward off the world and its torments. Finally, she was able to speak again.

"Pinkham, the calls will resume immediately. We shall be at home to all."

"Yes, my lady."

"It is what I expected." She drained the glass and set it aside. "Has Lady Trowbridge finished her second toilette?"

"She was coming downstairs when I was hastening to your summons, my lady. I would assume she has gone to the library, where Lord Trowbridge is. Shall I request that she come to you?"

"No, I shall go there myself. I wish to speak with both the earl and the countess." She rose. "Pinkham, I will thank you to reinstate a studied air of formality and deference. This house must be brought from such a . . . such a *shambles!* I hope I have come before things got too far out of hand. It is clear the new little countess is in dire need of my instruction."

"Yes, madam."

"Very well, you are dismissed." Before she departed, the dowager drifted across the room to stare out at the garden.

The beds boasted a riot of bright early summer colors, but they failed to cheer her. What she had dreaded had indeed come to pass. Davina Trowbridge was no more fit to be a countess than a common shop girl would be. And what of that odor of brandy? It had not come from the unstoppered bottle Adam had been so anxious to produce. He was hiding something. Had his wife been imbibing?

Things were worse than she had first thought. Apparently Adam was not going to help set the girl on the right course. That left only her. Yes, she had her work cut out for her, and she didn't relish it one bit.

Oh, why had her son insisted on wedding the chit? Merely because she was a novelty, of course. Eventually, he would be sorry.

Fustian! What a tangle! Shaking her head, she cursed all inappropriate marriages and walked wearily toward the door.

Six

Adam glanced up from his paperwork as the door to his library opened. He smiled at once when he saw it was Davina. Placing his quill in its resting place, he rose and crossed the room to greet her.

"I hope I am not disturbing you."

"Since when have you ever disturbed me?" he asked, then grinned broadly. "I take that back. You constantly disturb me, whether you are physically present or not. I live in a permanent state of disturbance, which is evidenced by—Davina, I am suddenly not interested at all in paperwork."

"Naughty!" Laughing, she placed her index and middle fingers across his lips. "We must behave. Somehow I doubt your mother would approve of our retiring in mid morning."

He looked into her dancing blue eyes and sighed ruefully. "Yes, we are rather scandalous, are we not?"

"Incurably so." She slipped her arms around his neck and gazed at him with pure adoration. As always, when he beheld her like this, he thanked his lucky stars he had found and won this marvelous woman. So easily could she have fallen for a more outgoing gentleman.

Davina cocked her head sideways. "You look pensive, Adam."

He gathered her into his arms. "As I have done hundreds of times, I am congratulating myself on winning your heart.

The competition for it was top drawer. I cannot believe I was victorious."

"Ha!" she scoffed. "I never looked at another. Had *I* not won *you,* I was resigned to become an old maid. And, oh, how I doubted my chances! You were so cool and sophisticated that I never dreamed you could want such a girl as me for your wife. I believed you would wed one of those serene, stately beauties of high birth and monumental dowry."

"At one time, I, too, thought I'd choose such a bride. Fortunately I came to my senses." He bent his head and swiftly and teasingly kissed her lips. "Now, back to the present. Did you come to me for anything in particular?"

"No." She shook her head. "I thought I'd embroider while you tended your business, if you don't mind."

"Have I ever?"

"No, but . . ." Her face clouded. "I thought you might wish me to seek out your mother."

"I imagine she's sound asleep. She had a long trip, and despite her seeming vitality, she isn't as young as she used to be. Don't concern yourself, darling."

"But I am her hostess."

"Mother needs no entertaining. I, on the other hand, greatly crave your company." He slipped his fingers under her chin, tilted back her head, and brought his mouth down to meet hers.

As always, Davina's body seemed to melt into his own, forming one perfect being. And as usual, he was swept by a sizzling, overwhelming desire, the like of which she alone had ever ignited. To hell with the details of everyday life. This molten fire demanded extinguishing. He'd either carry her up to his chamber or—

"Adam Trowbridge!" a commanding voice bellowed.

With a little squeal, Davina leaped backward, her face flooding scarlet.

"Mother?" Adam managed.

"Adam Trowbridge! I can scarcely believe my eyes have

rested upon such a . . . such a . . . such a *lowering* sight! To be sure, I have never witnessed such a scandalous scene." She turned her ferocious gaze upon Davina. "And you! Somehow I am not surprised to see you acting like a trollop. You sadly want culture, gel. How fortunate you are I have come to guide you."

With a cry, Davina lifted her skirts and fled.

"Coward," the dowager observed, her voice dripping scorn.

"Good God, Mother! What did you expect?" Adam railed, his own cheeks burning. "Who wouldn't be overset? I know I am!"

"At least you are ashamed, for you did not behave like a gentleman, Adam."

"A gentleman? Mother, kissing one's wife has nothing to do with being a gentleman!"

She clicked her tongue. *"Really,* Adam."

He took a deep breath and returned to his chair behind the desk, his body aching from unrequited passion. "Speaking of good manners, have you never heard of rapping on a door before entering?"

"On the door of a public room? Scratching on the door is the practice of servants. I would never engage in it."

"My library is not a public room."

She eyed him with haughty rancor. "All rooms, except bedchambers, are public to family members, who should have nothing to hide."

Adam muttered an obscenity.

"If that utterance was what I think it was, I am overcome with shock." She advanced toward the desk as purposeful as a ship under full sail. "What has become of your elegant manners, Adam? Have you forgotten your breeding?"

"Lord, Mother, I was kissing my wife in what I thought was the privacy of my library."

"When one accepts the privilege of employing servants, privacy is curtailed."

Adam rolled his eyes heavenward. "Mother, you just said . . ."

He fell silent. The last thing he wanted was to engage in a debate over privacy. The whole matter was awful enough.

"I have never been so humiliated," she went on. "Your wife did not exactly look happy with the situation, either. No young lady of quality is pleased with being mauled in such an offensive fashion, whether she is married to the perpetrator or not."

"I'm beginning to understand why I am an only child," he murmured to himself.

"What?" she demanded.

"Nothing, Mother. Just a fleeting analysis."

"This is not a moment for assessment, fleeting or otherwise." She dramatically lifted her hands in the air. "It is a time for action!"

Her stance—and, indeed, the entire circumstance—suddenly struck Adam funny. He burst into laughter. "Well, Mother, I was hoping for a bit more action, but you spoiled it."

Her face flushed crimson. "I have never been so ill-used! I cannot believe such vulgarity has crossed your lips. You, Adam, my perfectly well-behaved son! I await your apology."

"For what?" He chuckled. "Acting like a red-blooded male?"

"Oooh . . ." Her eyes seemed to turn backward in her head. With a long, drawn-out moan, she collapsed in a chair, her body and limbs draped lifelessly akimbo.

"Mother?"

There was no response.

"Mother!" He quickly skirted the desk and lifted her inert hand. For heaven's sake, she had fainted. He pinched her cheek to make sure. Totally unconscious. *Damn!* Now there'd be the devil to pay. He hastened across the room to pull the bell rope.

Pinkham swiftly appeared and surveyed the spectacle. "I'll fetch her abigail, sir. She'll have a vinaigrette."

Surely it was only a faint and not an apoplexy. Adam studied her. She seemed to be breathing with comfortable regularity, so probably it was nothing serious. But he shouldn't have deliberately horrified her so. He lifted her into his arms and carried her to the sofa.

"Oh, my poor lady!" her maid cried out, entering upon the scene. Kneeling beside Adam's mother, she opened the vial of smelling salts and thrust it under the dowager's nose.

The dowager's head jerked back. Her eyes popped open. "Oh, what has happened to me?" she moaned.

Adam stared at her grimly.

"You!" she spat out. "You gave me such a start, young man!"

He felt like a schoolboy caught up in mischief. "I am sorry, Mother."

"You should be," she scolded, sitting up and gazing around.

Drawn by the excitement, a small crowd of servants had gathered. Her abigail crouched center stage, the heroine in the farce. Pinkham, Mrs. Benning, a footman, and two housemaids hovered nearby.

Davina hastened in, her brow creased with worry. She did not speak or thrust herself forward, apparently preferring to remain on the fringe of the onlookers. It was obvious from her taut bearing and visibly trembling hands that she was as shaken as her mother-in-law, if not more so.

"Get out!" cried the dowager, waving her arms. "Am I an actress in a raree-show? Get out! Get out at once! You're all fired!"

All but Pinkham fled toward the door. Davina was nearly knocked down by the stampede. Bounced aside, she edged forward when the frenzy ebbed.

"Do not precipitate another incident, young lady," the dowager warned.

Biting her lip, Davina lifted a questioning eyebrow.

"Mother, maybe you had best retire to your chamber," Adam quickly advised. "You must be exhausted."

"Perhaps I shall." She rose unsteadily to her feet, leaning heavily on her abigail. "You will probably not see me at luncheon. I shall dine in my chamber, if my appetite has not forsaken me."

"That's a good idea," he seconded.

"Well, you don't have to act so happy about it," she snapped.

"Certainly not, ma'am. You have the wrong idea. I am solely concerned with your recovery."

She favored him with a suspicious glare, then turned to Davina. "You may come and read to me during the afternoon, gel." With that, she hobbled from the room.

"My lord, are those people sacked?" Pinkham asked. "Am I?"

"Definitely not," Adam assured him. "My mother is no longer the mistress of this house. Indeed, you may regard her as you would a guest. Domestic matters are to be handled by my lady and by me," he emphasized.

Pinkham look unconvinced, but he nodded his acknowledgment and departed.

"I do not think it will be easy for him to adjust to your mother's lack of command," Davina mused as the door closed. "He and the rest of the servants are too accustomed to following her orders. I suppose that is a normal state of affairs, however. Transitions must always be problematic in old, established homes."

"If so, you are managing magnificently." He slipped his arm around her waist and guided her to the sofa. "You may have made few physical changes, but the aura you have projected to this house is fresh and comfortable."

"I fear I've had little to do with it. The house runs itself.

All I've done is to request the servants be less starchy and stiff."

He grinned. "I actually heard a housemaid singing this morning. Her voice was perfectly frightful."

"Perhaps I've gone too far," Davina said worriedly.

"No!" he protested. "I'm glad to hear the servants cheerfully going about their duties. It makes me feel as though they are happy to be employed here."

"You are certain?"

"Yes."

She studied his face. "You aren't just saying that to avoid hurting my feelings?"

"No! Lightheartedness is one of your finest qualities, darling." He sat on the sofa and drew her down to his lap. "Because of it, you have wrought more change than you realize."

"I only wish to please you. You must always tell me if I go too far." Once more, she frowned. "What on earth brought about your mother's swoon? Did it happen because of our dalliance?"

Adam decided not to relate the entire story. Davina was already sufficiently distressed by their guest.

"We shocked her," he answered. "Remember that she is very old-fashioned. But more than that, I think it was pure weariness. She wasn't up to such a speedy journey. Don't fret about it, darling."

"I cannot help but do so." She shrugged helplessly. "I am so anxious that she like me and approve of my being your countess. Oh, Adam, if she despises me, what shall I do?"

"Hush." He cuddled her close. "She will soon be as charmed by you as I am."

"I hope so," she said doubtfully, resting her head against his shoulder. "But she is so very grand and formidable."

"She is that," he agreed and kissed the top of her head. He wished his mother had not put in an appearance so early in their marriage. Davina needed time to build confidence in her new role. So did he, for that matter. The dowager would crimp their period of adjustment. But she was here, and there was nothing he could do about it. If only she wouldn't choose to meddle. . . .

When Pinkham left the library, he immediately sought Mrs. Benning. She was just as anxious to talk about the contretemps as he. She led him to her office and firmly closed the door.

"What did you see, Jerome?"

He was only too eager to relay his part in the incident. "I was setting a footman to the chore of polishing the door brasses when I heard overly loud voices. Unfortunately, the words were not distinct enough for me to ascertain what was being said. Then the countess—Lady Davina, that is— dashed from the room, her face red with embarrassment. There was more loud talk, then evidently the countess—er, his lordship's mother fainted. Quite overset, she was, too, when her abigail brought her 'round, wasn't she?"

"Yes, but you were unable to distinguish what was said in the heat of the incident?"

"No, Hannah. I know nothing more of note, but I have my suspicions."

"So do I. Did you know the dowager Lady Trowbridge did the menus this morning?" she asked, seating herself and gesturing him to do the same. "In my opinion, she will not relinquish the reins of the house. She does not wish our young lady to rule the roost."

Pinkham nodded sagely. "Moreover, I think she dislikes our new countess. She has been testy ever since his lordship announced his plans to marry."

"How true," the housekeeper concurred, "and how unfortunate! Whenever the two are together, we'll all be at sixes and sevens. There will be a battle for control of the house. Just thinking of it makes me consider looking for another position."

He grimaced. "I, too. But you won't?"

"Of course not. I have served the Trowbridges far too long." She shrugged. "And you?"

"I won't leave, not as things stand now." He smiled crookedly. "But I anticipate a ghastly domestic storm."

"Undoubtedly. Such a shame! Alas, there is nothing we can do." She sadly studied her fingernails. "Although she has a lot to learn, I like our new little mistress."

"I hate to admit it, but she is like a breath of fresh air," Pinkham ventured, "even though she is a bit too informal for my taste."

"I feel the same way, but I've an idea we'll be returning to our old ways. Our new mistress is too young to stand up to the dowager Lady Trowbridge."

"Yes." He sighed. "She doesn't stand a chance."

"And I must make an admission." Mrs. Benning winced. "When orders are given, I cannot help but obey our past mistress. I vow I'm afraid of her!"

"I, too," Pinkham agreed grimly. "I, too."

As she had planned, Davina sat in a chair by Adam's desk, engaged in mending a frill on one of Adam's shirts, while he scanned the financial briefs sent by his man of business. It was his valet's duty to care for his clothes, but she liked to do these small tasks. It made her feel like an industrious wife.

Besides, in a day when young ladies were thoroughly taught sewing, painting, and music, her skill at fancy needlework was not as good as most. Recently, she had begun working an embroidered floral design on a set of pillowcases, but the tediousness of the stitching was too much of a challenge to concentrate on just now.

As she sewed, she turned her thoughts to the dowager

countess. She scarcely knew the woman personally, but she'd heard a great deal about her. She didn't know how much of the gossip was true, but it was enough to give her pause.

All of the talk could be best summarized by saying that Lady Trowbridge was a high stickler. Davina had certainly had a taste of that on several occasions. Now she knew Adam's mother believed in formality even in private.

Adam had probably been reared at arm's length from his parents. How did that affect him now? He was wonderfully affectionate, but could he be merely putting up with her overt tenderness? A youngster's environment, family customs, and teachings molded the adult the child would become. When she had first met Adam, he had been stiff and cool. Was that the real man? The thought was chilling.

Davina gazed through her lashes at her husband. He was so handsome, with a face and figure to make most girls swoon. She could hardly believe he was hers.

As if he felt her perusal, he looked up and glanced her way, catching her eye. He grinned boyishly. "Am I that interesting, my dear?"

She laughed lightly. "That and more. I love to look at you, Adam."

"That's a good thing, since you'll be doing it all our lives." He placed the quill in its holder. "Tell me your thoughts, my darling. You look very pensive."

"Other than marveling at your countenance, I was considering your mother and how I might please her."

He arched an eyebrow. "That might be an impossibility. Mother can be rather difficult. I doubt anyone has pleased her totally."

She eyed him curiously. "Not even you?"

"Especially not me." He chuckled.

Surely he could not be serious. If he was, she had no hope of satisfying her mother-in-law. In fact, she wondered if hers was a losing struggle anyway. Ruthlessly, she recalled Lady Trowbridge's response upon the few occasions of their meeting one another. At all times, the countess had given her *that* look, which was worse than a cut direct. Her blue eyes would become icy, her elevated nostrils would draw back, her lip would curl in derision. Adam's mother didn't like her. It was a certainty.

"I doubt I can ever delight her, no matter how hard I try."

"Don't be a defeatist, darling."

Davina shrugged. "I am accepting reality. If you can't please her, how can I?"

"You are serious, aren't you?" he asked.

"Yes." She solemnly nodded. "I suppose I must read to her this afternoon. If she allows me to select the material, I can predict with assurance I will choose wrongly. The whole business is vastly oversetting."

"Don't be negative, Davina," he begged. "You must approach this with an attitude of confidence. I am sure you read splendidly. If she does not recognize this, it is her own fault. Take the *Times* along with you. A newspaper is a neutral, logical choice. She cannot complain about it."

"Very well." Davina tried to force a smile, but she could feel her lips trembling. She bent her head to conceal her distress. Adam wanted her to do well, and the pressure of that was tremendous. She must make him proud of her.

After that interchange, they returned to their respective work. Then they passed luncheon, engaging in no more than small talk. Afterward, Davina went back to the library to await her summons, which occurred in less than an hour.

"Wish me luck," she said, picking up the newspaper.

"You'll be fine." He rose and came forward to kiss her forehead encouragingly. "Mother may find she likes having a daughter."

Davina held little hope for that miracle, but she lightly tossed off, "I'll wager she will."

She exited the library and climbed the stairs, softly treading down the hall to the dowager's room. There she faced a quandary. Should she rap gently like family, or scratch like a servant? Well, she was kin, even if the lady did not wish her to be. Taking a deep breath, she knocked quietly.

Her mother-in-law's abigail opened the door and curtsied. "My lady, do come in. She is expecting you."

Butterflies fluttering in her stomach, Davina entered and crossed the room toward the stately figure seated by the window. Once again, she was suddenly cast in the throes of a dilemma. Should she formally address Adam's parent, or should she call her Mother, as Adam did? She swiftly decided she would attempt to avoid a name by using the generic *ma'am*. If forced, she would refer to her as Mother. After all, she was her daughter-in-law.

She curtsied. "How do you do, ma'am?"

Lady Trowbridge grimaced. "I am still weary, and I am bored beyond belief."

Davina sank down in a nearby chair. "I hope I may relieve the day's tedium. I've brought the newspaper."

"Lud, I do not want to hear its babble!"

"Shall I fetch a book?" Davina asked anxiously.

She waved a limp hand. "No! I doubt your reading would suit me anyway. Being a Halderton, you've probably had only a modicum of education."

"I must beg to differ, ma'am," she objected. "I studied alongside my brothers until they went off to school. Then I had a governess who taught me well."

The dowager chortled. "Oh, yes, I imagine you've had the veritable equivalent of a university education! No doubt you're well grounded in the classics, decidedly versed in Latin and Greek, and capable of ciphering mathematics in its highest form."

"I did not claim such a capacity," Davina murmured, nibbling her lip. "I only asserted a respectable schooling. I do believe I can read any item you would request."

"Fiddlesticks!" Adam's mother cried. "I don't wish to hear you read. Instead, we will commence our new lessons."

"Lessons, ma'am?"

"You must learn what is expected of you, Davina," Lady Trowbridge announced in no uncertain terms. "I shall teach you to be a countess, and especially a countess in this august family. You must have already discovered you are entirely unprepared to step into the role without much consideration. Already you have made mistakes. I know. My friends have written me about your shortcomings."

A horrible fear seized Davina's stomach. What had she done wrong? What could those nameless correspondents have accused her of?

"It is not too late, I think, to remedy the errors," Adam's mother added breezily. "You and I will begin resolving the problems at once. You would not wish to disappoint Adam, would you?"

"No, of course not!" Davina fretted. "I was not aware of offending."

"I thought not, and my friends agree. You must admit my generation is quite socially prominent." She nodded, concurring with herself and forging forth before Davina had a chance to reply. "We are the arbiters of Society. It is we who make the rules and judgments—Almack's, for example."

Davina flushed. She had not been invited to Almack's, that sacred hall of acceptance into the best of the *ton*. Her family was just too boisterous and scatter-witted to receive that nod of decorum.

The dowager pounced on her embarrassment. "Just so. You should be overset. Think how it affects Adam! But you may redeem yourself and put period to the behavior that has compromised this family."

"I wasn't aware I had blundered," she said in a small voice. "I shall do anything to make up for it."

"I know. I know you will be most dutiful. You honestly did not realize what you were doing."

"I still do not," Davina said miserably.

"I will tell you. I'll tell all in due time, but we must work on one thing at a time." Adam's mother smiled with seeming relief. "First are your social obligations. I happened to see quite a stack of invitations this morning. All were marked as refusals."

Davina frowned. She and Adam together had decided to decline those requests. It was not her fault alone, but she didn't wish to implicate Adam. Also, there'd been the planned trip to Brighton.

"You are correct," she said, "but—"

"No excuses! Luckily, I saw the bids and changed your order. You will attend those parties. It is your family duty." Lady Trowbridge lifted her chin. "We have always been placed in the highest levels of Society. You will accept, you will attend, *and* you will stay a respectable time at each."

Once more, Adam's mother was blaming her for both their actions. Davina was torn. Adam did not want to go to those fetes, let alone stay forever. Disregarding his desires seemed rather high-handed. Like the dowager, she lifted her chin.

"Adam disliked going to those functions," she stated.

"That is no surprise," the elder woman trilled. "Many men are notorious in refusing invitations. They cannot understand the necessity. But before you were married, did you not see Adam at numerous functions?"

"Yes," Davina agreed.

"So, you see, he is remiss at present because he wishes to be with you. I must now speak frankly." She sighed. "Your family is not welcome in ever so many homes. You must face this, my dear, for it is, oh, so true."

Again Davina felt her cheeks suffuse with warmth.

"No doubt Adam is concerned about your reception. That probably explains his reticence to go on as he did in the past. But do not fear. I will help you rise to the challenge! Adam will be pleased and proud. Now, we shall begin by answering the invitations in the affirmative and entering them on your social calendar." She chortled. "Did I say *begin?* As a favor to you, I have already completed the task. Let us plot our attack. I am fully capable of making *anyone* the toast of the *ton.* Even you, my rustic gel!"

Seven

Fifi was just putting the final touches to Davina's glorious hair when Adam entered the chamber through the interior connecting door.

"My lord!" she cried insouciently. "See how fine *madame* looks?"

Accustomed to Fifi's flights of impertinence, he nodded. "Quite lovely, as always."

"Unfortunately, she has not the jewelry to be—how you say—a diamond of the first water."

"That will be all," Davina intervened, horrified by the maid's forwardness.

Giggling, the abigail sketched a curtsy and hastened from the room.

Adam frowned slightly.

"I know I should scold her for her sassy tongue." Davina bit her lip. "But she is such a good abigail."

Adam shrugged. "Fifi is one of a kind."

"Yes, she is that." She ventured a small smile at her husband through the dressing table mirror. "Do I truly pass muster?"

"You always do that." His forehead clearing, he bent to kiss her bare shoulder. "However, I must say you have outdone yourself this evening."

Her blue eyes twinkled. "I hope you are right. I've the feeling my lady mother-in-law might be difficult to please."

"Oh, you do? Fancy that!"

She rose, turning to face him. Adam was certainly in fine looks tonight. His evening attire fitted him faultlessly, accenting his pleasantly proportioned broad shoulders, narrow hips, and well-muscled thighs. The lustrous black fabric stood in sharp contrast with his pristine white shirt. A particularly large diamond pin winked from his neckcloth. His mother should find no fault with his appearance. From his gleaming gold hair to his spotless black footwear, he was absolutely perfect.

"I do believe someone else has dressed with extra great care tonight," Davina teased.

"Yes." He grinned ruefully. "After having my cravat pin fall to the floor this morning, I thought I'd best try to redeem myself."

"Well, you are certainly handsome, my lord." She laughed lightly, but her mirth was shallow. Fretting about herself, she crossed the room to the full-length pier glass mirror and critically assessed her appearance.

For the first evening meal with the faultfinding dowager, Davina had chosen one of her Parisian gowns, a costly garment of midnight blue. It was almost severely simple in cut, the gossamer sleeves barely touching her shoulders and the skirt flowing softly from a snug Empire waist. The dress had no adornments save a sprinkle of diamond chips across the bodice. It was highly fashionable and very sophisticated. Moreover, although the design was unembellished, the fluid cloth rendered the costume unwearable for any lady except one of exquisite figure.

With an unconscious nod, she turned toward the earl, who was frowning again. Panic twisted her stomach. "Is something wrong?"

"With you?" He shook his head. "Of course not. I am aggravated with myself. Our outspoken Fifi was right. I have yet to present you with the family jewelry. I wish you'd reminded me."

Davina flushed. She had only four pieces of precious jewelry: the lovely pearl necklace, bracelet, and earrings Adam had given her as a wedding present, and the pair of tiny diamond drops which had been her grandmother's and which she wore in her ears at present. The remainder of her baubles were only paste, and not very good replicas at that. Fearing to appear avaricious, she'd avoided asking her new husband if there were any Trowbridge gems. Besides, she'd had no real need of elaborate ornamentation.

"It isn't necessary," she told him. "Not for dining *en famille.*"

"Nevertheless, you shall have them. I remember a particular set of diamonds which would be perfect with your gown." He extended his hand. "Come. They're in a safe in the library."

Davina felt suddenly shy of parading the jewels in front of the dowager. The caustic lady might deplore seeing her in them. "Really, Adam, it isn't necessary. We can do this another time."

"Nonsense. Come along." He caught her hand and nearly dragged her from her chamber.

Davina made her final protest. "We haven't time."

"Yes, we do. Remember? The *earl* and *countess* are never late. Come on, Davina."

She relinquished her objections and hurried with him down the stairs and into the library. Adam retrieved a key from his desk drawer and removed several books from a shelf to expose the vault. She watched with anxiety as he brought forth several small chests. When he opened the first, she couldn't help gasping. The contents were like a king's treasure trove and probably just as valuable.

"The Trowbridge family has always been financially sound, so no one has ever been forced to sell off the assets," Adam remarked.

Unlike the Haldertons. But then, her family always prized elaborate practical jokes over possessions. Her spirits sank. All at once, she wondered if he would ever be sorry he'd married her. His in-laws were buffoons. And his wife— would she truly be an appropriate countess, or would she garner the veiled disrespect her family did?

Adam opened all of the jewel-filled caskets until he found what he was seeking. "There. These will be just right."

Davina studied the gems he brought forth. He was right. They would be perfect for her gown. The styling of the diamonds was simple, yet anyone with a modicum of intelligence could see the stones were flawless and impressively clear and glittering.

Her husband fastened the necklace round her throat. "You see? Ideal."

She looked down at the large diamond pendant nestling in the top of her cleavage. *Gracious, but it must be valuable!* It made her uncomfortable to wear such finery, but she did not recommence her protest. If he wanted her to wear these luxuries, she would do so.

"They're beautiful, Adam," she whispered, donning the bracelet, "but I hope I won't be overdressed."

"Put in the earrings," he directed.

She did so, the long drops weighing on her ear lobes. "How do I look?"

"Like a princess. No, you are more comely than our current royal ladies. You look like a fabled princess of legend, one whose beauty is renowned throughout the ages."

"Fustian!" she scolded, giggling.

He lifted her chin with his forefinger and carefully kissed her lips. "I don't know about the meal, but my eyes will certainly have a feast tonight."

"Your mother will have us both on platters if we don't cease this dalliance," she warned.

"Oh, very well. I suppose we must." He returned the boxes to the safe and locked it. "Let us hope Mother will still be weary from travel and grant us an early evening."

"I am beginning to suspect she has boundless energy," she mused as they strolled from the library. "Most ladies of her age would have spent the entire day in bed, especially after her disagreeable experiences."

They entered the salon to find the dowager countess standing by the window, tapping her foot and casting pointed looks at the ormolu clock on the mantel.

"Such tardiness," she admonished.

"The earl and countess are never late," Adam reminded.

She clicked her tongue with disapproval. "Where did you come up with that drivel?"

"From you, of course, Mother."

"I hardly think so!" She leveled an accusatory glare at Davina. "Perhaps it is a Halderton custom?"

"No, ma'am. My family is definitely never late for dinner." She smiled, visualizing the voracious appetites of her father and brothers. "They are enthusiastic trenchermen."

"I can well imagine," the dowager said sarcastically, her nose twitching. "Hogs at the trough, no doubt."

Davina's mouth dropped open.

"Really, Mother, that was uncalled for," Adam stated.

"I only meant to acknowledge a state of excellent health," the dowager muttered piteously, as if she were misunderstood.

She did not fool Davina. It was a sharp barb in what would probably become a habitual practice of disparagement. But Davina did not strike back. She would never be discourteous to Adam's mother. Sadly, too, there was an element of truth in the insult.

Adam departed to the sideboard, where he poured their customary preprandial drinks. "Sherry, Mother?"

"There isn't time," she denounced.

"I am *making* time." He delivered Davina's wine and repeated, "Do you wish a drink, Mother?"

"No!" she snapped and piercingly stared at him. "What is wrong, Adam? Only a short while ago, you were a man of polish and proper decorum. Now you have become akin to a tenant farmer. Nay, the *hired hand* of a tenant farmer!"

The earl snorted and rolled his eyes heavenward.

"I can scarcely believe it," she said unhappily and fixed her gaze on Davina. "Have you caused this? I have noticed you command a terribly informal household. I hope indifferent etiquette is not a part of it."

Davina colored, snatching her lip between her teeth. Her cheeks positively burned. She wished she could flee from this awful scene.

Stunned speechless, Adam froze with his glass halfway to his mouth.

The dowager smiled knowingly. "Do not mistake my words for criticism, Davina. A relaxed household can be quite comfortable, but it sometimes tends to foster derelict manners. It is very difficult to maintain a pleasant balance. I shall wholeheartedly throw myself into assisting you in implementing your philosophy—with, however, admirable behavior on the part of all. There now! I do look forward to our becoming quite close. I did always want a daughter."

Adam's mother's words were garbled in Davina's mind. Was the lady offering friendship, or was this another mode of attack? She decided to assume the dowager meant well.

"Yes, ma'am," she murmured and set aside her wine. It was rather lax to linger over sherry when the meal was ready and waiting. Good breeding did require promptness.

She rose. "Perhaps we should adjourn to the dining room."

"Excellent!" applauded the dowager countess.

Davina glanced at her husband and thought she saw a brief frown flicker across his brow before he set his drink aside and assumed an expression of cool, noncommittal poise.

After the uncertain beginning, dinner passed without incident. The dowager countess recalled the early days of her marriage, regaling her son and daughter-in-law with her first experiences as a newlywed hostess to the highest members of the *ton*. With her memories occupying her mind, she did not dwell upon the present. Following the meal, she briefly took coffee in the library with Adam and Davina, then retired for the night, leaving the young couple to their own devices. When they went to bed, her visit was far from their minds. The morning, however, was a different matter. Awakening in Adam's arms, Davina visualized her mother-in-law's dislike of slothfulness and promptly left the bed.

"Getting up so soon?" her husband protested, yawning.

"I have no wish to court your mother's disapproval," she replied, slipping into her ice blue satin dressing gown.

"To hell with it," he grumbled. "Come back. We were up late last night."

"I doubt she would judge that as a logical excuse." She crossed the floor to her dressing room to perform her morning ablutions.

"Oh, very well." The bed creaked as he arose. "I'll ring for breakfast."

"Maybe we had best not do that," she said worriedly. "I don't think your mother approves. She will expect us to dine in a proper fashion. Let us go downstairs."

"Darling, Mother never breakfasts in the dining room. She is always served from a tray while she languishes in bed."

Davina could not visualize the countess being slothful. Of course, her husband would never tell a falsehood, but he just did not realize the scope of his mama's beliefs. When she was a young bride, the lady had probably done everything correctly, including dining in the designated room with her spouse. Only in later years had she allowed herself to become indolent. Adam would remember that, not the early days.

She was certain the countess would spy on her, making sure she was living up to the Trowbridge family ideals. Yes, the lady would be certain to investigate. She would know if her daughter-in-law was behaving properly.

"Please, Adam," she murmured.

"I am going!" His voice contained a thinly veiled hint of irritation.

Davina felt like crying. It was the first time he'd ever spoken to her in a tone less than loving. She lowered her eyes and quickly blinked away the tears.

"It will only last until her visit ends," she pled. "Then we can return to our usual schedule and habits."

He did not reply. She heard him striding toward his own bedchamber. Unhappily, she pulled the bell rope to summon Fifi and began to prepare for the morning ahead.

After she finished cleansing her face and teeth, Davina sat down at her dressing table and began to comb her long, shiny hair, gently removing the tangles. It was a time-consuming occupation, but she didn't mind a minute of it. Adam liked her flowing tresses much too well for her to complain about picking out the snarls. Still Fifi hadn't come.

Frowning, Davina rose and tugged the rope again, then began to study her wardrobe, attempting to decide which gown would please the countess most. She had chosen a soft yellow muslin when her abigail arrived, breathless and slightly disheveled.

"I am sorry, my lady. I expected not to be called so early."

Davina knew she should have reproached her, but she was too kindhearted to do so. "I am up much earlier than usual, am I not?"

"*Oui,* my lady." The maid nodded, moving to help Davina don the dress.

"Tell me, Fifi, has the dowager countess arisen?"

"I know not, *madame.* I . . . I was rather in a hurry when I passed through the kitchen."

"Of course." Davina let the subject falter, watching her

reflection in the mirror while her dresser did up the tapes on her dress, shaping the garment to fit her to perfection.

"Fifi . . ." It was on the tip of her tongue to ask her maid if she'd heard any backstairs gossip about Adam's mother, but she held her tongue. Somehow, the countess might find out. Davina was certain the lady would highly disapprove of personal discourse with servants.

She returned to her seat at the dressing table, her thoughts still spinning as Fifi gathered her hair into a silky, becoming knot at the nape of her neck. She must prove she was eminently suitable to be a Trowbridge countess. She couldn't let Adam down. She would make him proud of her, no matter what she must do to impress his mother.

Right now he might not seem to care, but deep down inside he did. He would want to prove he'd made an excellent choice of wives. She would demonstrate not all Haldertons were buffoons.

Adam shrugged into his coat and readjusted his neck-cloth. Staring into the cheval mirror, he saw a well-dressed *tonnish* gentleman reflected within. His powder blue coat was exquisitely tailored, as were his pale pantaloons. His cravat was white as snow and styled in his own adaptation of the popular waterfall. His Hessians were blacked and shined by his valet's secret method. No one, not even his mother, could fault his appearance today. Unfortunately, he was damned uncomfortable. This was no way to start the day. He was spoiled by his and Davina's cozy, informal breakfast room.

When she had presented him with the idea of turning the abigail's room into a private sitting-dining area, he had been secretly shocked. No gentleman in his family had ever lazed about in his dressing robe. One was either up and dressed or in the process thereof, or one was in bed.

But Davina had other, quite risque ideas. Once her bridal

shyness had worn off, she wished to postpone their making an appearance below stairs. Wanting to grant his wife her every heart's desire, he readily acquiesced.

Soon, he succumbed to the pleasure of this and other manifestations of her bubbling, informal manner. Life seemed as if she had created a warm, private island where they could remain alone together while the rest of the world flowed past them, a safe distance away. That was how he wished to spend the rest of his days—with her, alone.

Now his mother, as usual, had managed to overturn his quiet routine. He sighed, frowning.

"Is something wrong, my lord?" Turnbull, standing behind him, met his gaze in the looking glass.

Adam started, grinning self-consciously. "No, I was woolgathering. Everything is fine. Everything, that is, except having to go downstairs this early. I've become pleasantly accustomed to my wife's relaxed attitude."

The valet blinked and arched both eyebrows in surprise before quickly reschooling his expression to blankness.

The earl was rather dumbfounded, too. He'd never ventured into such commentary with the staff. His parents never would have approved. Servants were placed on the earth to serve, not to chat. He abruptly turned away from the mirror and strode from his dressing room, leaving Turnbull feverishly and unnecessarily folding a parcel of unmentionables.

When Adam entered his wife's bedchamber, she was still at toilette, her abigail smoothing the final touches to a wispy Grecian knot. He decided to try once more for a reprieve. "My dear, are you certain you wish to breakfast downstairs?"

"Yes." She nodded anxiously. "I do so wish to make a good impression. Yesterday I fear I did not."

"Mother will not attend breakfast this early," he told her again, "and she will not appear in the dining room until luncheon."

"I cannot be sure of that. She might . . ." Her voice trailed off.

The conversation promised to become too personal to continue in the presence of a servant. He fell silent until the girl finished, then gave her a speaking glance. Understanding the unspoken order, the maid departed.

"Davina, you are the mistress of this house, not my mother. You can order all breakfasts to be served on trays," he told her.

For a moment it seemed as if she were considering doing just that. Then she asked, "What did your mother do?"

"She dictated both options," he admitted.

"What did she herself do when guests were present?" she probed further.

He couldn't fabricate. "She took her meals in the dining room."

"Then that is what I must do."

"Darling, Mother ate very late nevertheless, unless there was an activity planned for early morning," he protested. "Besides, we aren't precisely entertaining at the moment. This is immediate family."

She lowered her gaze, her long lashes fanning the delicate cheeks below. "Please, Adam. Please allow me to do this."

When she pleaded so prettily, he couldn't resist. "Very well, but mark my words. She won't be joining us."

She smiled. "At least I will know I have tried."

"Yes, you will know that." Adam offered his arm to escort her from the chamber.

"I want her to like me," Davina stated, her voice cheery with relief. "Even more than that, I want her to *approve* of me."

"How could she keep from doing that?" he asked.

"Very easily!"

They descended the stairs into the main hall and turned toward the dining room. Adam was surprised to see no footmen present. Had his and Davina's morning habit become so predictable that the staff had shifted their working times until later?

As they entered the dining room, he saw why the footmen were elsewhere. Every man was hastening to and fro, bearing breakfast food to be placed on the sideboard. Not merely directing, Pinkham had even lowered himself to carry a huge platter of sliced ham, sausages, and rashers of bacon. Adam drew a deep breath.

At the foot of the table, in the seat reserved for the mistress of the house, sat his mother, a look of disdain on her face. Before her was an empty plate. Adam had the impression that if it were not improper, she would have her knife and fork in each fist, pounding them on the table. Beside him, Davina quailed.

"Goodness, Mother, this is a surprise!" he blurted.

She lifted a single, imperious eyebrow. "Obviously."

He struggled for a way to remind her that she sat in Davina's chair. It was an exercise in futility. Knowing he was making a gross error, he said nothing, drawing out a chair catercorner from his for his wife.

Davina sank down, looking miserable. "We . . . we are not in the habit of breakfasting below stairs, ma'am," she tried to explain.

"I am well aware of that, but I thought you would have provided for your guest's meal. It was rather inconsiderate, Davina, but I can scarcely say I expected better. You are young and . . ."

What she left to the imagination seemed worse than what she actually stated. Tears trickled down Davina's cheeks. Covering her face with her hands, she wrenched toward the door.

"Sit down, gel!" the dowager countess commanded. "This is no cause for vapors. I am merely instructing you on what is expected of a countess in this family."

"I . . . can't . . ." Davina jerked open the door before a servant could attend to it and dashed from the room.

"Damn it!" cried Adam, starting after her.

With lightning speed, the dowager turned her attention to him. "You will sit down, young man!"

He hesitated just long enough for a footman to cross his path. The two collided, sending a bowl of scrambled eggs flying into the air. With a mouthwatering aroma, the golden mass descended, pelting Adam and the footman with delicious curds. The pretty porcelain bowl crashed to the floor and broke into smithereens. Adam halted, gaping at the mess.

"Well, I never!" gasped his mother.

Pinkham speedily took up a crumber and began to flick the eggs from the earl's coat.

"Let me pass," Adam muttered with grave aggravation.

"But, sir—"

Adam darted aside, flinging eggs in all directions and wishing his mother was close enough to receive a share of the mess. Ignoring her continued commands, he strode from the room, but Davina was nowhere to be seen. He climbed the stairs two at a time and halted before her door. It was locked.

"Davina!" He pounded frantically.

"Adam?" Her voice quavered so softly he could scarcely hear her. "I do not wish you to see me like this."

"Darling, open the door."

When he did not receive a response, he continued on to his room. There were no locks between the master and mistress's suites. Throwing off his soiled coat, he went through the passageway and saw his wife lying facedown on her bed, her shoulders heaving with sobs. Lying down beside her, he gathered her into his arms.

"Oh, Adam!" She buried her face in his chest. "Oh, Adam, I never should have married you. I am not good enough!"

"Davina, darling, you are the only woman I wanted, the only woman I would *ever* want! I love you above all else, as I thought you loved me."

She lifted her tear-streaked face. "Sometimes . . . sometimes I think love just isn't enough."

Panic seized his breast. Was he going to lose her because of his parent? Of course, there could be no divorce, but she could leave him just the same. Even if they continued to share a home and even set up a nursery, she could shut him out of her heart. The pain that thought caused was almost overwhelming. He held her closely to him.

"Love *is* enough, Davina. I will show you it is. Just don't . . . don't . . ." He couldn't put his fears into words. Besides, at the present, she probably wouldn't listen to him anyway.

Eight

As soon as Davina was comforted and settled, Adam left her chamber to return to the dining room. His mother had finally been served. She sat eating, her nose drawn up haughtily and a rather smug smirk on her face. Her expression infuriated him, but he held his tongue. Long ago, he had learned there was no gain in arguing with her, although sometimes he became so irritated he forgot that fact. This threatened to be one of those times. Clenching his jaw, he seated himself and beckoned the butler to fill his cup.

Elevating her left eyebrow, the dowager laid down her fruit spoon and eyed him with curiosity. "Has Davina regained control of herself?" she asked coolly.

His cheek muscles twitching, he took a sip of the hot tea. "Mother, that incident was too bad of you."

She lifted a shoulder. "The gel must learn."

"If there is blame, it should fall on my head. I informed Davina you seldom rose for breakfast," he readily admitted.

"Ah!" She raised a finger, interrupting him. "That is the key, do you not know? *Seldom,* not *never.* Davina should have noted the discrepancy."

"Oh, for God's sake!" he said tightly. "Really, ma'am, are you trying to trap your own family?"

"I do not understand what you are talking about, Adam." She frowned. "I am not trying to trap anyone. I am endeavoring to *teach*. In my opinion, learning by observation is far more effective than learning by lecture."

He sighed and shook his head. Rising, he crossed to the sideboard to fill his plate. "Perhaps I am a slowtop, but I fail to see a lesson in this."

"Why, it's perfectly plain! Davina will never again slothfully keep to her chamber on mornings when guests are present in the house."

"This is ridiculous," he tossed over his shoulder. "Davina would not commit such an error."

The dowager chuckled without mirth. "She just did."

"But, Mother, you are family!" He returned to his chair. "Can you not see the difference?"

"I may be related, but I am no longer the mistress of this house or even a permanent resident. Therefore, I am a guest, and I deserve to be treated as such by my hostess." She pursed her lips. "I was ill-used. That was a fact that needed to be pointed out. I am very hurt by this lack of respect, but I am not surprised. Those Halderton people were always rackshambles. I knew the daughter would have difficulty adjusting to her elevated status. Oh, Adam, life could have been so much easier if only you would have been guided by me."

"Maybe for you," he growled. "I remember those two insipid, pie-faced young ladies you attempted to foist off on me. They may have been daughters of the upper peerage and possessed with handsome dowries, but they were the greatest antidotes I have ever encountered."

"How you do run on," she twittered. "Lady Hortense and Lady Elmira might have been somewhat plain, but they were not antidotes. Moreover, they were knowledgeable in all the ladylike arts and skills. They could have stepped into the role of countess without batting an eye. One never need have been concerned about their grasp of correct deportment."

He stabbed a slice of ham. "There are more things in life than etiquette."

"Oh, yes, a pretty face! That is all you thought of when you asked Davina to marry you. Men are so shallow and single-minded. I thought that, being a Trowbridge, you would be different."

Adam was finding less and less appetite for his breakfast. He wished he was taking the meal in the ease and comfort of his and Davina's private room. Why did his mother have to arrive and ruin his idyllic existence?

"Beauty fades quickly," the dowager went on. "Decorum and strength of purpose last a lifetime. I'll grant you Davina is beautiful, but she lacks the essential grace of good form that is so important to a lady of high quality."

"At least there is one thing on which you feel able to compliment my wife," he said sourly and laid down his knife and fork. "Indeed, there is not one flaw in her countenance and figure."

"Well, that is the only asset she possesses."

He abandoned the effort of eating. His cook was superb, but today everything tasted like sawdust. He gestured the butler to remove his plate and refill his cup. A meal with his mother in one of her moods was a dyspeptic affair. He longed for none but Davina's company. If only he had the insolence to order his mother to return to the country—but that was too improper to contemplate.

"Pretty *façade*," she mused. "I shall forever marvel that you would be so superficial in selecting a countess."

"First of all, Mother, I was choosing a *wife*," he parried. "Davina and I are much alike. We—"

"What?" she cut in, aghast. "You are not like the Haldertons, Adam! You are cool and refined and polished. That gel is a hoyden."

"No, she is not. She is merry and bright. She is the most charming lady I have ever known. I admire her lightheartedness." He gritted his teeth. "Inside, that is the way I have always felt. I needed her to bring it out."

"Flummery! You and the Haldertons are different as night and day."

"Mother, I do not know why you constantly assume Davina is as intemperate as her father and brothers are rumored to be. She is not like them."

She snorted. "Of course she is. Just wait and see."

"You, madam, will be the one who is surprised." He folded his napkin and laid it on the table. "Now, if you will excuse me?"

"You've scarcely eaten a bite, Adam," she chided.

"I find I have better appetite if I begin my morning by breakfasting upstairs," he informed her. "In fact, I believe I shall do so in the future."

"What about me?" she whined.

"I suggest you do so, too. Besides, you know you seldom descend the stairs at this hour."

"Seldom, but not never," she reminded him disdainfully.

They were back where they started from. Dreading a continuation, Adam hurriedly rose. "I shall leave you now, Mother, and go to the library. I've business matters to attend."

She pursed her lips into a pout. "Very well, Adam. I suppose I must finish my meal alone, pondering this very sad circumstance."

He hesitated. "Mother, there is nothing lamentable about this situation. You are judging Davina by her family. If only you would renounce this prejudice and open your mind to her, you would see her merit."

"Nothing but a pretty face," she muttered.

He was wasting his breath. She was just too obstinate and set in her beliefs. As he already knew, there was no point in quarreling with her. Once she had her mind made up, there was no changing it. He could only hope for a truce between the two ladies. Shrugging his shoulders, he strode toward the door.

Davina had scarcely washed the tears from her cheeks and neatened her hair before there was a tentative scratch at her chamber door. Answering the summons, she gazed at an unsmiling footman who was shifting from foot to foot in obvious anxiety.

"The countess wishes to see you in the formal drawing room, ma'am," he conveyed.

Davina sighed. Shouldn't he have said *dowager* countess? After all, she was the current Countess Trowbridge. But there was no point in remarking on it. The young servant was probably as terrified of her mother-in-law as she was.

"Very well," she acknowledged. "You may inform her I will attend her shortly."

He grimaced. "Madam, if I may—you'd best hasten."

That was impertinent, but Davina decided he was only trying to be helpful.

"All right." She left the room immediately, without taking time to scan her appearance again. It was difficult to know which was most important to the dowager, instant presence or flawless appearance. Both, no doubt.

That was clear as soon as she entered the drawing room. Adam's mother harshly looked her up and down. "Surely you might have freshened yourself."

Catching her hands behind her back, Davina peered at the floor. "I did."

"You certainly don't look it."

Davina's temper rose, but she choked it back. "My abigail was otherwise occupied. I did for myself."

"Your hair looks like a bird's nest. You should have rung for her," the dowager pronounced.

"I did not wish to interrupt."

"Fustian! She is a servant," Lady Trowbridge spat out. "Gel, do you not know your station in life?"

Davina bit her lip.

"Well? Speak up, gel!"

"I wish always to be thoughtful and kind, ma'am." She glanced hopefully at her mother-in-law. Surely the lady could not dispute those qualities.

"Misplaced kindness defeats all semblance of order within a house. For what you give, servants always want more," she lectured. "They grow lax and insolent. Without discipline, there is no respect. Affability has no place in a well-run establishment. I will expect you to remember that."

"Yes, ma'am, but fairness . . ."

Lady Trowbridge gave her a look that would instantly melt an iceberg. She peremptorily jerked the bell rope and stared at her daughter-in-law until a footman arrived.

"Send Lady Trowbridge's dresser up to her chamber," she commanded. "She is needed immediately."

"Yes, my lady." He fairly flew.

Again, she turned her attention to Davina. "Go make yourself presentable. Callers should be arriving at any moment."

Davina managed a small smile. Adam's mother need not be concerned about that. "Oh, we seldom have callers, especially in the morning."

"That will change today, I imagine. I have advised my friends of my arrival in town." She clapped her hands. "Go on! Be about it! And bring down your sewing basket. You must be seen partaking in a genteel pursuit."

Davina fled, unsurprised to find Fifi waiting. "I'm sorry to interrupt."

The lady's maid lifted a hand. "Serving you is my occupation and desire, my lady. What do you wish?"

"Lady Trowbridge believes callers will arrive and wants me to be ready to receive them," she said.

Fifi stood motionless, a rather perplexed look on her face.

When the servant did not respond, Davina smiled with chagrin. "I must look a fright."

"In my opinion, *madame,* you look lovely, but I shall do whatever you request."

Davina helplessly racked her brain to think of some request so the interruption of Fifi's schedule would not have been in vain. "My mother-in-law did not like my appearance. Perhaps she dislikes my dress."

"She does not know fashion." The maid shrugged. "Maybe the peach one? It brings out the pretty color of *madame's* complexion."

"All right," Davina said, relieved. "That is the one I will wear."

Davina changed gowns and sat while Fifi restored her coiffure. Minutely studying her reflection in the mirror to make certain no hair was out of place, she rose. Hopefully, the lady would now be satisfied.

"Thank you, Fifi." She smiled. "I should not be bothering you until evening."

The servant nodded. "My lady?"

"Yes?"

"Good luck, my lady." Fifi smiled confidently.

Davina drew a deep breath. "I fear I will need it."

Departing her chamber, Davina hurried downstairs and along the hall to the library to fetch her workbasket. Adam looked up and grinned as she entered.

"I shall not disturb you," she said, picking up her basket. "I've come for my sewing."

"I thought we might go for a ride in the park."

"Oh, no." With the turmoil of the morning, she knew she could not cross the dowager again. Disappointment flooded over her. Why must she boringly sit awaiting nonexistent visitors when she could be with him? But she was too afraid to dispute her mother-in-law's wishes. Adam would understand.

She smiled ruefully. "I fear I cannot go. Your mother seems to expect callers. She wished me to be ready for them."

"Let *her* greet the callers." He rose and came round the desk to cup her jaw in his hands and tilt her head for a kiss.

"Oh, Adam, please do not muss my hair."

As soon as the words were out, she wished with all her heart she had not spoken them. A flash of pain briefly flickered in his eyes. He curtly dropped his arms to his sides.

"Do excuse me, Davina."

"No . . . I . . ."

"I thought you liked my kisses." He returned to his seat behind the desk.

"I do! Adam, I didn't mean—" She followed him, but there suddenly seemed to be an invisible, awful barrier in her way. "Please understand."

"Go along to your callers."

"I don't want to go to any callers!" she shrilled. "I much prefer to be with you!"

"Then what is all this about?" he asked, busily shuffling papers.

"Your mama wants me to join her. She thinks it is necessary to wait upon callers. Maybe you could come with me," she finished lamely.

"I have no interest in that. Do not expect me to dawdle in the drawing room with Mother's noxious friends."

"Adam." She laid her hand on his shoulder.

He absently patted it. "Go along, my dear. Perhaps I shall see you at luncheon."

Perhaps? Her heart aching, she went to the door, then turned. "Could we go to the park after luncheon?"

He didn't even look up. "People make calls in the afternoon, too."

It was a dismissal. Tears prickling her eyes, Davina retrieved her basket, left the room, and wandered down the hall, so deep in her upset that she didn't even see a housemaid pass her without smiling. Was this a quarrel? Why didn't he understand? He, of all people, should know how his mother was. Didn't he also bend to her wishes?

As she passed the bottom of the stairs, she had a notion to go to her chamber and plead a return of her headache. That would eliminate being present for callers, and maybe it would set up the need for fresh, soothing air in the park. But the ruse wouldn't work. The dowager would probably have her dragged down to the drawing room, or Adam would send her off in the carriage with her abigail. She could not win.

The dowager scrutinized her as she entered the grand salon. "That is better."

A compliment? Davina could scarcely believe her ears. "The gown is from Paris, ma'am."

"Quite becoming, although I much prefer to provide employment to our own countrymen. I cannot forget that wicked Napoleon." Lady Trowbridge laid her embroidery on her lap and patted the seat beside her. "Join me on the settee."

She obeyed, glancing at the lady's stitchery. "How beautiful!"

Adam's mother brushed the praise aside. "It is nothing. Just a piece of scrap."

"It would be ever so pretty set into a bodice," Davina observed.

The dowager gasped. "For Heaven's sake! I am not my own modiste!"

"No, ma'am, of course not. But you could give it to your dressmaker to be inserted into your next gown," she persisted. "It would be lovely."

Lady Trowbridge laughed shortly and with little humor.

"Mayhap, but whatever would I say if someone asked me the origin?"

The mood was broken. Davina opened her basket and removed the shirt she was mending. She quickly found the small rend under the arm and threaded her needle.

"What is that?" the dowager countess asked.

"It's Adam's shirt. I am going to repair this slight tear." She pointed to the spot.

"Adam's shirt?" she screeched, startling Davina. "You cannot do mending!"

Davina looked at her helplessly. "It does not require great skill. Look. I can make as fine a stitch as the tailor."

Lady Trowbridge ripped the garment from her hands and threw it to the carpet. "I am totally disgusted! What is wrong with you, gel? Do you not know ladies do not refurbish clothing? This is a task for Adam's valet."

She bent to retrieve the apparel. "I am quite capable of doing it."

"It is beyond belief." Adam's mother collapsed against the back of the settee. "If I were frequently given to taking smelling salts, I would do so now."

Davina eyed her with puzzlement. "I'm sorry, ma'am. I just do not comprehend what you are trying to tell me."

"Did your mother teach you nothing?" the dowager cried. "No, probably not. Not in that haphazard household!"

Davina bent her head and bit her lip.

"Goodness, gel, must I instruct you in every tiny facet of everyday life?" Again, the dowager answered herself. "I suppose I must. First of all, Davina, you will turn over that torn shirt to Adam's valet, whose duty it is to mend it. Gad, but I'll wager the servants are laughing their heads off at your misguided domesticity."

"Surely it cannot be that bad," Davina murmured. "What's wrong with mending my husband's shirt?"

"What's that? Do not talk back to me!" snapped her

mother-in-law. "Gel, you will do as I say! From this moment forward, you will sew nothing but pretties. A countess, particularly the countess Trowbridge, stitches only fancywork."

"Yes, ma'am." She carefully folded Adam's shirt, laying it on her lap and smoothing out the wrinkles.

"Let's see what you have in here."

Davina's heart sank as the dowager opened her basket and began to rummage through it. Her needlework was passable, but she did not excel at delicate stitchery. At a time when other little girls were learning the fine points of embroidery, she was playing outside with her brothers. Her mama had never forced her to practice the feminine arts. As a result, she had not paid much heed to it until she had come to London to live with her aunt. Then, recognizing her ineptitude in such feminine arts, she had begun to rectify the matter. But she had a long way to go.

Arching an eyebrow, Adam's mother drew out the pillowcase that she'd begun decorating when she and Adam had returned from their honeymoon.

"I suppose this is passable," the lady muttered, "but your work is not good, gel."

"I know I need practice," Davina admitted.

"I cannot imagine what your mother could have been thinking when she instructed you in a lady's responsibilities," she mulled. "Gad, but you are so unsuited to your role."

Davina felt like dashing from the drawing room, but she knew she could not flee every time her mother-in-law was nasty. If so, she might as well remain in her chamber twenty-four hours a day. Besides, she was the mistress of this house now, not the dowager Lady Trowbridge. If only she had the nerve to tell her so.

But doubt niggled at her mind. Lady Trowbridge was a countess, and a grand one. She moved in the very highest circles. She knew how to conduct herself in a plethora of social predicaments. There were things Davina could learn from her. For a young lady uncertain of her role, the dowager could be a godsend. Of course, Davina would super-impose the position with her own brand of kindness, eliminating the countess's coldness. But she would not have to ask Adam or grope in the dark for the proper way to go on.

"Now hide that shirt." Adam's mother thrust it into the bottom of the basket as the front door knocker clapped. "Just in time!"

Davina knew her mother-in-law was a social arbiter, but still she could scarcely believe her eyes when three ladies of the highest *ton* imaginable entered the drawing room. These elegant matrons, contemporaries of Lady Trowbridge, had never acknowledged her existence, let alone sought to grace her presence. Of course, she didn't fool herself into thinking the women came on her accord. They were Adam's mother's friends. But to see them in her home was gratifying nevertheless.

"My dearest companions of old!" the dowager cried, rising to greet them.

Davina stood, watching the elders exchange chaste kisses on cool cheeks.

"Have you met my new daughter-in-law?" Lady Trowbridge asked with noticeably less enthusiasm.

She curtsied to them, even though Lady Castleford was of lesser rank in the peerage than she. "How do you do?"

They responded politely, though studying her with the same critical gaze Lady Trowbridge usually employed.

"Won't you sit down?" she implored, satisfyingly before her mother-in-law issued the invitation.

They nodded, spreading out so they occupied all the seating in the conversational area. Did they do that purposefully to exclude her? Momentarily nonplussed, Davina drew a chair from alongside the wall. This was her house. Truthfully, she was the real hostess, but this time, the dowager outdistanced her. With a smile like a cat at the cream, the older woman rang for a servant and requested refreshment, then peered at her.

"Fetch Adam, Davina. I know he will enjoy seeing my bosom friends."

Her heart skipped a beat. Her previous interview with him had been bad enough. If she went to Adam with that request, the results would be just awful.

She hesitated, scrabbling for a plausible excuse. "He is closeted with his man of business. He informed me that he must not be disturbed under any circumstances."

"Strange." His mother lifted a brow. "I heard no person arriving."

Davina shrugged vulnerably. "I did not either, but he is there. I saw him."

Lady Trowbridge eyed her with disbelief.

Countess Ellsworthy chuckled. "Ah, you know men! They do abhor interruption when tangled in business matters."

Davina smiled with relief. "It is so kind of you to understand."

"Hmmph!" said the dowager. "We'll see."

The seemingly compassionate Countess Ellsworthy switched the topic. "Never mind that, Eleanor. We are most interested in you. What brings you to Town?"

"Well, of course I missed the company of my friends." She narrowed her nostrils and elevated her chin. "Most of all, however, I have come to advise my new daughter-in-law in her social obligations. Being a countess is an altogether alien occupation for her, as you all may have guessed."

Davina quickly lowered her gaze against the sudden tears in her eyes. Lady Trowbridge professed proper manners? Humiliation was not polite. What the dowager was doing was just as bad as the Halderton practical jokes. She bit her lip.

Pinkham arrived with the large silver tray and set it with a flourish on the tea table.

"Do pour for us, Davina," Adam's mother requested.

Her heart leaped to her throat. She wished she could flee. Looking up, she saw all eyes peering at her. With a deep breath, she began the task. Of course, the worst thing happened. China rattled.

Nine

Davina had never been so thankful than when Pinkham announced luncheon, thus terminating the calling hours. The grand dining room seemed like a cozy haven after the debacle of the drawing room. Happily, too, Adam was present. But although she was greatly relieved of the strain, she did not feel like her usual cheerful self. The morning had taken a toll on her.

Her mind reviewing the past events, she absently stirred her turtle soup, taking few sips and merely watching the swirls of rich broth separate, then mingle together. In all likelihood, the ladies' visit had lasted only thirty to forty-five minutes. It had been longer than the average call, but it had seemed like an eternity. Fortunately, Lady Ellsworthy had continued to be benevolent, but the other two ladies had regarded her with little address and high, arrogant noses. Lady Trowbridge had registered great shock at the rattling china and then had retreated behind her cold, self-possessed front.

Davina knew she would hear much, much more about the clinks of the cups and saucers. That was a major social crime. There would be definite repercussions.

Worst of all, the misfortune would reflect back on Adam. Those ladies were probably chattering madly about the unsuitable chit he had married. Davina sighed. Could she ever make up for it? How could she ever please Lady Trowbridge?

"Cease playing with your food, gel!" the countess said sharply.

She startled. "I'm sorry. I confess I was woolgathering."

"Let us not enact a scene," Adam muttered.

His comment drew his mother's attention. "Whatever are you prattling about? There will be no *scene,* as you call it, unless your wife decides to perform another Cheltenham Tragedy."

Davina laid down her spoon. The whole situation had caused her to lose her appetite, but she was determined the dowager would not overset her. Hopefully, she would soon have some distance from her unwelcome guest. Lady Trowbridge could wait for afternoon callers. Surely she could wheedle Adam into going out.

"It would be a lovely day to ride in the park," she said wistfully.

"Indeed," agreed Lady Trowbridge. "A carriage ride in late afternoon would be most pleasant."

Davina's spirits fell. Her mother-in-law envisioned the fashionable hour, when carriages moved at a snail's pace as their occupants paused to greet each other. It was highly stylish, but in the company of Adam's mother, it would be a nightmare. Something awful would be sure to happen. Then there would be another nail in her societal coffin.

"I was thinking of a refreshing horseback ride." She optimistically glanced at Adam.

"Horseback?" cried his mother. "How gauche! No, you cannot do that, Davina. It is not elegant."

Davina persisted. "If you saw my new Parisian riding habit, you would not think so, ma'am. It is remarkably dashing."

"Out of the question," pronounced her adversary. "You must take pains to obscure your hoydenish background. Horseback riding would only remind people you lack polish."

"Mother!" Adam interjected.

"May we not admit the truth among ourselves?" she fired back. "Davina is well aware of her family's reputation. I'm sure she wishes to overcome it in order to be the perfect countess for you, son. Is that not true, Davina?"

The old shrew had neatly boxed her into a corner. Davina nodded. "Of course I wish to be the perfect wife for Adam."

"You already are," he said quietly.

She wished she could leap from her chair and throw her arms around his neck. He'd forgiven her for their earlier quibble. But if she did as she wanted, the dowager would certainly faint again.

"Hmmph!" Lady Trowbridge threw up her hands. "Just like a man! Cannot see beyond the end of his nose."

Adam arched a brow and looked every bit as formidable as his mother when she executed that gesture. "Mother, I know you set great emphasis upon Society, but I married Davina because she makes me happy. The opinion of the *ton* can hang."

"Oh? Is that what you will think if you have daughters who reach marriageable age? Tell me, Davina, do you know how to launch a young lady into Society? Can you single-handedly plan a ball or even a large rout party for the cream of the *ton?*"

Davina glanced quickly at Adam and saw the brief uncertainty in his eyes. He had his doubts. In all honesty, so did she. Once again, the reality of her social position battered her. No, she wasn't prepared to do such a thing. Her aunt had managed the details of the small party given in her honor. She'd been dreaming so much of Adam that she'd scarcely paid heed to the details. The dowager was right. She was socially ill-equipped to be Adam's hostess or even to be the chaperon of her own daughters. Could her mother have felt the same way when she'd placed Davina in the hands of her aunt?

"I shall assume your silence answers my questions," said her mother-in-law with grave finality.

During the lull, the soup course was removed and the main entree set in its place. Seeing and smelling the strong-scented lamb and mint sauce, Davina felt her stomach rebel with queasiness. Ovine concoctions had always repulsed her. She would never have allowed that suggestion to remain on the menu, which brought to mind that Mrs. Benning had not presented her with the day's culinary plan. Had Adam's mother intercepted it? Come to think of it, yesterday's menu had been changed, too. At the time, Davina had decided quality ingredients must not have been available, so Jacques had substituted. But two days in a row? No, it was impossible.

Her patience wavered. Lady Trowbridge might make her life miserable with her social prodding and verbal affronts, but she would *not* usurp her role as mistress of this house. After all, Adam had stressed that Davina was in domestic command.

Gritting her teeth, she watched Adam carve the nasty joint. To be purchased by the Trowbridge chef, the dark meat must be of the finest quality, but it still looked dry and grainy. He presented a portion to his mother and turned to serve her.

"My dear?"

"No, thank you." She firmly shook her head.

"Come, darling. You've scarcely eaten a thing all day." He carved off a small slice. "Surely you can manage this bite."

"No," she said flatly.

"She is being contrary to gain attention," surmised the dowager.

"Please, darling," Adam cajoled. "You'll make yourself ill."

She watched the repulsive meat come closer to her plate.

Nausea filled her throat. Impulsively, she pushed Adam's hand away.

"I do not want it."

"Don't be stubborn," he said.

Her temper flashed like ignited gunpowder. "I hate that abominable fare!"

Adam started.

"If I had been shown the menu," she snapped, "I would have struck out such an abhorrent selection. I cannot bear the odor, let alone the taste, of lamb. I would starve before eating it!"

"My goodness," breathed the dowager. "What a display."

Lips pursed, Davina turned to the butler. "Pinkham, I want to know why I was not consulted about the menu. Please ask Mrs. Benning at once."

"Such a tempest in a teacup," Lady Trowbridge interjected. "It isn't necessary to go off on such a chase. *I* approved the menu. What difference does it make? I thought to save you the time and trouble."

Davina glanced at Adam, but he was studying an ornate ceiling medallion from which hung a crystal chandelier. Obviously he was not going to stand up for her. That angered her even further.

"Lady Trowbridge," she stated, obliviously admitting that she herself was not *the* Lady Trowbridge, "when Adam and I returned from our honeymoon, he directed that I was the mistress of his house. Until he instructs me differently, that is exactly who I intend to be."

"What a silly to-do," the dowager purred, "over a slice of lamb."

"Mutton is not the issue," she hotly began.

"Lamb, my gel," her adversary corrected. "Perhaps you do not know there is a difference."

"Not to me! Besides, as I said—"

"There is a great difference to those who dine above the salt and those who feed below it," she went on, her haughty

distinct voice overriding Davina's. "In case you are confused, I refer to social class, of course."

Knowing she should not be so disrespectful as to continue to argue with her elder, Davina drew a deep breath
and, nevertheless, carried on. "Ma'am, I know you are a
veritable arbiter of propriety; therefore, you, of all people,
should be aware that the wife of the master of the house
is its mistress. I'll thank you not to pilfer my role!"

Adam awoke from his daydream and had the audacity to
laugh.

"What is so amusing?" she demanded, her indignation
reaching no bounds.

He sobered.

"Why do you not support me, Adam?" Davina challenged.

"I do, darling. With all my heart." He reached under the
table and caught her hand, squeezing it. "You are the mistress of my house. Isn't that so, Mother?"

"But of course." The dowager threw up her hands. "I
was only attempting to help. Davina has so much to learn
that I thought to take the everyday cares from her shoulders.
And this childish temper tantrum is all the thanks I receive!"

Adam's touch had caused Davina's wrath to flee. She
should not have lost her temper, especially in front of the
pensive Pinkham and two avidly listening footmen. It did
seem childish and disrespectful. But she had done it and
could not take it back.

Adam did not comment on his mother's statement. Instead, he directed his next words to Davina. "My dear, I
do believe a horseback ride in the park is just what you
need. Shall we? After nuncheon?"

"It is not seemly!" wailed the dowager.

"Mother, you know there are many ladies of the *haute
ton* who ride," he replied. "I like to ride with Davina, and

I see no reason to deprive myself of her company and to prevent her from her pleasure."

"Fiddlesticks," muttered his mother. "What of afternoon calling hours?"

"I know you'll enjoy greeting those who may come. My lady and I will merely be out."

"From what I've heard, you are always out." The dowager clicked her tongue and leveled her gaze at Davina. "Just be sure to return promptly. We have an important ball to attend tonight."

"What?" Adam cried.

His mother bristled. "How is the young Lady Trowbridge to take her place in society if she remains at home?"

He exhaled long and irritably.

Davina laughed.

"Damn!" Adam protested, as they rode through the park. "She is totally oversetting our life, and she has scarcely arrived! What are we to do?"

Davina wished she could advise him to banish the lady to the country. She wanted to tell him to order his mother to cease harassing her. But no matter how close she and Adam had become, she couldn't divulge what she really wanted to say.

"I don't know, Adam. I am scarcely acquainted with her. I cannot counsel you."

He shrugged powerlessly. "Perhaps she will weary of her so-called lessons. Davina darling, can you strive to behave exactly as she says? Then maybe she'll leave us in peace."

Her fingers tensed on the reins. "I do behave properly, Adam."

"I know. I didn't mean that." He grinned crookedly. "But if you became a high stickler like she is, it might do the trick."

"I don't want to be a high stickler." Her horse began to prance, made nervous by the tautness of her hands.

"For God's sake, can't you pretend?" He frowned as her gelding skittered sideways.

One benefit to having been a youthful hoyden was an equestrian ability equal to that of many men. Davina moved easily with the fractious creature. She knew the horse was reacting to her own restiveness and tried to calm her handling of him, but one didn't fool an animal. With this added to his normal high spirits, he decided to enjoy himself by misbehaving. With a snort, he lunged and half bucked.

"What is this?" queried her husband, who was well familiar with her expertise. "Another scene?"

"What?" she cried.

"I'm trying to speak seriously."

The gelding pitched again. "Do you think I delight in having my bottom bludgeoned by this saddle?" she fired back.

"*Davina,* shh!" he cautioned, glancing about to see if anyone had heard.

It did not take long for her already smoldering temper to fully ignite. "Today, Adam, I have had just about enough of you and your mama and all your criticism of how I behave! And I am certainly vexed by this horse!"

"Calm down, Davina." He reached for the bridle. "Let me ride him."

That insult to her equestrian ability was outside of enough. "Do not touch him! I know this horse, and he is relishing my discomfort." She rode out another heave. "He is taking advantage."

From the corner of her eye, she saw several wags, watching and chuckling at her predicament. The rogues! They were probably hoping to see her fall.

Long ago, her father had instructed her and her brothers on how to discipline a horse. If one smacked him with a crop, one did not hold the bit tight and chasten him on the mouth as well. It made logical sense, and the subsequent reaction discouraged unnecessary chastisement on the part of frustrated riders. Taking good hold of his mane in one hand, she cracked her whip across the horse's hindquarters. The gelding took off at a gallop.

"Davina!" Adam shouted.

Deciding not to rein in the animal, she laughed to herself as she raced through the park. That would show those annoying bucks—and her husband, too. If Adam was worried about scenes, let him take snuff at this one!

She heard approaching hoofbeats and glanced over her shoulder. Her lord was hard upon her, looking frightened out of his wits. *Fiddlesticks!* She was enjoying the madcap pace. Seeing his pallid face, however, she skillfully drew up.

"My darling!" he cried. "I thought you'd be killed!"

She sobered, quickly determining not to tell him her dash had been deliberate. Adam apparently had not had the same equine instruction. She had terrified him.

"I am all right." She reached out and squeezed his forearm.

"Thank God." He covered her hand with his.

"The horse is very fresh. I haven't ridden him in quite a while. But all is well now. See? He's docile as a . . ." She started to say lamb, but thought better of the reminder. "He's as docile as a kitten."

He exhaled with relief. "I'm glad you are as good a horsewoman as you are."

"A Halderton trait. You see," she couldn't help adding, "there are *some* good things about being a Halderton."

"I know that. I know it very well." His eyes soft with love, he brought her hand to his lips. "I am sorry we had words. I did not intend to criticize you."

"It's all right."

When he looked like that, she was lost. How could she

remain annoyed with him? She briefly closed her eyes, languishing in his touch.

"Mother is a strain," he said unhappily. "I know she is making things difficult for you. I'm sorry. I am well aware of what a trial she can be."

"Say no more," she interjected, feeling his pain and striving to make things easier for him. "I will be fine. I'm sure there are many things I can learn from her."

He seemed greatly relieved. "She's demanding, I know, but can you adjust to her manner?"

Was he pushing her to learn from his mother? Her thoughts returned to that moment at the dining table when the dowager had questioned her social competence. Yes, she did need to learn. Unfortunately, the knowledge must come from a harsh tutor. There was no one else.

"Davina?" He squeezed her hands. "Are you all right?"

She nodded, searching his eyes for encouragement.

"Let us go home, my darling." Flushing slightly, he gazed at her through his long lashes.

"Yes." Holding his gaze, she smiled. "We've had a sufficient outing."

He grinned. "We've been out long enough to avoid any drawing room summons."

"Just so." She giggled. "Also, before we could entertain callers, we must change clothes."

"That is exactly what I was thinking of. Shall we use it as an excuse to be naughty?" He grinned.

She shyly stared at her hands. "My lord, you may be as naughty as you wish."

That was enough to kindle his devastating slight flush. "What a bewitching invitation."

Turning their horses, they left the park and rode directly home. As they entered the house, they came face to face with Lady Trowbridge and two departing callers. Davina's light heart sank. There had been visitors, so her mother-in-law would probably ring a peal over her head for not being present.

The two ladies paused for introduction. Davina recognized them both. Of very high *ton,* Lady Warren was as great a stickler for propriety as Adam's mother. Her daughter, Lady Gail, now Lady Hartland, had been considered a diamond of the first water during the past Season. Neither woman appeared to remember Davina, but both were exceptionally cordial in making her acquaintance.

"I am sorry to have missed you," declared Lady Gail, "but I can understand how you would have preferred riding with your husband to remaining indoors. I, too, would have favored it."

"How is Hartland?" Adam inquired.

"Quite well, my lord. You and Lady Trowbridge must call on us sometime."

When they departed, the dowager turned to Adam. "Well, there is a gel who set her cap for you in the not too distant past, and she was certainly not an antidote."

"Indeed?" he asked. "I didn't notice. I suppose I was blinded by Davina's starshine."

His mother clicked her tongue in censure.

"Did Lady Gail really cast sheep's eyes upon you?" Davina questioned, sparked by faint jealousy.

"I have no idea whatsoever. As I said, I was too busy falling in love with you." He kissed her gloved palm. "There was never anyone but you."

She forgave Lady Gail. After all, any young lady would be attracted to handsome Adam. She even forgave him his aggravating mama.

"You are the sweetest man in all England," she whispered.

"Oh, for heaven's sake!" the dowager said disgustedly.

Davina and Adam met up with Lady Gail halfway through the ball that evening. This time, the attractive young matron was accompanied by her darkly handsome husband, Earl Hartland. Perceiving from their touches that they were in love, Davina totally exonerated Lady Gail for throwing herself at Adam.

"I am exceedingly pleased to see you so soon, Lady Trowbridge," Lady Gail said with genuine pleasure. "Let us all go in to supper together."

"I would enjoy that very much," Davina responded, glancing about to locate her mother-in-law. "I must tell Adam's mother."

"Oh, let us escape our elders!" the countess begged.

"An excellent idea," her husband agreed laconically.

Davina wondered if the earl had experienced difficulties with his mother-in-law. Lady Gail's mother, Lady Warren, was as high a stickler as Lady Trowbridge. But Lord Hartland was *haute ton*. His decorum was probably above reproach. He'd surely been welcomed with open arms.

Lady Gail truly did intend to hide. She led them to a table behind a miniature grove of potted palms. "There! I shall have some relief at last."

Davina eyed her with surprise.

She shrugged and mischievously grimaced with guilt. "I know I must seem to be perfectly awful, but my mother is driving me up in the boughs. William, *please* can we not leave for Brighton?"

"In due time," he said amiably.

"That is all well and good for you to say. You flee to your club when you see her coming. What of poor little me?"

He laughed and signaled to Adam. "Let us fetch plates for our ladies. My mother-in-law is a dangerous subject right now, and I would just as soon avoid it."

Lady Gail watched them go. "My mama is the most interfering lady in all creation. She visits me every day to ascertain I am governing my household to her standards. If I do not have some respite, I shall surely go mad."

Davina absolutely could sympathize, but she merely smiled kindly.

"She preaches and preaches upon my social obligations. I must do this; I must do that! If not, I shall insult Lady Such-and-such, or make an enemy of Lady So-and-so. Do I not remember that someday I might have daughters for whom I must arrange brilliant matches?" She rolled her eyes. "Sometimes I wish my unborn girls would be satisfied with simple country squires."

Davina laughed and couldn't help nodding.

"I detect a kindred soul," Lady Gail sensed. "Tell me, am I alone in my misery? Do you have such troubles with the dowager Lady Trowbridge?"

"It is doubtlessly difficult for our elders to adjust to changes of circumstance," Davina replied carefully. She did not know Lady Gail. If she were to acknowledge her own problems, it might get back to Adam's mother.

The young woman sighed. "With the exception of William, I feel so alone in my affliction."

"You should not," Davina stressed, allowing some commiseration.

"Thank you for saying that. I am greatly relieved." She smiled conspiratorially. "I know Mama is right. Social position is very important. But wouldn't you just love to bolt to Brighton?"

"We were planning to go when my mother-in-law arrived from the country," she murmured. "Naturally, our preparations were canceled."

"I'm so sorry." Lady Gail morosely propped her elbows on the table and cradled her chin on her hands. "Perhaps we shall both soon achieve our goal. The Season won't last much longer."

That was true. Davina swiftly reviewed her own adversity. Society was extremely important. Surely she could bear with Lady Trowbridge's foibles for such a short time.

"But how I long for the seashore," Lady Gail breathed.

"If only Mother doesn't want to accompany us when we go."

"Adam's mother does not like Brighton."

"You lucky lady! I'm sure Mama would go to the ends of the earth to plague us. Unfortunately, she dearly loves Brighton." She cheered. "But she does have my younger sister to prepare for the Little Season this Fall. Perhaps that will soon occupy her!"

The gentlemen returned with the plates.

"Are you still protesting your mother?" Lord Hartland chuckled. "Very well, Gail, you have made your point. We'll leave for Brighton as soon as we can pack."

"I cannot believe what I am hearing." His wife actually bounced in her chair. "I shall cause the servants to work all night! We'll leave tomorrow morning."

"As you wish."

Davina stole a glance at Adam, wishing he would follow suit.

Lady Gail saw her pensive expression. "Why don't you come with us? William owns a house in Brighton. There's plenty of room. We'll have a regular house party!"

"I wish we could," Adam stated, "but my mother has only just arrived."

Davina's small spark of hope vanished in a flare of disappointment, but she nodded loyally. "Leaving just now would be decidedly rude. But thank you for inviting us."

The countess smiled sympathetically. "Wouldn't it be wonderful if honeymoons did not have to end?"

"Yes," she concurred, biting her lip. "But they do."

She caught Adam's swift look of query. Any thoughts of honeymoons lasting forever was nonsense. Ordinary life held just too many responsibilities. Life with a lofty peer held even more. Realistically, she might as well put a period, for both of them, to any more such dreams of endless bliss.

Ten

"Good morning, my love." Adam gently kissed the top of Davina's hair as she lay curled against him, her head on the hollow of his shoulder.

She stretched with unconscious feline sultriness. "Is it morning already?"

"It is, but we don't have to get up yet."

She suddenly tensed. "Your mother! We have to get up and go down!"

"No, we don't." He held her close. "I do not intend to participate in her games of whether we'll see her or not. We have our breakfast room, and that is where we shall eat. I will not allow her to occupy all of my time with you. We have to have some time alone."

"But . . ."

"Hush, darling. This is what we are going to do, and there's an end to it." He tried to speak adamantly, but the words came out softly. She seemed quite willing to comply, however.

"If you say so." She giggled deep in her throat. "She is your mother, so you shall do the answering for our transgression."

"Do you really think you will escape?"

"Alas, no, but it is fun to pretend I might." She yawned and sat up, modestly gathering the sheet about her. "However, we must rise. I will enjoy our morning relaxation, but I must be ready in time for callers."

He felt a sharp jab of irritation. "Do you relish visitors?"

"It is my duty," she said mildly. "I missed yesterday afternoon. I cannot do so again."

He recalled how he'd asked her to comply with his mother's ideas and did not complain, as he wished to do. "Very well, Davina."

With a quick smile, she slipped into her dressing gown and climbed from the bed. "I shall join you in our breakfast room. My, but I am famished!"

He watched her disappear into her dressing room and reluctantly left her bed. Donning his robe, he proceeded to his own room, where Turnbull was busy laying out the day's attire. The valet bowed.

"Good morning, my lord."

"Good morning, Turnbull. The countess and I will be dining in our breakfast room. Do send for our meal immediately."

"Yes, sir." He left, but only after a brief pause when the servant glanced at him as if to question whether he was truly serious or not.

Again, Adam was miffed. He was the earl, the master, the head of the family. Did everyone from his wife to the servants mistrust his command just because his mother was resident? Was she that powerful? He sighed ruefully. She was. Only recently had he begun to dispute her.

He attended his morning ablutions, but put off shaving until after the repast. No matter what his wife might do, he was in no hurry to appear downstairs. He had finished his current matters of business the preceding day and had nothing planned with which to occupy himself. One thing was certain. He wouldn't await a passel of chatterboxes in the drawing room. Perhaps he would go to his club.

The thought astonished him. He hadn't been to White's since his marriage. He'd spent all his time with Davina.

But he wasn't interested in doing so now. She and his mother could entertain the callers.

Turnbull returned. "My lord, I feel I must inform you that the dowager Countess Trowbridge is in the dining room."

"She may dine wherever she likes," he said. He had told her he'd be breakfasting alone with Davina.

"Yes, sir." His valet nodded worriedly. "I merely thought you might wish to know."

"Her presence changes nothing."

"No, my lord. Footmen are setting your table as we speak."

"Good." Adam strode to the private room as the servants were leaving. He dismissed his mother from his mind as the delicious aroma of ham assailed his nostrils. He was hungry, too.

Davina joined him as soon as the footmen had left the room. "It smells so good."

"Yes." He waited while she served herself. "And speaking of food, that supper at the ball was surprisingly hideous."

"It was not very top drawer, was it? But the ball was quite lovely."

"What?" He couldn't believe she'd said that—Davina, who preferred to spend her time at home with him?

"Lady Gail made the difference," she went on. "Perhaps when I become acquainted with more people, I shall not dread social life so much."

"You were acquainted with many people before," he remarked, filling his plate.

"That was different."

"Oh?"

"I am your wife now."

Adam nearly questioned what difference that made, but he held back his query. It probably had to do with his asking her to pretend to be a high stickler. The subject was best left alone. He didn't want her to take offense. He did, however, want to reassure her.

"I rejoice every day that you are my wife, Davina," he said quietly.

Her cornflower blue eyes seemed to glow.

He grinned. "You are so very precious."

"Adam." She leaped from her seat and into his lap. "I do love you so very much!"

He sought her lips, which parted sweetly beneath his own. Once again he marveled how lucky he was to have found such a wife. No matter what his mother thought of her, she was perfect.

But after only a fleeting moment of the stirring kiss, she touched his cheek and lifted her head, flushing. "Oh, dear, here I am in dalliance when I should be breakfasting. Just like a Halderton! But now I am a Trowbridge, and I must conduct myself as one."

"I happen to like Haldertons." *Better than Trowbridges,* he thought as he regretfully let her scramble off his lap. "I find Haldertons to be thoroughly delightful. After all, I did marry one."

She giggled. "I will not make you sorry you did."

"That would be impossible."

She lifted an eyebrow. "Don't be too sure."

Since she was in such a damned hurry, he poured the tea while she helped herself to a minuscule serving of eggs and a slice of toast. "I thought you were famished."

"I was, but I think my nerves are getting the best of me."

He leaned forward and took her hand. "Slow down, Davina. There is no reason for you to overset yourself."

"Receiving callers with your mother is not easy, Adam," she said, her blue eyes appealing. "I am determined to do it properly today."

"You set too great a price on it. Everyone knows you

are a newlywed, and thus your life has greatly changed."
He kissed her fingers.

She lowered her gaze. "Yesterday when I poured tea, the
china rattled."

He grinned. "Just toss the damned stuff on the floor.
Become the *eccentric* countess."

"I can just picture your mother's expression." She
laughed, then sobered. "I want to be a *proper* countess."

"You already are. You married an earl."

Before she could reply, there was a faint knock at her
bedroom door. She shot Adam a questioning look. "Come
in, Fifi!"

"I do not know who Fifi is," said an imperious voice.

"Lady Trowbridge!" Davina cried.

"God damn," muttered Adam.

In horror, they heard her cross the chamber and enter
the dressing room. "Where are you, Davina?"

"Oh, no, no, no," his wife wailed softly, dropping her
head in her hands.

Adam rose and stalked into Davina's room. "We are
breakfasting, Mother. I told you we would continue our
habit of greeting the morning in private."

"Ooooh!" Framed in the dressing room door, she swayed
and grasped the jamb for support. "Adam, you cannot be
en déshabillé!"

"Why not?" he declared ruthlessly.

"It is not proper!" she gasped.

"Mother, I am not exactly out for a stroll on Rotten
Row."

"Impertinent!" She recovered herself enough to shake a
finger at him. "I can scarcely believe this is really you.
You were such a dutiful son."

"Oh, God damn."

"For shame, Adam Trowbridge." She advanced on him.
"Taking the Lord's name in vain! Enacting bordello behavior! What is next? You are the head of this family and you

are conducting yourself like a total rakehell. A Trowbridge! Oooh . . ."

"Mother, the door is in the opposite direction."

"Let me see this scandalous parlor."

He tried to block her way to spare Davina's sensibilities, but she evaded him. With stiff back and jutting chin, she marched into the breakfast room. Following, he expected to see his wife cowering in the corner, but she was nowhere in sight.

"Where is Davina?" his mother demanded.

"She probably ran for it." He took her arm. "Come, Mother, I know you are not comfortable here. Do await us downstairs."

She seemed to deflate, but she still pursed her lips in disapproval. "Very well, but I do not wish to see you, Adam. Send Davina to me at once. I shall be in the morning room."

"Yes, yes." He hastened her from the suite and firmly closed the door, sliding the bolt before he hurried back to the breakfast room. "Davina?"

"I am here." Trembling, she slipped from behind the drapery. "Oh, Adam!" She flew into his arms.

"It's all right, darling," he soothed.

"No it isn't! She will *murder* me!"

He held her gently, stroking her back. "I'll speak with her first. I will remind her that I told her we would breakfast alone. She grossly ignored propriety by coming in here. She is the one who behaved scandalously."

"No." She stepped back, laying her hands on his chest. "I must stand up for myself."

"Darling, that's what husbands are for. I want to protect you. Allow me to do my duty."

Davina managed a smile. "We are speaking as if I were in mortal danger. She is only an elderly woman. I could doubtlessly knock her down if I had to."

They both burst into laughter.

When they were able to be serious, Davina squared her shoulders. "I shall face her, Adam. If you go, she will believe she has intimidated me. Then things could become worse for me."

"If you are sure." He wasn't so positive. He needed to speak seriously with his mother and inform her, in no uncertain terms, to use a more gentle approach with Davina.

"I am certain. And now I must dress."

"Finish your breakfast first."

"You must be jesting, my lord." She stood on tiptoe and kissed his cheek, then fled to her chamber.

Adam grimly returned to the table. Davina was being very brave. She must be quaking inside as she prepared for the future encounter. He doubled his determination to speak with his mother, and he would give her an ultimatum. She would treat Davina kindly, or she must return to the country. And he didn't give a hang for the scandal it might cause. This was it!

Davina dressed in haste and was almost ready before Fifi arrived to attend her. "I've completed the fundamentals," she said, smiling, "if only you will add the finishing touches."

"I came as quickly as I could, my lady," the dresser said anxiously. "I thought you were dining with his lordship, but then I learned the old lady ruined it."

"Please do not be impertinent," she gently reminded.

Fifi snorted, tossing her head. "Truth is not impudence, *madame*. I do not like that old hag, no matter the opinion of others."

Davina knew she should have sharply corrected the girl, but her curiosity was piqued. "What do the others think of Lady Trowbridge?"

"That the *dowager* Lady Trowbridge is superior to all.

Fah!" Fifi snapped her fingers. "She is nothing. Just a bitter, devil-tongued snob. I think—"

"That will be all, Fifi. I am well aware of your opinion."

"Madame should stand up to her." She painstakingly began to arrange Davina's hair.

Davina bit her lip and decided to speak plainly with her abigail, even though she knew she should not confide in a mere servant. "There are things I can learn from her. Fifi, you must know my family is not among the highest echelon of society. In order to be a good countess, I must adapt to the Trowbridge way."

"To his lordship's way, yes, but not to hers!" Fifi arrested her hands in mid curl. "You are kind to all, *madame.* You care about people and want all to be happy! The mistress I had before you, she was cold and lofty like that old shrew. I hated her. You are so good to me. You talk to me and treat me like a human being. I love you, my lady!"

Tears prickled Davina's eyes. "What a lovely thing to say."

"It is true."

Davina reached back to squeeze her hand. "I believe I am about to face a most unpleasant interview. What you have said will make it much easier."

"Do not allow her to trample you, *madame.*"

Davina did not reply. Lady Trowbridge would doubtlessly do just that, but she would not meet her with force, as she had when the lamb had been served. Fifi's words, and Lady Gail's, too, had given her pause for reflection. Adam's mother probably felt she was doing the right thing. Davina would treat her with kindness.

Her toilette complete, she bid Fifi farewell and descended the stairs. An unsmiling footman, mysteriously knowing where she was going, escorted her to the morning room and opened the door. Lady Trowbridge, in conference with Mrs. Benning, looked up from the desk.

"Well, Davina, you have at last arrived. In light of your

tardiness, I have taken the liberty of issuing the day's household orders. I must speak to you before calling hours, so there is no time for you to instruct Mrs. Benning." She pursed her lips. "There will be joint of beef, sole, and roast pheasant. No lamb."

She smiled. "Thank you, ma'am, for remembering."

"Hm." She clicked her tongue. "However, you must know you will be compelled to eat food which you may not like when you visit the homes of others. That is only polite."

"Yes, ma'am."

Mrs. Benning curtsied and fled, leaving them frighteningly alone.

The dowager arched an eyebrow. "And now, Davina, I must speak plainly about this private breakfast room. It, and the conduct it creates, are altogether too vulgar. You cavort there in your dressing gown like a—I am sorry I must say it—like a common doxy."

Davina gasped.

"You are shocked," observed the dowager. "I am glad to see that, for it proves you possess a healthy decency."

"But Adam is my husband," she protested weakly, sinking into a chair.

"What about the servants?"

"The meal is waiting when I arrive! Only once did a servant enter the room, and that was to announce your arrival, my lady. I interpret that as a sort of emergency."

"Nevertheless, it did occur." The dowager waved her finger. "And it could happen again."

"But . . ."

Lady Trowbridge continued. "Nor should you exhibit yourself in such a fashion to your husband. It is crude."

Davina could scarcely believe what she was hearing. Adam had seen her in all stages of dress—and undress. Wasn't that part of marriage? Granted, it had taken her quite a while to grow accustomed to it, but now she had nothing to hide. He knew her, all of her, and he thought she was beautiful. Besides, her dressing gown covered her more thoroughly than a large number of her dresses. Lady Trowbridge was a prude. And she was wrong.

"Adam likes our casual mornings," she defended, hoping that would dissuade his mother from further lecturing.

"Of course he does. What man wouldn't? That is why so many of the gender have mistresses."

Davina gaped.

"I have scandalized you again." She chuckled. "You are probably vastly surprised that I have the temerity to admit to the existence of such women, but we both know they exist, do we not? Unfortunately, due to your behavior, I am forced to disregard propriety and speak of them. Davina, don't you realize you are behaving as Adam's mistress instead of his wife?"

"I don't understand."

"I doubted you did. That is why I have brought up the subject." She settled back in her chair. "Do fetch us a glass of sherry, my gel. We are going to have a very earnest talk, and I believe the bracing effects of wine are in order."

"Yes, ma'am." Stunned, Davina rose and walked woodenly to the sideboard. What could Lady Trowbridge mean to say to her? This was awful! She thought she'd merely be scolded for ignoring her "guest," but this? Why was this so wrong?

She returned with the drinks.

"Are you ready to commence?" asked the countess.

Davina nodded. "But I cannot understand what I am doing wrong."

"Haven't you even a hint?" the older woman shrilled. "I mentioned your lounging about in your dressing robe and encouraging Adam to do the same. That is the behavior of a gentleman's mistress! A respectable wife does not parade herself *en déshabillé* in front of her husband. Where did you get that idea? From your mother?"

"No!" Davina said hotly. "Mother dresses and comes down for breakfast every morning."

"Then where did you get the notion?" she demanded.

"I don't know." She shrugged weakly. "We just fell into the pattern in our hotel rooms on our wedding trip."

"You were served in your suite?"

"Yes. It seemed ridiculous to leap up and dress first." Davina was certainly not going to tell her mother-in-law she and Adam sometimes returned to bed after the meal.

The dowager shook her head. "Bad habits."

"People have breakfast in bed," Davina dared. "What is the difference?"

"A great deal. They dine alone, or a servant of their own gender might be present."

"But, ma'am, I assure you there are no servants about when we breakfast. The meal is already on the table."

"But your husband is there." Lady Trowbridge glared at her. "Can you not understand? How can he respect you when you are flaunting about *en déshabillé?*"

"I don't flaunt," Davina defended.

"Gad, you are dense." She made a moue of exasperation. "Suffice it to say that respectable people do not frequently go about in mixed company in their dressing gowns, whether they are married or not. It just isn't done. Adam knows this. He is treating you like a mistress, certainly not like a wife he respects. The same is true for kissing in public, such as I witnessed in the library."

Davina's cheeks burned.

The dowager smiled in smug delight. "Yes, you are right to blush. You were caught behaving improperly. You should never have welcomed an intimate embrace in such a location."

"We thought we were private," she murmured.

"A library is a public room. Moreover, when one employs servants, one can never be certain of privacy. The busybodies listen at doors and peek through keyholes. Have you ever noticed how speedily Pinkham comes when summoned? It is because he is eavesdropping."

Davina couldn't believe the Trowbridge staff spent much of its time engaged in clandestine activities, but she didn't voice her skepticism. Adam's mother would only argue. There was no point in debating her words.

"Intimacy can only be ventured very late at night," Lady Trowbridge expounded. "That eliminates stolen expressions of ardor *and* all other secluded enterprises, such as your breakfast behavior."

Davina sighed and slowly took a sip of her sherry. "Adam likes our leisurely mornings."

"Of course. What man wouldn't? But mark my words, he will not respect you for it. It makes you too familiar." She lowered her voice. "There are no bounds of propriety between a man and his mistress. He expects things of her he would never dream of asking a lady. He wants her to tease and exhibit herself in bedroom attire. She must always be available for his caresses. Can Adam be replacing a mistress with you?"

The thought that Adam might have had a mistress before marriage had never occurred to Davina. She knew he could not have one now, purely because he spent all his time with her. But what if—horror of horrors! What if Lady Trowbridge was right?

Adam's mother was studying her closely. "Men are frail when it comes to . . . certain pleasures. They wholly embrace loose behavior, but in their hearts they do not respect it."

Davina could scarcely believe Lady Trowbridge was saying these things. Advising her on social skills was acceptable. This was outside of enough!

At the same time, however, she'd given Davina cause to ponder. She and Adam were becoming more and more casual with each other, and she did respond to his lovemaking in what must be a very unladylike fashion. It certainly wasn't a duty, as her aunt had professed when advising her upon marriage. Maybe she *did* act like a mistress.

"A lady," went on Adam's mother, "is modest and virtuous. She is not forward and does not initiate amorous advances. She exudes an aura of delicacy, tenderness, and gentility. She incites a gentleman's sense of reverence."

Davina groaned inwardly. She had abandoned reserve on her honeymoon. Alone in her chamber with Adam, she did not behave like a lady.

"Enough of that!" Lady Trowbridge threw up her hands. "I shall speak on another topic, that of doing your duty to provide an heir."

Davina's mind swam. In a sense, the two subjects seemed at cross-purposes with each other. Not so, evidently, to the dowager.

"May I assume you are not presently in the state of fulfilling that obligation?"

She bent her head. "I don't think so."

"Well, you should be. You've had long enough." The dowager frowned. "You had best get busy, gel. That is your primary function to this family."

Her spirits fallen, Davina remained silent. She couldn't do anything right. It seemed there was nothing in the role of Countess Trowbridge she could perform. By now, she should be carrying Adam's child, but she wasn't. For that and the other reasons, maybe she did seem more like a mistress than a respected wife.

"Do you hear me, gel?" demanded Adam's mother. "You must do your duty."

"Yes, ma'am," she whispered.

"No more horseback riding. That creates more problems than I can bear to relate. You must trust me. Even your mother would say the same."

"Yes, ma'am," Davina repeated.

"No dancing."

"What?" she gulped. No more frisson-filled waltzes in Adam's arms? That seemed somewhat extreme.

"Dancing jolts one's system."

"Surely not a waltz!"

"All dancing," she said severely. "Do you want to be a dancer or a mother? Do you want to be a mistress or a wife? You had best heed me, Davina, for I am right."

Davina sighed.

"Well, I have given you a great deal to think about, haven't I?"

"Yes, ma'am," she nodded.

"Now we had best proceed to the drawing room, but I would like to say this, Davina. You pleased me last night on your friendship with Lady Gail. She is a delightful gel."

Davina's heart leaped with triumph from the unaccustomed praise. "I liked her very much. Unfortunately, she and Lord Hartland are leaving today for Brighton. They invited us to join them, but we politely declined because you had so recently come to visit us."

"Very good. I quite approve of your response." A ghost of an actual smile astoundingly flitted across her mouth. "You see how easy life is when you adhere to my philosophy? You will learn. Ah, yes. I do believe you will eventually become a true Trowbridge countess, one we will be proud of."

Eleven

Adam deliberately lunched from a tray in the library to throw his mother off balance, then carefully orchestrated his intended meeting with her. Where she was concerned, it was impossible to gain the upper hand, but at least he could physically set himself on an equal footing.

The interview would take place in his own arena without prior warning. When the hour arrived, he moved a chair to the opposite side of his desk. There she would sit, like a subordinate. He took his usual working position, shuffled papers to give the appearance he was a busy man, and sent Pinkham to fetch her.

After a long wait that clearly bespoke her attitude to his summons, she arrived. "What do you want of me, Adam? I am occupied. Davina and I are readying ourselves to make calls this afternoon."

"I wish to speak with you on a matter of importance," he said, half rising and waving her to the chair.

She pursed her lips. "Had you attended luncheon, you could have done so then."

"I wanted to address you alone."

She inclined her head, settling herself. "Do be brief. As I have explained, I am going out."

"Yes, Mother. I am busy, too." He made an issue of setting documents aside. "I want to speak to you about Davina."

"Naturally. What else could I expect? I must say I am pleased your wife has taken up friendship with Lady Gail."

"She's all right, I suppose," he allowed.

"Adam, she is more than all right. She is impeccable *ton*." She clicked her tongue. "My goodness, can I not compliment Davina on her choice of companion? She has made an important step to her goal."

"And what is that?" he was compelled to ask, though it gave her an opportunity to control the conversation.

She shrugged. "Why, to become a good wife to you, of course."

"Mother, she already is," he began, but she overpowered him.

"You know an important part of being your wife is being socially adept. You are not an ordinary man. You are an earl, and you are a Trowbridge. I wish you would not continually try to deny it."

Neatly, she had placed him on the defensive. "I do not take my responsibilities lightly, madam."

"No? You give the impression of having embarked upon a fantasy. You want to hide in your rooms with that gel and ignore duty and proper etiquette." She leaned forward, frowning. "When have you visited your estates? What of your seat in the House?"

He set his jaw. His planned discourse had disintegrated into nothing but an argument, as always!

"The wife you have chosen must take her proper place. She does not know what she is doing, and you are not guiding her. You are doing her a grave disservice." She stuck out her chin. "If you refuse to direct her, you should allow me to do so, and stay out of my way."

"For God's sake!" he erupted. "Anyone can interact with Society!"

"That is easy for you to say. You grew up with it. Davina did not."

"There is plenty of time for all that."

"No, there is not!" she cried. "People are judging her. Adam, she is so overset by Society she cannot even pour tea without rattling the china! Why do you think I came up to London? Because people are gossiping about your inept countess!"

"Mother, please! Must everything always become an altercation?" he shouted. "Cannot we maintain a modicum of calm deliberation?"

She sat back in her chair, twitching her nose. "Apparently not. Not when you insist upon burying your head in the sand."

He took a deep breath and tried to speak softly. "Cease meddling in my marriage, Mother."

She, too, lowered her voice. "I am only trying to help."

"I do not need it."

"You will, when you find yourself cast beyond the pale. And then what?" She slowly shook her head. "Maybe you don't care about yourself or your wife, but what of your children? You know how important Society will be to their futures. They will never forgive you this nonsense. Why are you being so stubborn?"

He sighed. "I just want to be left alone."

"You gave up that right when you were born the heir to the earldom," she said severely. "What has that gel done to you?"

"She has shown me there is more to life than duty," he said morosely.

"Not for an earl, Adam. Not for an earl."

Blushing deeply, Davina backed away from the library door, knowing that the hovering footman was well aware she was eavesdropping. Even if she had the nerve to continue, she couldn't have heard without pressing her ear to the keyhole. The voices were dropping too low. She glanced surreptitiously at the servant. He was staring up at the ceiling, but otherwise standing alertly, awaiting her direction.

"Evidently, they are in serious discussion, so I will not disturb them," she explained, hoping to excuse her spying.

He lowered his gaze.

"I shall walk in the garden." She darted down the hall. The footman attended a pace behind.

Davina glanced back. "I know the way."

He recognized the dismissal and bowed, turning back.

She hastened out into the afternoon sun, but she could not enjoy the balmy breeze and the sweet scent of flowers. The discourse between Adam and his mother had worried her more than she could say. Adam might bravely defend her, but Lady Trowbridge was right. They had great responsibility of position. They were ignoring it.

She wandered down myriad brick paths and found refuge on a stone bench under an arbor of early roses. Dear Heavens! Could she get her jumbled thoughts in order?

From the beginning, she had known that she must learn her new role of countess. She was not really prepared for it. Thinking of some of her behavior with Adam, she wondered if she was even a lady. In retrospect, it seemed she had made so many mistakes. She must correct them and accept her noble status. Everyone, even Fifi, seemed to tell her different things. It was time to sort it all out.

First, Adam was an earl. Their honeymoon was keeping him from his duties. That must cease. Hadn't she and Lady Gail, a kindred soul, agreed honeymoons couldn't last forever? It was time to go on with life.

Secondly, she was his countess. She had her duties, too. She must be his hostess and social adjunct, manage his household, and bear his heirs. So far, she'd done nothing but haphazardly reorganize domestic arrangements. She was neglecting her responsibilities.

Now, what to do about it? She nibbled her lip. The grand Lady Trowbridge was here. She may as well graciously allow the dowager to lead her through the social labyrinth of the *haute ton*. Her learned grace would reflect prettily back upon Adam. No longer would she cause china to rattle or create any other embarrassment for the Trowbridge family, and she would know how to direct her own daughters, when and if the time came for that.

Hopefully, there soon would be a son or daughter, but there did not seem to be much she could do to accelerate that event. Oh, yes, she would refrain from riding and dancing and any strenuous activities. She longed to know her mother's thoughts on the subject, but she would never benefit by that. The new Countess Trowbridge would certainly never stoop to visit Halderton Manor. That would be one sure way to lose her husband's love and respect.

Adam. *Respect.* She must withdraw a bit and test the waters. She had probably been too forward. She remembered his slight flushes. Yes, that must be it. He was embarrassed by her passion. Well, she would behave in a more ladylike fashion.

"My lady?" Fifi's voice floated through the shrubbery.

"I am here!"

Fifi burst into the bower. "A footman said I'd find you here."

"Yes." Davina forced a smile. "Isn't this a pleasant spot?"

Fifi bobbed her head in the affirmative. "I'm to tell you the old countess is looking for you. She is waiting to go visiting."

"Yes, I am ready." She stood. "Am I presentable?"

The abigail surveyed her simple willow green ensemble. "You are beautiful."

"Then we shall hope I pass Lady Trowbridge's scrutiny."

"That one does not know fashion!" Fifi impulsively severed a white rose with her sharp fingernail and inserted it in Davina's Grecian knot.

"It isn't too much?" Davina asked worriedly. "I do not wish to appear maidenly or gauche."

"It lends *madame* a nice delicacy."

"Very well. Let us go then." She walked swiftly to the house, her maid trailing behind her. As they entered, Fifi made a slight adjustment to the flower, then bid her adieu.

Adam and his mother were awaiting her in the hall.

"I have found the most lovely place to sit in the garden," she told them.

"Indeed?" said her husband with interest. "I should like to join you there."

"We have no time for trifling," pronounced the dowager.

"Not now, I know," he acknowledged. "Perhaps when you return."

"This is a busy time," said the dowager. "We have an enormous number of rout parties to attend tonight. Why do they plan them all for the same evening?"

"There is always much planned for every evening," Adam said brusquely. "I thought we might stay home tonight."

"My goodness, no!" she cried. "It is impossible."

"Perhaps Davina would prefer . . ." he ventured.

Davina smiled sadly. "I would love an evening with you, but alas, duty calls."

"That is the spirit!" applauded his mother.

When they arrived home, Davina was weary but pleased with the results of her efforts. They had actually called upon the fearsome Mrs. Drummond Burrell and had been well received. Well, the dowager had been well received, but the haughty matron had deigned to nod with a distant acceptance upon closely examining Davina from head to toe.

"So I see, Eleanor, you have taken this young lady under your wing. That is commendable, I assure you," she proclaimed in her high, haughty voice. "And you, dear gel, will pay close heed to what your mother-in-law tells you. She is of magnificent *ton,* you know."

"I am honored by her interest," Davina managed to say.

"Oh, but she must take concern," came the nasal, top-lofty tones. "Whatever would happen to the Trowbridges if she did not?"

Davina supposed that was a setdown aimed at her Halderton antecedents, but instead of angering her, it strengthened her will to become the perfect countess. She would show Mrs. Drummond Burrell. She would show them all! When tea was served, she concentrated very hard and avoiding rattling her cup as she returned it to her saucer. If nothing more was accomplished this day, that was enough.

"Mrs. Drummond Burrell seemed to approve of you," Lady Trowbridge mused as they removed their bonnets and gave them to Pinkham. "I am pleased. While I would not deem it a conquest, she did speak directly to you."

"Yes, ma'am." Spirits high, Davina took a deep breath. "Lady Trowbridge, might we have a glass of sherry together before retiring to dress for dinner? We could discuss the afternoon. Maybe Adam could join us, too."

Her husband's mother seemed taken aback. "Yes, I suppose there is time. Pinkham, you will serve us, and see that Lord Trowbridge is informed of his lady's request."

The dowager chose the informal salon for the venue. She sank, half reclining, onto the sofa. "La, I am quite fatigued. I am not as young as I used to be!"

Davina laughed politely, her hopes rising. Perhaps the lady was too tired to make the rounds of the rout parties. Maybe they could stay at home.

"But never fear, I shall revive by this evening," the countess pledged.

"Do not overtire yourself for my sake," Davina begged.

She narrowed her eyes. "Do not think to get 'round your duty by feigned concern for me, my gel. I know you don't want to go."

Davina couldn't help smiling.

"Trickster!" accused Lady Trowbridge, but she actually chuckled.

"Do I hear Mother laughing?" Adam asked, entering the room. "My ears must be failing me."

Davina giggled. "I do believe you did."

"Very well," his mother responded in a mock snap, "I will admit to the mirth."

"If the two of you are in such fine moods, the afternoon must have been a success."

"I think it was," Davina said, accepting a glass from Pinkham. "Ma'am, do you agree?"

The dowager thoughtfully sipped her sherry. "Yes, it was. Davina is well on her way to becoming acquainted with the cream of the *ton,* and they are acknowledging her presence. In time, they will come to accept her wholeheartedly, if she does not err."

Davina saw Adam's jaw begin to tense and reached over to squeeze his hand. "I am very pleased with the day's events. Mrs. Drummond Burrell truly conversed with me."

"If talking with that old harpy makes you happy, then I am delighted for you." He kissed her fingers and turned to his brandy.

"Adam Trowbridge!" scolded his mother. "You know how important Mrs. Drummond Burrell can be in a young woman's future."

He rolled his eyes. "If you say so. I am only glad to see the two of you pleased with the outing."

Davina perceived how difficult for him it must be when his wife and his mother were at swords' points. It was part of her responsibility to make him comfortable in his home. She would try very hard to get along with the dowager.

"I am delighted to have garnered attention from Mrs. Burrell," she said, "but I am even more proud to have gained approval from you, ma'am."

"Ha!" the dowager said merrily. "Do not think you will escape those rout parties."

Davina laughed. "I *want* to go. I want to repeat my success."

"With that attitude, I believe you will."

Adam looked suspiciously from one to the other. "I suppose I can bear this nonsense. The Season is almost ended."

"Then will come the house parties," his mother advised.

"I am going to take Davina to Brighton."

Lady Trowbridge groaned. "I despise that place. It is too muggy and salty. It causes my lips to crack."

"Of course, you do not have to go," he said quickly. "I would not force you, Mother."

"There will be social activities, and Davina will need my sponsorship."

"Lady Gail will be there," he tantalized. "She and Davina will go on nicely."

"Yes, but still . . ." She contemplated. "I will think about it. I can always put salve on my lips."

"I wouldn't dream of asking you to discomfit yourself," Adam rushed on. "No, I will not allow it."

"We'll see," she said.

Davina, hoping to elude her mother-in-law, struggled to disguise her disappointment. But she must make the best of it. If Lady Trowbridge decided to go, there was nothing anyone could do about it.

Adam stood and strode to the sideboard to replenish his glass of brandy, returning with it and the bottle of sherry to freshen the ladies' drinks.

"This will be all, Davina," the dowager advised, "and partake very slightly of wine at dinner. You will be drinking champagne at any number of homes tonight, and you must not have too much. Few things condemn a lady's reputation more swiftly than having too much to drink."

"Davina does not overly imbibe," Adam declared.

"I know she does not. But no amount of little reminders

ever go amiss. You will realize that when you are rearing children."

He sighed.

"Moreover, champagne can sometimes slip up on one and intoxicate very speedily. Remember that, Davina," she finished.

"I shall," Davina promised. She wondered if the countess was hearkening back to the morning of her arrival, when Adam had given Davina the brandy-laced coffee for her headache. Did Lady Trowbridge really know? She would take care nothing like that happened again.

They soon finished their drinks and proceeded upstairs to prepare for dinner and the evening ahead. Adam accompanied Davina into her chamber and took her in his arms.

"Darling, we do have some time to spend together before dinner."

"Not much." She briefly rested her head against his shoulder. "In addition to bathing, I must wash my hair. It takes so long to dry. I suppose it would be more practical to cut it."

"Don't you dare!" he exclaimed. "Your hair is your crowning glory."

"I do not need that now," she quipped. "You have provided me with a tiara. I wonder how it will look on me?"

"For a moment, do forget about being a countess and promise me you won't bob your hair. I love it just as it is."

"I forget about being a countess all too often." She stood on tiptoe to kiss his cheek. "But I vow I will not cut my hair."

"Thank you, my love. Would you like to see the tiara now?" he offered.

"I would, but I really haven't the time." She kissed him again and stepped out of his embrace. "I must ring for Fifi."

"Come now, Davina," he softly cajoled. "It is early."

Her stomach began to knot. It took so long for her hair

to dry. Why couldn't he understand how momentous it was that she looked her best? Mrs. Drummond Burrell and people like her would be watching. She had made much progress today, and she couldn't afford to lose it.

"Help me pick out what to wear, Adam." She took his hand and led him to her dressing room, catching the bell rope as she passed.

"This wasn't what I had in mind," he muttered.

"I know." She touched his cheek. "But I have no choice. Please understand."

He looked for a moment as if he were going to press her further, then relented, grinning. "I'll tell you the gown I like. The sapphire Parisian one. Among the Trowbridge jewels is a diamond-and-sapphire parure that will look well with it."

She smiled brilliantly. "Oh, thank you. That will be just the thing! And I will wear my white velvet cape. I'm glad you have a favorite, Adam."

"Sincerely, I like all your gowns. You are very special in each one of them." He brought her hands to his lips. "You will be beautiful, as always, but we'll make an early evening of it?"

Davina doubted that was possible, unless his mother became too tired to continue. "I hope so."

The door clicked as Fifi entered the chamber. Davina drew her hands away from Adam's caress. "I must begin my preparations."

"If you must." He reluctantly left her.

She slumped, suddenly overwhelmed with exhaustion. "Fifi, do send for my bath. There isn't much time, for I must wash my hair as well."

"Yes, my lady." The maid peered at her. "You are tired. Why not get into bed while you wait?"

"That is a good idea." Fifi removed Davina's dress and tucked her into a dressing gown. Davina debated following Adam into his room. They could lie down together.

She thrust the thought from her mind. More would occur than she bargained for, and she would be even more worn out afterward. She sought her own bed, crawling beneath the cool sheets.

Almost before she knew it, Fifi was waking her up. "Your bath is ready, my lady."

Davina agonizingly rose, actually wondering how she would get through this evening. "I wonder where Adam's mother gets all her stamina?"

"That old hag tires you out by making you nervous," Fifi opined.

"Perhaps that is so." But even if it was, there was still the frantic schedule to take into account. "I must begin getting more sleep."

Fifi lifted an eyebrow, giggling. "Good luck at that, my lady!"

Davina blushed and busied herself with her bath. Adam wanted an early evening so they could be together. She would be too tired for lovemaking, and how could she tell him that? Oh, Lord. Today she had begun trying to be all things to all people. How would she ever keep up the pace?

A tear slipped down her cheek. Adam must understand. He was her husband, lover, best friend. Surely he could be patient while she learned to do what she must. It wouldn't last forever.

Twelve

It was a late night. Arriving home exhausted, Davina wondered how Adam's mother could be so indefatigable. Vaguely she heard Adam instructing the dowager that he and Davina would be breakfasting in their private dining room. She started up the stairs, not hesitating to listen to the lady's reply. Of course, she recalled the countess's interpretation of the mornings *en déshabillé,* but she didn't even care about that. She was just too weary. All she wanted to do was to get out of her gown and collapse in bed.

Fifi was waiting for her. "How did it go? Were you a success?"

"I think so."

She had received a friendly nod from Lady Sefton, another of the formidable Almack's hostesses. This did not possess the level of difficulty of garnering approval from Mrs. Drummond Burrell, for Lady Sefton was noted for her sweetness and kind heart. Still, she had never attracted the countess's attention until Lady Trowbridge had gone into action.

"I just want to go to bed." Davina yawned. "I am spent beyond all belief."

Fifi hastened to aid in the undressing. "Poor lady. You must sleep late in the morning. The old shrew will probably not leave her room until afternoon."

"I feel as if I could sleep all day." She slipped into a

white negligee and wearily performed her nightly ablutions. "As if I could!"

"You must take care of yourself." Fifi bundled her into bed and pulled up the sheets. "Good night, my lady."

"Good night, and thank you for being here, right when I needed you most." She was asleep almost as soon as she spoke the words.

Later, she was remotely aware of Adam getting into bed and taking her into his arms. "I am just too tired," she murmured and slept again.

Then before it seemed possible, he was waking her up. "It's morning, darling."

"That isn't possible," she mumbled, turning away.

"It is. In fact, it's late in the morning." He kissed her hair and drew her close.

"I don't care. Your mama can dine alone."

He caressed her back. "I wasn't thinking of breakfast."

"Oh, Adam, please leave me alone." She turned over and pulled the sheet over her head.

When she awakened again, he was gone. The bed wasn't even warm where he'd lain. He must not even be breakfasting, for she heard Fifi humming and opening and closing drawers in her dressing room. The day had long started without her. She didn't even care.

There was a soft rap at the door. Fifi tiptoed to answer it. *"Oui, madame?"*

"Who are you?" came the demanding voice of Lady Trowbridge. "Where is Draper?"

"The old prune? I take care of my lady now. My lady fired that ancient, stupid excuse of a dresser."

"What? Draper was a highly skilled lady's maid!"

Fifi snapped her fingers. "That one knew nothing of fashion. Dressed my lady like an old woman!"

"How dare you, girl?" Adam's mother screeched. "I will not tolerate your impertinence. You are fired!"

"Ooh, la, you can't do that. Now go away. My lady is sleeping."

With a stab of dread, Davina sat up. "No, I'm not."

Lady Trowbridge pushed past Fifi and strode into the room. "You will get rid of this sharp-tongued urchin."

"I am not an urchin, whatever that is!" the maid asserted. "I am French lady!"

"You are a French peon, and you should have your mouth washed with soap for your cheekiness!" The countess clicked her tongue.

"Please!" begged Davina. Momentarily surprised she was still clad in her nightrail, she swung over the side of the bed, feeling for her slippers.

Fifi rushed to slide the satin, feather-trimmed confections onto her feet. "What a way to wake up. That old . . ."

"Hush!" Davina commanded in a forceful tone that astonished them both. Apologetic for her intensity, she tried to temper it with a smile. "Fifi, please fetch tea, won't you? Lady Trowbridge, will you join me in some refreshment?"

"Very well, if this saucy hireling will get out."

"Fifi, please," Davina interjected to head off a tart rejoinder.

The servant minced from the room, twitching her hips.

"Prissy minx," the dowager denounced. "Why did you let Draper go? She was a very experienced, talented dresser."

"We didn't suit. Please excuse me, ma'am, for a moment." Davina crossed to her dressing room to enact her morning routine. She had hoped to avoid controversy concerning Fifi. With great luck, she could smooth over the matter, especially if Adam's mother was pleased with the results of last night's rout parties. She said a quick prayer that Fifi would keep her mouth shut when she returned.

"Do not take the time to dress!" Lady Trowbridge called. "I wish to converse with you, and there are only the two of us."

"Yes, ma'am." Davina donned her dressing gown and returned to the chamber. "Shall we sit in the breakfast room?"

"Certainly not! I refuse to set foot in that brothel!"

"Ma'am," she said gently, "I think you would find the room is done up in good taste. There are soft tones of paint and fabrics, pretty watercolors, and—"

"It's not what it looks like. It's what goes on there!" she barked. "But that, of course, has come to an end."

Davina sighed and led her to the sofa by the hearth.

"When I came here, I ascertained Adam was not hanging about, so I knew we would be alone. He has gone to his club." She sat down, fastidiously arranging her skirt.

Davina felt a wave of disappointment. "I fear I failed him by sleeping so late."

"Fustian! You are a busy woman, so I'm sure you were weary," she pronounced. "You must have your beauty sleep if you are to become the toast of the *ton*."

This was a new development. "I only wish to be a proper countess," she reminded her mother-in-law.

"You shall. We are making great strides in a very short time. Do you see how easy it is when you heed my instructions?"

"Yes, ma'am," she said honestly. "I am truly amazed."

"Hmmph!" The dowager tossed her head. "You underestimated my power. But I have not finished speaking about that servant of yours. I have fired her, and you must accept that."

Davina's heart raced. No, she would not. Fifi was instrumental in her modish appearance.

"Lady Trowbridge, I grant you Fifi was very bold this morning. She is unusually protective of me. Do you not prize loyalty in a servant?"

"Absolutely, but I do not admire impudence. The girl is above herself."

"I am working on that," Davina lied. "I wish to give her

a second chance. She has a sense of style that is invaluable. And if you wish me to be the toast of the *ton . . .*"

The countess worked her jaw. "I do not approve of insolence."

"I'm sure Fifi is sorry. The quick French temper, you know. Oh, Lady Trowbridge, I want to work so hard to make my mark in Society. If I must install a new abigail, it will be a definite distraction."

Adam's mother considered. "Very well, but I shall hear no words of effrontery from that French mouth."

"No, ma'am. I shall scold Fifi fearfully," she vowed. "It will not happen again."

"See that it doesn't, or the girl must leave," she declared. "Now, Davina, we shall plan our day."

Before the dowager had launched into a flurry of plans, Fifi returned with a tea tray and placed it on the table beside Davina.

"Go on with you, girl." Lady Trowbridge flicked her fingers.

The servant squared her shoulders.

Davina hastily intervened. "Fifi, please press the yellow muslin. I shall wear it this afternoon."

"That plain English rag?" the dresser asked.

Lady Trowbridge snapped her fingers. "Do it, girl, with no sass!"

Muttering to herself, Fifi strolled toward the dressing room.

The countess shook her head. "You will never change that one."

"But I must try." Davina eyed the teapot and cups. She must also try to pour the brew without clinking the china.

Adam's mother noticed her hesitation. "For heaven's sake, get on with it!"

"Yes, ma'am." Concentrating very hard, she managed the feat. Relief flooded over her.

The dowager's nod of sanction was as gratifying as a gift of jewels. "You'll do . . . eventually."

"Everything is becoming easier."

"That is because your attitude has improved."

That must be true. Everything seemed brighter today, except that she missed Adam's company. Well, she would see him at nuncheon. Maybe then they could go for a carriage ride in the park. His mother could not object to that.

"We will be at home to callers today," pronounced Lady Trowbridge, throwing cold water on that idea, "so our day will not be so tiring. Tonight is a very important ball. Everyone who is anyone will be there. You must have your wits about you, Davina."

"I shall." She was disappointed, but somehow she would squeeze in some time with Adam. Since the plans weren't quite so frantic, she would not be as weary when they returned from the ball.

"Well, then." Lady Trowbridge finished her tea and rose. "I shall see you at nuncheon. I assume the yellow gown is suitable for afternoon entertaining."

"Yes, ma'am."

"Do be sure it is. One flaw can cause you a great setback."

Davina stood. "You will not be dissatisfied."

"Hmmph!" Adam's mother snorted. "That girl whom you think is so knowledgeable about fashion did not like it."

She smiled. "Only because she knows it isn't French."

She accompanied her mother-in-law to the door and bid farewell, with relief. Things were improving in their relationship, but there was still great stress. She thought of the day ahead, and again longed to be with Adam. She would make time after lunch for a coze with him in the library. If callers arrived, she could hurry to the drawing room. Yes, that would do perfectly! Surely Lady Trowbridge would have no objections.

She returned to the sofa and poured herself another cup

of tea. Fifi should be returning soon with the dress. She *must* caution the Frenchwoman to bite her tongue when it came to Lady Trowbridge. That was the first thing she'd do. Then she would prepare for what, hopefully, would be a pleasant day.

"Adam!" the gentleman who had been his best friend before he married Davina hailed him from across the card room.

"Charles." He made his way among the tables to join him.

"I'm finished here." The viscount tossed in his cards and stood. "My luck's no good today. Besides, I'd rather talk with you. My God, I haven't seen you in an age! Let's have a drink."

They proceeded to the bar and ordered up brandy.

"I wonder who's won the wagers," Charles Draycount mused. "There's been spirited betting on when you'd finally grace White's with your presence. Things rather died down until your mother arrived in town, then wagers picked up again. Someone, no doubt, has won a vast amount of money on you, Adam."

He arched an eyebrow. "I am overjoyed."

His friend chuckled. "I'm sure you are. What caused your flight from home? Too many women?"

"You might say so. Since Mother's arrival, the emphasis has been on social events. Utter boredom, Charles." He turned to lean against the bar and survey the room. "It doesn't look much more interesting here."

"Maybe not, but it's better than dancing attendance on the grand old arbiters of the *ton*. I can provide more entertainment than that," he offered. "Stay for lunch. Then go with me to Holyoak's mews. I'm trying out a team he's been trying to sell me."

"The grays?"

"No, it's a pair he brought up from the country. He'd never part with those grays, more's the pity. I've been trying to buy them this century."

"I know." Adam grinned. "Maybe these will be just as good."

Charles shrugged. "I doubt it, but they're worth a trial. Do say you'll come. I could use another opinion."

Adam hesitated. He hadn't seen Davina all day. She had been too sleepy to get up for breakfast, so he'd dined alone and hated it. For a short time, he had amused himself in the library, but she still hadn't joined him. She'd be present for luncheon, but so would his mother. The talk would be filled with social engagements. He almost wished he hadn't told Davina to cooperate, especially since she seemed to be enjoying it so much. Where did that leave him?

"Come on," Charles pressed. "It'll be fun."

"All right," he decided. One of White's beefsteaks and a bit of male company would provide a change.

"Excellent—though I don't want to be accused of stealing you from your lady's company."

"Davina will forgive you."

"I hope so. Good God, I suppose I'll have to get myself leg-shackled someday. Tell me, how is married life?" He signaled the barkeep to refill their glasses.

Adam smiled, slightly flushing. "I highly recommend it."

"She's everything you thought she would be?"

"And more." He thought of Davina's sensuous curves and almost resolved to go home instead of spending the day with the viscount.

"You're lucky. How many men do you think would agree?"

"Not as many as there should be." He shrugged. "Finding the perfect mate is a matter of taking one's time."

"Prittle-prattle!" Charles chortled. "After one glimpse of Davina, you were head over heels! Take your time? Ha!

You were off on the chase as hard as a hound on a five-minute trail."

Adam laughed good-naturedly. He couldn't dispute it. After seeing Davina, he'd had only one thought in his mind: to wed—well, actually, it was more basic than that.

His friend whacked him on the shoulder. "Damme, I'm glad for you, but I miss you, too. Don't play least in sight. The honeymoon's over."

Adam was beginning to tire of hearing that, but evidently it was true. Other matters were intruding upon their togetherness. Surely, however, the sweetness would never end. They were too close for that to happen. He didn't want to think about it.

"Let us have lunch now, Charles," he said quickly. "I'm famished."

Adam didn't come home for luncheon. Dining alone with the dowager and chattering of social trifles, Davina had been miserable. He didn't come home before callers came, either. Thank goodness they'd had a throng of visitors. The crowded drawing room had cheered her and taken her mind off his absence, but she still missed him dreadfully. When he didn't come home when it was time to prepare for dinner, Davina was totally overset. As she dressed, she sent Fifi to the window every time she heard carriage wheels. When that was not enough, she was compelled to go herself.

"He is gaming with his friends," Fifi said airily.

Chewing her lip, Davina fidgeted in the dressing table chair. "It's so late."

"Gentlemen." Fifi made an elaborate Gallic shrug. "They pay no attention to time."

"Adam does . . . I suppose. At least, I thought he might." She jumped to her feet as she heard the ring of horses' hooves and ran to the window. Below, Adam leaped from his curricle, tossed the reins to his tiger, and dashed into the house.

"He's home!" she cried and rushed into his room, thoroughly startling Turnbull, who dropped a parcel of unmentionables he'd been putting away.

"Adam!" she shrieked as he entered the chamber, and threw herself into his arms.

"Darling!" He stepped back, off balance, then caught her. "What is this?"

"I missed you!" she told him. "It has been an eternity."

"Not quite." He grinned, kissing her quickly on the lips. "But I am sorry. I didn't realize it was becoming so late. I'll dress quickly for dinner, though. I won't be tardy."

She giggled. "Didn't you once tell me Lord and Lady Trowbridge are never late?"

"Indeed so, but I'll be speedy. We'll have a drink before dinner. Then afterward, we'll have an early evening. Mother can entertain herself."

"Oh, Adam." She bit her lip. "There is a ball tonight."

"Damn!" He frowned.

She winced. "I know. But your mother says it is most important."

He dropped his hands to his sides. "Very well. I don't suppose I can do anything about it. Is it possible to leave early?"

She lowered her gaze. "I doubt it."

"All right. Now go about finishing your toilette, darling, while I commence mine. I'll meet you downstairs." He kissed her forehead and strode to his dressing room.

"To Hades!" whispered Davina and returned to her chamber. This was difficult. She wished she could stay at home with him and let Lady Trowbridge go to the ball. But that was ridiculous. It would accomplish nothing.

Adam's irritation continued through dinner, ruining a particularly delicious roast pheasant and causing conversation to flounder. With the exception of his mother, everyone from his wife to the lowliest server was on edge. Davina wished they could abandon their social plans and stay at home.

"I hope you will resurrect your charm before we arrive at the ball," Lady Trowbridge told him dryly, after dessert was dispensed.

He coolly lifted an eyebrow. "Doesn't a Trowbridge always know how to behave?"

"Indeed so," she replied just as frigidly. "That is our purpose. To make Davina just as experienced."

"I hope it doesn't take very long."

"That is up to your wife, isn't it?"

Davina kept her gaze low and picked at her cream puff. This wasn't the time to utter a word. Both of them could very well pounce on her. It wasn't fair. She was trying so hard.

She was glad when the awful meal ended. She accompanied Lady Trowbridge to the informal salon for coffee. Adam remained in the dining room for his port.

"It was pleasant when Adam took his port with us," she ventured.

"I am glad he has ceased that practice. It was not proper." Her mother-in-law motioned her to pour.

She smiled wistfully. "It's just family, and we haven't been together all day."

"If appropriate etiquette is not cultivated every day, it withers on the vine."

"But . . ."

"No buts, young lady. That is the way it is." Lady Trowbridge studied her closely as she managed to serve without incident. "Well done, Davina."

"Thank you, ma'am." She sipped the warm brew and hoped the port would put Adam into a better mood.

It didn't. At the ball, when he discovered his mother had prohibited his wife from dancing, he disappeared into the card room. As a result, Davina spent the evening beside

Lady Trowbridge, with no respite from the tension of chatting with the dowager's haughty friends. At supper, she found herself stressfully seated at the side of a portly duke, and at the table of Mrs. Drummond Burrell. Before she had taken her first bite of salmon patty, she felt a hand on her knee. Careful to maintain her agreeable expression, she pushed it away.

The assault continued throughout the repast, until Davina plucked a piece of the skin over the lofty peer's knuckle and pinched it hard between her fingernails. His Grace choked on his champagne and had to leave the table. He did not return.

"Poor man," noted Mrs. Burrell. "Such an unfortunate event."

Davina was furious, but she took care to hide her true feelings under a mask of polite composure. Duke or not, the old knave had it coming to him. That he was of very high *ton* made no difference to her. It was Adam's fault, too. If he had stayed by her, the ancient reprobate might not have attempted his familiarity in the first place.

The whole evening had given her an immense headache. After supper, she told the dowager of her malady, adding, "I must go home, else my face will register my affliction and cause comment."

"Very well, Davina," she nodded, surprisingly genial. "The hour is late anyway. Find your husband, and we shall take our leave."

She located Adam in the card room, playing whist with other gentlemen. She bent to his ear. "I must leave. I have a brilliant headache."

"In a moment, my dear."

She watched him finish the hand and begin another one. "Adam, please, I must go."

"Soon, Davina."

Half an hour passed before he rose from the game. By then her head was pounding harder, and her temper was short. She took his arm and managed to smile graciously to those in the room, as they left.

"You knew I was miserable," she hissed. "How could you put me off like that?"

"Duty, my dear." He smiled coolly.

She set her jaw. "To whom?"

"To my fellow card players," he said. "Don't you understand?"

"No! What about me?" she demanded.

"The countess Trowbridge worships duty above all else."

She bit her lip and murmured, "But what of your wife?"

"My wife *is* the countess Trowbridge," he said coldly.

They rode home in barbed silence, with his mother looking curiously from one to the other. Upon their arrival, Davina reminded them of her headache and immediately fled to her chamber. Adam did not follow.

For the first time since they had wed, Davina and Adam slept alone.

Morning brought a sense of strangeness. Waking alone, Davina reached drowsily for Adam in the hope he had joined her after she had fallen asleep, but she knew in her heart he hadn't.

Unhappiness washed over her. This couldn't be happening. Discord befell other couples, not them. She sat up, staring at the expanse of white bedclothes. This big bed was not intended for one person. It was meant to be shared.

What had happened? With a heavy ache in her chest, she swung over the side of the bed and dangled her feet, staring at the floor and wondering what she should do. The clock struck eight. According to past scheduling, she and Adam should be breakfasting. She looked longingly toward the breakfast room door, but it was firmly shut. Of course, she wasn't supposed to give in to improper desires and dine there at all, but if he had been there right now, she would have cheerfully joined him.

She slid from the bed, donned her slippers and dressing gown, and padded to the forbidden door, pausing to listen. All was quiet, and there were no delicious aromas of ham and bacon wafting from within. To be certain, she peeked in. The room was empty, the chairs neatly placed against the table. Davina bit her lip. What should she do now?

She walked hesitantly to Adam's chamber door and laid her hand on the knob. Though she had no idea if he was within, she seemed to perceive his presence like a palpable entity. There was no lock. She could enter. But would he dislike her intrusion?

This was Adam! This was the man she loved, the person she was closest to in all the world. Why did he suddenly seem like a stranger? She lay her cheek against the sleek wood, breathing in the faint fragrance of polish. She couldn't go in there. He might not want her. She wished she could cry, but the tears wouldn't come. Only a pounding ache evidenced her distress.

Why hadn't he come to her? If she went to him, she would feel like a discarded mistress pleading for the restoration of her position. She could not go.

Turning away, she walked to her dressing room and rang for Fifi, then began her morning routine. Things would sort themselves out. She and Adam loved each other. All would soon be well. He would come to her.

Thirteen

Adam was miserable, but he wasn't sure he blamed himself for the results of the foolish little tiff he and Davina had the night of the ball. He had been aggravated by her insistence on doing the social whirl that evening, especially since they'd been spending so little time together. He'd probably reacted to the outing like a spoiled brat.

But he hadn't liked her ordering him to drop out of the card game before its conclusion. She may have had a headache, but bearing with it was just as much social responsibility as attending the blasted gathering in the first place. She'd best learn to take the bad with the good.

Then, when they had returned home, she had made it plain she was terminating his company for the night. He'd hoped to go to her room, treat her headache with brandy and coffee, and tenderly cuddle her until she slept. But no, she wanted to be left alone.

In the morning, everything seemed worse. He was afraid to go to her for fear of rebuff. Davina was suddenly like a stranger. He didn't know what to do, so he went to his club.

When he returned home, Davina and his mother were entertaining callers. Then suddenly it was time to prepare for dinner and the evening's damned social events. And afterward . . . afterward, she looked very tired, strained, and pale, positively drooping by bedtime. He stayed in his own room.

And so it continued day after day, night after night. Davina slept, ate very little, and socialized. Adam went to his club and waited for the Season to end, wondering if he then would be subjected to endless country house parties. He knew he must do something about this unhappy state of affairs, but somehow it was just easier to maintain the status quo.

Davina was miserable. Awakening alone again, she looked wistfully at the closed breakfast room door. Those meals she had shared with Adam had been happy ones, even if they were risqué. At least they had been together, which was more than she could say now. According to the dowager, she was on the verge of being a wonderfully proper countess. She was readily acknowledged by Mrs. Drummond Burrell. But did Adam even notice?

She dragged herself from bed as Fifi entered with tea and a ewer of warm water. Nowadays it seemed she was always weary. Perhaps she should curtail her schedule, but she didn't want to disappoint Lady Trowbridge, who was working so tirelessly on her behalf.

"Good morning, Fifi." She forced a smile. "I trust you slept well?"

"*Oui,* my lady. Good morning." As she poured her pitcher of water into the basin, the Frenchwoman cast another peep through the door at the bed. "And you? Are you sure you wish to rise? You look weary, *madame.*"

Davina nodded. "I may as well. I did not sleep well, but I've a busy day ahead."

"Ladies should listen to their bodies," Fifi scolded.

"I shall, after the Season. Then I'll rest and rest and rest."

"I am glad, Madame, but . . ." Fifi arched an eyebrow, then bobbed her head. "It is no matter. *Madame* does as she wishes."

Davina washed and dried her face. "I think I shall wear the pink dress with the mint sash and embroidery this morning."

The gown was very light and feminine. It flattered her elegant curves and gave her an almost ethereal air. Adam would like it—if he happened to see it.

While her abigail sorted through the apparel, she sat down at her dressing table and poured herself a cup of tea from the tray Fifi had brought. A glimpse of herself in the mirror told her the worst. She looked as run-down as she felt. Her face was pallid and almost ashen. It seemed to hold nothing but forlorn blue eyes. Her heart wrenched. She looked like a ghost. It was just awful.

She stood for Fifi to clad her in the blush colored garment. "This will be a good choice for a day that promises to be quite warm."

The dresser scowled slightly.

Davina, too, frowned. "What is wrong?"

Fifi cocked her head. "Too pale."

"Yes, it is very soft, but for the heat—"

The abigail returned her to the dressing table and rummaged in her cosmetic case, the contents of which were a complete mystery and a source of fascination to Davina.

"You are colorless, *madame.*" She extracted a jar and a hare's foot brush and applied a touch of rouge to Davina's cheeks and lips. The effect was magical. Her skin took on a complimentary glow, and her eyes glistened.

"There." Fifi nodded to herself. "Is not that better?"

"Yes." She wonderingly eyed the transformation. "I've never worn cosmetics."

"There was no need, *madame.*"

"No." She lowered her gaze. "I suppose there was not."

The Frenchwoman skillfully brushed and knotted her hair. "Shall I buff *madame's* nails?"

"Not now. I shall go down to breakfast." She rose and

started toward the door, then paused. "Thank you, Fifi, for your expertise."

She shrugged a shoulder and curtsied. "It is nothing."

"I think it is something akin to a miracle." Davina smiled and left the chamber. Her pulse throbbing, she descended the stairs, hoping as always that Adam was in the dining room and everything would magically be normal between them. But when the footman opened the door, there was no one, not even the dowager. Adam's place setting had been removed. He'd already been there and gone.

Pinkham was fussing at the buffet, rearranging dishes. He turned and bowed. "May I serve you, my lady?"

"Just tea and fruit, thank you." She walked with leaden feet to her place, while the footman drew back the chair. "Has everyone dined?"

"Only his lordship, ma'am," the butler replied.

"Is he at home?"

"I believe he has gone riding in the park, my lady."

Her heart fell. How wonderful it would have been if he had asked her to go! But she wasn't supposed to ride anyway.

She sipped her tea and picked at the fruit. Pinkham had been so bold as to add a muffin to her request. Seeing him surreptitiously watching her, she spread it with jelly and tried to eat it, but her appetite failed her. She just wasn't hungry. To force it down would be impossible. She returned it to the plate.

"That is all." Abruptly, she folded her napkin and pushed back from the table.

"My lady?" Pinkham took one step forward.

She hesitated. "Yes."

He shifted from foot to foot. "If I may be presumptuous . . ."

"What do you wish to say, Pinkham?"

"My lady, I know it is not my place to comment."

She waited momentarily, watching him fight a great mental battle between proper servile behavior and forthrightness. "Please go on."

He took a deep breath. "My lady, you are not eating enough to keep a bird alive," he said in a rush. "You grow thin. I worry for you."

"I am all right." She started to rise, then saw his distraught countenance. "I shall try a bit harder."

She replaced the napkin on her lap and compelled herself to finish the muffin and fruit, although it all hung rather nauseatingly in her throat. She signaled for more tea to push the mass down. Maybe now he was satisfied.

"I never did have a big appetite, Pinkham." She finished the tea.

"No, ma'am," he intoned, but he looked better pleased.

She got up from the table. "Pinkham, please send Mrs. Benning to me in the morning room."

She felt alien seating herself at the mistress's desk instead of sitting there beside Lady Trowbridge, but this was her rightful position. Now that she was becoming socially adept, it was time she resumed the reins of the household. She hoped Adam's mother would not be angry.

She opened the calendar. How could it have been such a short time since she and Adam returned from the Continent? It seemed like a lifetime.

She studied the dowager's squiggly handwriting. From the looks of things, they were engaged in a strenuous social schedule until the very last day of the Season. She hoped she could rise to it.

She briefly closed her eyes. She felt decidedly ill from stuffing herself with the fruit and muffin. She had almost decided to return to bed when the door opened.

Her attendant was Pinkham, not Mrs. Benning. As usual, he bowed gravely. "My lady, his lordship is home and wishes to see you in the library."

Davina's heart lurched and began to hammer, making her light-headed. The summons sounded so formal, but at least he had requested her presence. She unsteadily got to her feet.

Pinkham leapt forward as she wavered and caught her arm. "Are you all right, my lady?"

"Quite so." She braced herself on the desk. "I was just a bit dizzy for the moment. Now I am fine."

Nevertheless, he stayed close by as she traipsed from the room and down the hall.

Drat! Davina thought. He would blame the spell on lack of food and not nervousness. She would feel guilty every time she sat down at the table.

"I am fine," she repeated as he opened the door to the library, but her knees suddenly seemed made of water, and she was forced to clutch the molding.

"My lord," Pinkham said helplessly, taking her elbow.

"Davina, are you all right?" Adam asked coolly, striding across the floor.

"Yes." She shook off the butler's aid and crossed to the sofa, ignoring the chair across the desk from Adam's.

"Are you sure?"

"Yes, and I wish everyone would quit asking me that," she stated, sitting down and smoothing her skirts. "You wished to see me?"

Adam saw the little flash of temper in her eyes and was dismayed. He longed to take her in his arms and beg her forgiveness for his chilly behavior, but he was hesitant. She might take his apology as a sign of weakness and mount a defense for what he was about to say. It was too important to risk. Hopefully, he could hold her when he was finished.

His long ride had cleared his head and allowed him to reason. If he was to have his sweet wife again, he must get her away from London and his mother's stiff influence. He must do it before it was too late, if indeed it was not so already.

He'd seen it happen so many times. The husband and wife went their separate ways and the marriage became one in name only. That couldn't happen to him! He wouldn't live like that, and he was going to do something about it.

Going to Brighton was too great a risk. There would be frantic social activity there. Besides, the dowager might decide to set aside her dislike of the place and accompany them so she could continue the education of her daughter-in-law.

He had to take Davina out of his mother's reach—preferably to the country, where they could have long walks and talks and reignite the love that had sparked their marriage. But where? He couldn't go to one of his estates. It would be too easy for the dowager to find them. The same held true for one of his friends' houses, and he didn't want the bustle of another trip to the Continent.

Luckily, the post gave him the answer when he arrived home. Along with the copious invitations was a letter from Davina's father. He cordially bid their presence at a family reunion at Halderton Manor and beseeched them to come as soon as possible so they could enjoy a nice long visit.

It was a perfect idea. His mother would not set foot at a Halderton gathering, and only family would be present, so Davina would be comfortable. Furthermore, house parties usually provided ample time for a couple to be alone if they so desired. He leaped on the notion. Already he had written to his father-in-law, replying that they would travel immediately.

Adam anticipated sharp opposition from Davina and his mother. They probably had a very full social schedule, which would last till the end of the Season. He was going to have to stand up to them, forcefully if necessary, but he'd do it as shrewdly as he could.

"Davina?" He seated himself on the edge of the desk. "Would you like to take a trip, just you and me?"

Excitement filled her blue eyes. "To Brighton?"

Damn! He wished that destination had never been mentioned. "I had a more secluded location in mind."

"Oh? Where?"

"Somewhere without Mother." He grinned ruefully. "We must go away alone, Davina."

"Yes," she pertly agreed. "After the Season—"

"Not after the Season. Now."

Her eyes widened. "Adam, I do so want to be with you, but how can I leave London instantly? There are commitments. There are accepted invitations."

He gritted his teeth. "We will cancel them."

"We *can't!*" she cried softly. "It would be just awful. Think of what people would say!"

"I don't care, Davina," he said firmly. "We will tender our regrets. I have already made arrangements."

She gaped at him.

He chuckled. "I will handle Mother."

"But . . ."

"To all others, we will claim family considerations,"

"No one will believe it," she said anxiously.

"Of course they will, for it will be true." He hugged her. "We are going to visit your parents."

Davina literally shrieked and sat up ramrod straight. "No! We cannot! Adam, you do not know what you are about! We cannot go to Halderton Manor."

"Certainly we can." He took her hand and patted it patiently. "I just received a letter from your father inviting us to your annual family gathering. He informs me it is quite a tradition, and he is very anxious for us to attend."

She savagely bit her lip. "We'll tell him we cannot come. It is impossible."

"That's a lie, Davina."

"No, it isn't! We have social obligations."

He felt like shaking her. She was becoming more immersed in this mania than he had thought. Didn't she care about being with him?

"We can easily send our regrets to our would-be hostesses. Darling," he cajoled, "you cannot wish to fib to your own family."

"I don't care! Moreover, it is a *polite* falsehood. We just can't go to Halderton Manor. You must trust me on this, Adam." Her nibbled lip quivered. Again, she caught it between her teeth.

"You're going to make your mouth bleed." He tenderly touched her lip causing her to relax her bite. "Don't you want to see your family?"

"No!"

"Not even your mother?"

She eyed him pitieously. "Adam, this visit would make you miserable."

"Wouldn't I be the better judge of that?" he asked. "Truly, Davina, we must get away from London for a while . . . and away from my mother. Halderton Manor is ideal. Country house parties provide ample opportunity for long walks or, yes, even rides. Mother is being ridiculous about forbidding you to ride, especially when you love the sport."

"Couldn't we go to one of your estates?" she appealed.

He felt he had made some progress. Her statement indicated she was willing to abandon her social schedule without further struggle, and she did not insist on Brighton.

"At one of my estates, I would be hindered by duty," he explained. "I want you to see my properties, but that can come later. I want time without responsibility."

"There are other places we could go."

"Davina, I am interested in seeing your childhood home. I scarcely know your family. I'd like to become better acquainted."

"No, you wouldn't," she said flatly. "They are Haldertons."

He chuckled. "I am very much in love with one Halderton."

"And you will hate the others!" She turned toward him, her face twisted with apprehension. "You have heard what others say about the Haldertons, and every word is true. They are ridiculous, boisterous buffoons. I am not like that, or you would never have given me a second look. Frankly, they are an embarrassment."

"I know what is said, but I also believe it is my responsibility to be familiar with my wife's family." He played his last card before becoming lord and master and setting down an ultimatum. "Additionally, do you not think it is your obligation as daughter, wife, and *countess* to be gracious enough to acknowledge them?"

"I wish you wouldn't put it that way," she wailed.

"It is true." He caught her hands and squeezed them. "Now, I have sent word to your father that we will be arriving promptly. We'll leave the day after tomorrow. Will that give you time to pack and write letters of regret for our engagements?"

"No," she said sullenly, jerking her hands away. "You do not know what harm you are causing."

"Davina—"

"If you think we shall have time together, you are wrong." She bounced on the cushions and crossed her arms. "This will be the most odious interval you have ever spent in your life."

"No doubt, if you are intent upon making it so." His temper was becoming short. "I do not understand your pigheaded disregard for my wishes."

She suddenly stood. "Me, Pigheaded? Look to yourself, my dear lord. You would not forsake this notion if God advised you to."

He set his jaw. "Davina, we are going to Halderton Manor, and that is final. Maybe I will find the girl I married there."

She pursed her lips like the dowager. "All you will find is a headache, Adam."

"Well, we'll see about that!"

"Yes, we will." Turning on her heel, she left the library and shut the door very hard behind her.

Adam flinched. She definitely didn't want to go to Halderton Manor, but go she would. He would not back down. And they would leave on the date he specified. There would be no procrastination.

Sighing, he shook his head. He'd have to do battle with his mother, too. She would rail against their having anything to do with the Haldertons. Like Davina, she would lose. He was set on this. He was going to get out of London, and he was going to do it as soon as he could.

Rising, he crossed the room to the sideboard and poured himself a stiff glass of brandy. Women! They were wonderful, but they did give a man nightmares. He drank deeply.

Fifi left her weeping mistress and softly withdrew into the hall, scratching on the door to Lord Trowbridge's dressing room. Turnbull poked his head out, saw her, and grimaced.

"What do you want, pest?"

She eyed him severely. "My lady is weeping her heart out. What did your master do to her?"

"How the hell do I know?" he growled. "Don't blame me! It isn't my fault, and I'm not having anything to do with it."

"He ignores her for days. Now she is sobbing."

Turnbull threw up his arms. "His lordship does not exactly ask my advice on female affairs."

"Is he in his chamber?" she hissed.

"No. I haven't seen him since he changed from his ride."

"Good!" She pushed him inside and followed, closing the door behind her. "I do not wish servants to eavesdrop on us."

"You can't come in here!" Turnbull cried.

She shrugged eloquently. "I am already here. Listen, you. I want to know why his lordship is treating my lady so badly. Is there another woman?"

"He's never been interested in anyone but her."

"I didn't particularly ask that. Does he have a mistress?" she demanded, strolling around the room and glancing at the earl's collection of garments. She opened a drawer.

"Stop that!" Turnbull flew across the room and smacked her hands. "You are the nosiest—"

"Does he have a *fille de joie?*"

"No! Not that I know of, and I think I would know. I knew about the other one."

Fifi glared. "Are you telling the truth?"

"Yes, I am!" He took her elbow and propelled her to the door. "Leave me alone, wench."

She stuck out her lip. "I want to know what has happened between my lord and lady."

"Well, whatever it is, it's not his fault!" the valet loyally declared. "She's probably being a bitch like you. No man can stand that. I know *you* certainly couldn't attract me."

"Who would want to?" Fifi spat back. "Find out what is going on. I'll be back later."

"Leave me alone! I'll lock the door!"

"Ooh, la." She waved a saucy hand over her shoulder and departed.

Fourteen

The luxurious carriage slowed and squeezed through the narrow entrance of Halderton Manor. Good Heavens! It was even worse than she'd thought it would be. Davina couldn't believe how run-down and shabby the estate looked.

The double iron gates, which stood open in a welcoming fashion, were probably left that way because they sagged onto the ground. The bolts that should have held them up had pulled from the crumbling mortar of the stone pillars. Leaf drifts and scraggly vegetation informed the onlooker that they had been that way for some time. Davina had never noticed that.

My, but the gateway was a disgrace! She anxiously stole a glance through her eyelashes at Adam, but his face registered no reaction.

The perfectly matched team of blacks picked up their smart trot again down what Davina had remembered as a lovely avenue of oaks. Now it seemed unkempt, too. At least the parkland had been scythed and tidied, but the servants' efforts had not included clipping around the bases of the trees, leaving long stems of grass growing in uneven disorder. She had spent many happy hours playing in those pleasant branches, but today they seemed only sad.

The house hove into clear view. Davina held her breath, hoping that seeing it through her different perception would not be devastating. But it was.

Halderton Manor was very ancient. Built in the Elizabethan time, it had experienced no additions and few modernizations. It still had the little diamond-shaped windowpanes, thick plank doors, and old-fashioned, half-timber construction. Designed in the form of an E to honor the magnificent Tudor queen, its wings had once seemed to embrace Davina in its warmth and hominess. She didn't feel like that as they approached. She felt only dread.

She was relieved to see her father had caused the walls to be painted, freshening the exterior. Moreover, the sunlight reflected like sparkling jewels off the windows. But moss had grown in the slate roof and some of the tiles were damaged, hinting of leaking within. Several timbers looked rotten.

A raven perched on a corbel suddenly ducked down and entered the attic.Davina gritted her teeth and prayed Adam hadn't seen that. As fastidious as the Trowbridges were, what on earth would he think? She turned her head slightly and looked at him.

Her husband was thoughtfully perusing the place as if it were a sight in a guidebook. He would miss nothing. He'd quickly summarize the manor's glaring faults, pass horrible judgment, and wonder why he had ever married into such a seedy family.

Davina was just a breath away from crying. Why couldn't she have come up with a way to change his mind about coming here? But she knew if the dowager had failed, she couldn't have hoped to succeed.

She had not heard Adam inform his mother that they were coming here, but from the lady's reaction, it hadn't been pleasant. Davina could sympathize. *She* certainly hadn't been able to change his mind. He was determined to come here. Oh, what disaster would fall?

Adam broke the strained silence. "Your childhood home is very interesting, Davina. I did not realize it was so old."

"Yes, ancient," she acknowledged uncomfortably, "and

rather outmoded, I fear. None of the Haldertons have ever been interested in bringing it up to the mark."

"In many aspects, that's all for the better," he mused. "Such pure examples of Elizabethan architecture are becoming increasingly difficult to find."

Her mind was assaulted by an awful recollection of her chamber draperies puffing in the winter wind. For sure, Halderton Manor was unadulterated by renovation. She was glad it was summer.

They entered the courtyard, the horses tripping and the coach lurching so on the uneven stone paving that the coachman was obliged to bring them quickly to a walk. The solid manor door opened and Davina's family spilled out to welcome them. For brief seconds, her spirits rose with happiness to see them again, but swiftly were dashed as she remembered how mortifying her father and brothers could be.

"Oh, I don't want to be here," she murmured.

Adam faintly frowned. "You know the social whirl was winding down soon, my dear. You won't miss much."

She started to protest his interpretation, but it was too late. The carriage rolled to a halt, and Jeffrey, her youngest brother, leaped ahead of the footman and jerked open the door.

"Welcome to Halderton Manor, Trowbridge! Welcome home, Dini!" He grasped her arm to haul her out.

Davina twisted free. "Do not call me that," she sputtered. "I told you not to call me that."

Jeffrey chortled and bowed dramatically. "My God, aren't we grand? Well, dear sister Davina, *Countess* Trowbridge, allow this poor mortal to assist you from the coach."

Her cheeks burning, she started forth. "Can't you behave properly? Please, Jeffrey."

"But I am overcome with joy to see you!" Instead of taking her hand, he caught her round the waist and lifted her down, spinning her wildly through the air. "Look at her, fellows. She's slim as a reed. I win the wager!"

Davina did not have time to digest that remark before each of her other brothers raised her off the ground and twirled her in dizzying circles. She was almost staggeringly giddy when she found herself in her father's bear hug. She avoided watching Adam's reaction.

"It's been too long, daughter!" Sir William Halderton boomed. "I thought I'd be gaining another son and not losing my only girl."

"Papa, please," she begged.

Either he didn't hear her or he ignored her. "But now we've got you both here, and I intend to make the most of it!"

Davina detached herself as he directed his attention to Adam. She gently embraced her tiny mother. "Mama, can you not entreat them to conduct themselves as gentlemen? I am absolutely mortified."

"Darling, you know how they are. Nothing can dampen those high humors. Now let me look at you." She stepped back. "Jeffrey is right, my sweet. You are dreadfully thin."

"Not really," Davina denied.

"I beg to differ, but we shall speak of that later. I must greet Lord Trowbridge." She slipped her arm through her daughter's and stepped forth to receive her new son-in-law.

Adam was yet under siege by her burly brothers. When he shook Seth's hand, Davina saw him wince and knew immediately what had happened. Her eldest brother had once possessed a trick ring with a small pinpoint expertly hidden in the band, designed to prick the hand of his victim. Obviously, he had worn it today.

She set her jaw against her rising temper. *Damn him! Damn them all!* Why couldn't they conduct themselves as respectable people?

"There, there," her mother soothed, evidently feeling her

tension. "Adam will learn to contend with their playfulness."

"Is that what's it's called?" Davina hissed, noting a drop of blood on her husband's palm. "I call it vulgarity! And, no, Adam will not combat it! He is far too civilized."

"We're glad you've arrived, Trowbridge," her father said. "Hell's afire! I do believe you've snagged yourself on something."

"So I have. Sorry, sir." Glancing down at his outstretched hand, Adam removed his handkerchief, dabbed at the blemish, and completed the handshake.

"Outrageous bumpkins!" Davina muttered nastily.

"Control yourself, darling," her mother whispered and walked forward to join her husband.

Control myself? Davina thought viciously. *What of them?* Why did her mother chide her? She wished she could dash to her room, bolt the door, and never come out until it was time to leave, but she couldn't abandon poor Adam to this merciless slaughter.

No, she would not control herself! If this went much further, she was going to tell them off. She followed her mother and aligned herself protectively at Adam's side.

"The architecture of the manor is magnificent," her husband was saying, having received his welcome from her mother. "I was intrigued from the first moment I saw it."

"You were?" her father asked, surprised. "No one's ever said that to me. People have called it a screaming old relic."

"Then they must have been blind. I wish I owned such a jewel."

"Good God." Sir William looked up at the edifice, chuckling. "I'd best get the roof fixed. Seems to me that a chambermaid or two might've complained about wet beds!"

"Papa, really," Davina said with disgust.

"Oh, cheer up, young lady!" he laughed. "You've grown too serious by half! Can't you recognize a joke anymore?"

"I don't know that it is a joke," she mumbled.

Her brothers guffawed.

"What?" Her father cupped his ear. "Speak up, girl!"

"Never mind." She possessively took Adam's arm. "Let us go in."

"Yes," Sir William agreed. "If you're so interested in this house, son, I'll give you a grand tour."

"Not now," Davina objected. "We are weary from the trip. We shall retire for a rest."

"Balderdash!" said her middle brother, Lionel. "We're set to offer restorative drinks! I imagine Adam—you're our brother now, so we'll call you that—would like a big glass of brandy. And you, little sister, might want the same!"

"Really," protested Davina with contempt.

"Ha-ha!" He chucked her under the chin. "You sure put away a large cupful of port when you fell off in that point-to-point. I thought you might be ready for brandy."

"Disgusting," she sputtered.

Her husband eyed her curiously. "You rode in a point-to-point?"

Davina flushed. "It was a long, long time ago."

"Was not!" Lionel countered. "It was just before you went up to London."

"No, it wasn't," she snapped, seeing Adam's grin.

"Was!"

"Mother," she beseeched.

Lady Halderton came to her rescue. "Let us go in. The gentlemen may have their spirits. You and I, Davina, will go up to your chamber and chat."

But the preliminaries of the visit had not been completed. Just inside the front door, many of the Halderton servants waited to meet their much cherished young miss, now a real countess, and her husband, the earl. With their accustomed informality, they offered effusive greetings and, in the case of some individuals, embraces and handshakes. Successfully managing to keep from cringing in embarrassment, Davina couldn't help comparing this staff with the sober, restrained Trowbridge employees. Couldn't anyone strike a happy medium?

"Let us go upstairs," suggested Lady Halderton, when Davina had exchanged a few words with each one.

Unwilling to leave Adam to his fate with her father and brothers, she shook her head. "I do believe I would prefer refreshment, Mama. Let us go with the others."

The self-effacing lady inclined her head.

Halderton Manor's drawing room was reminiscent of a medieval hall. A vaulted ceiling, which might have been impressive had it not been so dingy from the two oft-smoking fireplaces, rose overhead. Wrought-iron chandeliers hung from chains. The walls were of dark paneled oak, with deeply recessed, red-velvet-padded window seats. Upon the walls hung timeworn broadswords, painted shields, a gnarled battle ax, a grisly spiked mace, and a tired, dusty old banner. Over one hearth was the portrait of a venerable ancestor clad in an elaborate ruff.

In the distant past, a Halderton forebear had refurbished the house by installing wood plank flooring over the original stone. Upon this lay a threadbare Turkey carpet. The furnishings incongruously ran the gamut from the Elizabethan period to the eighteenth century. Gazing at it from the standpoint of the mistress of the beautiful, meticulously decorated Trowbridge House, Davina could have cried.

"It's awful, Mama. You must make Papa modernize."

"It's marvelous!" enthused Adam. "Priceless things! My word, Sir William, you are sitting on a fortune of treasures."

His statement left everyone, including Davina, speechless.

"I know several gentlemen who would pay a fortune to own just one of those two Tudor chairs."

"You do?" croaked her father.

"This old rubbish?" ventured Seth.

Adam nodded vigorously. "But if you sell them to anyone but me, I'll never speak to you again!"

Davina gaped.

"Good God." Sir William sank into a creaking wing chair. "I won't sell them to you. If you want them that badly, you can have them. I wouldn't take money from my little girl's husband."

"I couldn't do that," Adam demurred. "They're far too valuable. I'd feel like a thief."

"No," stated Seth, the heir, "you take them. Consider them a wedding present."

Davina's emotions were thrown in conflict. Her family might be buffoons, but they were generous. She wished Lady Trowbridge could have heard the offer. That would have set her straight in her accusations of the Haldertons being grasping. But, no doubt, she would have turned up her nose at the sight of the old chairs.

Adam smiled and crossed the room to examine his bounty. "I scarcely know what to say, except to thank you. No one has ever given me such a fine gift."

"Well then, you and Dini shall sit in them while you enjoy your drinks," Seth exclaimed and tucked her hand through his arm, leading her to one of the chairs and bending to her ear. "They're uncomfortable as hell, you know."

Davina was well aware. As the youngest, she and Jeffrey had frequently been stuck with sitting in them when there were guests. "Thank you, Seth," she said dryly. "May you receive ample compensation in the afterlife for your generosity."

He howled with laughter. "That's more like our Dini!"

"Do not call me that," she declared once again.

While Lionel and Jeffrey poured brandy and sherry, their butler Carson and a footman entered with heaping trays of refreshments and arranged them buffet-style on an old trestle table which stood against the wall.

"Do we serve ourselves?" Adam whispered to her.

"Yes." She rose, taking his hand. "You will find Halderton Manor to be extremely unceremonious."

"Good! That is much more relaxing."

Was he criticizing her household management? Even when the dowager had pointed out the folly of staff familiarity, she had continued to attempt to ease the atmosphere as much as she responsibly could. Oh, what did the Trowbridges want of her?

She helped herself to half of a ham sandwich, which didn't even have the crust removed, and a macaroon. From the corner of her eye, she saw Adam filling his plate. She hoped he wouldn't be disappointed by the Haldertons' simple country fare.

"No wonder you are so lean," Lady Halderton tsk-tsked. "Davina, I do pray you will eat more and gain a bit. Even during your Season, you looked like a good, healthy, robust country girl in the prime of her age."

"I do not wish to resemble a rustic," she stated. "Besides, I think I look nice."

Lionel, overhearing, laughed. "I'll wager Adam would prefer something he could get hold of."

Davina blushed deeply. "What do you know of it?"

"I'm a man," he defended, setting their drinks on a low table between the two Tudor chairs. "I could explain further."

"Don't trouble yourself." She proceeded to ignore him, sinking down and smoothing her skirt.

"It's no trouble. Adam, wouldn't you prefer—"

"Don't sit down!" Davina shrilled at her husband, spying, just in time, a particularly large, plump earthworm squirming in the seat of his chair.

"Balderdash," said Lionel in disappointment.

"You did that!" his sister accused.

"Me?" He shrugged disarmingly. "How could I? I had a glass in each hand."

"You had it in your pocket!"

"A worm? Good God, Dini! I wouldn't soil my clothes with that thing."

"No? I've seen you with all manner of wildlife in your pocket," she asserted.

"Oh? Like this?" He promptly reached into his coat and tossed a grasshopper at her.

Davina screamed as the large, green insect landed on the bodice of her dress.

"Darling, don't be afraid." Adam handed his plate to Lady Halderton and reached for the offending creature. "I'll get it."

As his fingers closed on the narrow body, the grasshopper took exception and sprang into the air, disappearing down Davina's decolletage. Davina shrieked.

Adam grinned sheepishly while the Halderton males burst into laughter.

"He'll bite me!" she cried, pulling at her gown. "Help me!"

"Do excuse me, darling." Her husband plunged his hand down her dress and retrieved the insect.

"Oh!" she wailed, more embarrassed than she had ever been in all her life.

"I'm sorry, darling. I—"

"Just get rid of it!" she snapped, glaring past her husband at Lionel, who was laughing so hard he had to sit down and hold his sides. "You uncouth beast! I hate you!"

"Oh, Lord, I never dreamed it would be *this* good!" he managed. "Dini, you should have seen yourself."

Davina's response was a shrill of outrage, followed by, "I will never show my face again in this deplorable house!" Jumping to her feet, she threw her plate to the floor and dashed from the room.

Uncertain of what to do, Adam strode to the window to release the hapless grasshopper. He wanted to go to his wife, but he didn't know where she had fled, and he wasn't sure she would be happy to see him. After all, he had forced her to come here, then grinned at her distress.

"You're a good sport, Adam!" Seth shouted across the room. "Too bad Dini has turned into such a namby-pamby."

Adam suddenly felt like calling him out, though of course he would not. But Davina's eldest brother and the rest of the Halderton men were laughing heartily and all too long. Enough was enough.

"Perhaps Davina has merely grown up," he said bitingly.

"Ouch!" moaned Jeffrey. "Do I detect a setdown?"

Adam refrained from further comment. He had no desire to bandy words with the youth. He crossed the room to his wife's unhappy mother.

"Where might I find Davina, my lady?"

"She is probably in her chamber. Come." She took his arm and accompanied him from the room. "My lord, I must apologize. Sometimes . . . sometimes things get out of hand. My husband and sons are full of banter."

She led him to an imposing carved oak stairway. "This way, my lord."

"Thank you, ma'am." He eyed her sideways as they climbed the steps. Lady Halderton was still quite pretty in a dainty sort of way. He wondered how she stood up to the rigors of life with the Halderton men. She seemed too delicate to belong to such a batch.

She caught his eye and smiled. "One develops a thick skin around here," she said, as if she had read his thoughts.

He grinned.

They reached the top of the stairs and turned down the hall. "The door on the end," she said, halting.

"Thank you." With a half bow, he left her.

He was relieved to hear no sobbing as he paused at the door, suddenly in a quandary about whether to rap or to enter. He decided to do as he once did at home. He turned the knob and stepped in.

Davina was standing at the window, her hands clasped behind her back. "Adam?"

"How did you know it was me?"

"You didn't knock."

He came up behind her and slipped his arms around her waist. She remained stiff. "Are you all right, my dear?"

"I suppose so."

"The grasshopper didn't bite you?"

"No."

He felt ridiculous holding her when she was so obviously unresponsive. He let his hands drop to his sides. She didn't want his cuddling.

"It was bad of me to smile in the face of your distress, Davina. I am very, very sorry."

She lifted a shoulder. "Many people find their antics amusing."

It was difficult to curb his frustration, but he took care to keep his voice gentle. "I don't care about the opinion of others. Are you angry with me?"

She avoided a direct answer. Turning, she stepped away from him, placing herself out of arm's reach. Her face was a carefully schooled blank. His mother would have applauded the chilly lack of expression, but it made him almost sick. Where was the emotion-filled woman he married? He had seen her, in her anger, downstairs. Now she'd regained her control and was a veritable replica of the dowager countess.

"I didn't want to come here," she said coldly, "but you insisted. Can you be deaf to what people say about my family and their disgusting ways?"

"I told you I'd heard what people say. I've heard what people say about a lot of things," he maintained. "That is why I have found it best to discover the truth for myself. I don't trust the judgment of others."

She pursed her lips in a perfect imitation of his mother.

"I am referring to the convictions of the premier arbiters of the *ton*."

"So am I." He fought against his rising temper. "In the past, I have found these high sticklers to be very wrong."

She tossed her head. "I think not, Adam. Not really."

"No?" he blurted. "I married you, didn't I?"

Davina lost the battle to retain her newly acquired Trowbridge control. Tears sprang to her eyes. "You certainly made a mistake, didn't you?"

"No!" Adam could have kicked himself. Why must she take his statement the wrong way? "Davina, I love you with all my heart. I don't care what anyone else says about it."

"You shouldn't have married a Halderton." A tear slipped down her cheek. "I am not good enough for you, no matter how hard I try."

"You are perfect for me when you are being yourself." He stepped toward her.

She lifted a hand to halt his progress. Shaking her head, she drew a deep breath. "We both know that isn't true. But please, Adam, give me time. I am doing quite well at learning to be the kind of countess you deserve."

"You already are! You *were!*"

She shook her head.

He closed the distance between them and took her in his arms. For a moment, he thought she was going to melt against him, but she held her reserve. At least she didn't make a lame excuse and extract herself from his embrace.

"I love you, Davina," he whispered.

"I love you too, Adam."

But why wouldn't she show it as she used to do? However, this impassive caress was better than nothing at all. His wife would have to struggle through her false feelings of inadequacy. He could only reassure her and continue to tell her she was ideal just the way she was. Surely she would come to believe him and be herself again. If only the vibrant, affectionate woman he married did not become lost along the way.

Fifteen

"Mother?" Davina took up her after-dinner cup of coffee. They had just finished a bracing meal which featured a Halderton favorite of sirloin of beef, roast potatoes, and a selection of fresh garden vegetables. Lady Halderton was glad to see her daughter ate a hearty meal. Hopefully, the girl's palate had simply become jaded by city fare, and she would quickly regain the small amount of weight that made her vastly more attractive.

"Mother," she went on, "I should have spoken of this earlier, but because of the grasshopper plot, I did not have the opportunity. I am sorry to overset your house party arrangements, but I must request separate chambers for Adam and me."

Lady Halderton stopped with her cup halfway to her mouth, and looked at her daughter in disbelief. "All is not well?"

"Oh, yes. Why would you think that?" She daintily sipped the hot brew.

"Because happily married couples usually share a room."

"Don't be ridiculous, Mother." Davina averted her eyes. "Shared bedrooms are not *haute ton*."

Her mother lowered her cup without drinking. "I did not realize that was the kind of marriage you envisioned. I thought you and Adam were deeply in love."

Davina continued to gaze off in space. "Adam is an earl of very high status."

Lady Halderton tried to pierce the young woman's bland expression. "Does that make a difference?"

"Very much so." As if relieved to have broached the subject, Davina finally eyed her directly. "Propriety must be observed in all facets of life, you know."

"In the bedroom?" Her mother couldn't help laughing. "Really, my darling, Adam may be an earl, but he is also a man. When a man and woman are in love, I think separate chambers are rather redundant. Wherever did you get this idea?"

"We have separate chambers at Trowbridge House. Moreover, Lady Trowbridge believes too much informality between husband and wife fosters lack of respect. She is quite knowledgeable, you know. She is helping me learn what is expected of me."

Lady Halderton was immediately on her guard. She knew Lady Trowbridge was very grand and considered to be the pinnacle of decorum. She also guessed the dowager countess was as cold and tough as yesterday's mutton.

"Since when has Lady Trowbridge become your adviser?" she asked.

"She came up to London not long after we returned from our trip." Davina sighed. "One of her friends had written to her, complaining we were not fulfilling our social obligations. I was mortified."

Her mother smiled. "I imagine anyone would be mortified to have that virago ring a peal over one's head. What did she think you were doing wrong?"

"Avoiding invitations. Even when we attended the parties, we left too early. We wanted to be alone together." Davina shrugged. "She was right. We were in error."

Lady Halderton didn't agree, but she was pleased to see her daughter break that bland expression and show some animation in their conversation. She wondered if the girl's carefully schooled countenance was the product of the dowager's teaching. Davina was a sweet, kind, and loving girl. That old icicle had no business trying to make a haughty society matron of her.

She narrowed her eyes. "What did Adam have to say of his mother's opinion?"

"He did not agree, but of course, that is a man's point of view."

"You'd best learn from your husband and forget about his mama!" Lady Halderton chuckled, then sobered, perceiving how serious her daughter was. "Davina, are you certain of what you are doing?"

She nodded. "You are aware of what a high stickler Lady Trowbridge is. She knows what is proper."

"Perhaps so, in social affairs. But in this matter of bedrooms and husbands and wives, I am not so sure."

Davina murmured unintelligibly.

A cold chill descended upon Lady Halderton. She and her husband, no matter how outrageous and sometimes mortifying he could be, were very much in love. They would never have dreamed of separate bedrooms. She thought her daughter had also found such bliss. No, she was sure of it! Had something happened to douse the fire? She probed further.

"My darling, are you certain you and Adam are profoundly in love? Do you feel the same way about each other as you did before the wedding?"

Happily, Davina's cool expression faded and was replaced by a girlishly dreamy appearance. "Oh, Mother, it is even greater. I never imagined it was possible to love him more, but I do."

"I am so very glad to hear that."

"Still . . ." Davina squared her shoulders and regained her controlled countenance. "Still, proper conduct must be observed. I fear . . ."

"Yes?" Lady Halderton prompted, draining her cup.

A faint frown flitted across her daughter's face. Her cheekbones tinged with pink. "Such topics cannot be discussed in polite company."

"We are mother and daughter. This is hardly a mere social relationship." She paused to refill both cups. "I believe an intimate talk is in order. I sense something is wrong."

"It's just that . . ." A flush suffused Davina's cheeks. "It seems like . . ." She helplessly shook her head.

"Have you discussed this with the dowager Lady Trowbridge?"

"Good heavens, no!" she gasped.

"With Adam?"

"No! I could not."

Lady Halderton lifted her eyebrows. "I cannot help you unless you speak frankly."

"I know," she said miserably. "I think that . . ."

Lady Halderton waited. At least her daughter had again lost that cool expression. Whatever this tangle might be, it was enormously bothering the girl.

Davina drew a deep breath. "Mother, I think Adam tried to treat me like a mistress!" she burst forth.

Lady Halderton hid her shock. What did she mean? Had he treated her with disrespect?

"You must explain further," she urged. "You must be candid."

The girl's face could not become more scarlet. "In bed. He . . . he . . . Mother, what happens there is not a duty!"

Lady Halderton's heart soared. "You find pleasure in your husband's lovemaking?"

Davina nodded shyly. "And so does he."

Her mother smiled. "Then it is altogether wonderful."

"What?" she cried. "I don't think it's proper!"

"Propriety stops at the bedroom door," Lady Halderton firmly advised.

"But it's not only there! One time Lady Trowbridge came

upon Adam kissing me in the library. She was horrified! She actually fainted, then scolded us soundly."

Lady Halderton held back her mirth with great difficulty. She would have given anything to have witnessed the dowager coming upon such a scene. Oh, what a wonder that would have been!

"And he tried it again one time." Her daughter nibbled her lip. "But I put period to it."

"Davina." She reached out to take her daughter's hands. "Lady Trowbridge may be a respected social arbiter, but I think she's a cold fish who knows nothing of love. I am sorry for those couples who find mutual lovemaking simply a duty. It seems you have a very warm and affectionate husband. Treasure what you share with each other. Unfortunately, it is not a common commodity."

"You don't think he treats me like a mistress?"

"I think he loves you, and he is showing you that. You must show him, too, Davina. Don't hide your feelings of pleasure."

Davina frowned. "But also . . ."

Lady Halderton smiled encouragingly. "Yes?"

"Well, lately we haven't—never mind that." She exhaled a long, drawn-out breath. "Thank you, Mother. You have given me much to think about."

Lady Halderton did not feel comfortable with her response. The dowager countess seemed to have so much power over the girl. Her interference wasn't right. In fact, it was downright dangerous to the couple's life together. The woman could ruin their marriage. Something must be done. Davina and Adam must rekindle their unconstrained affection.

Their *tête-à-tête* was interrupted by the men joining them after their port, but Davina whispered urgently in her ear.

"Mother, what about the additional chamber?"

"I am sorry, Davina," she replied amiably. "I scarcely have enough room for the number of guests who'll be coming. All the couples will be sharing. Now, won't you pour the coffee for our gentlemen?"

It was very early morning when Davina awakened in her husband's arms. The past night, when Adam had initiated lovemaking, she had tried to behave as a dutiful wife, but passion had swiftly assumed control. She had acted like a mistress.

Although absolutely wonderful at the moment, it was now depressing. She just did not possess enough willpower to resist her own ardent response. Perhaps when she became in a delicate condition, Adam would cease this activity, but she doubted it. He greatly seemed to enjoy the practice.

She shrugged into her dressing gown and slipped from bed, tiptoeing to the window. A light fog rested on the shrubbery, forming grotesque, ghostly shapes. Overhead, the sky was the palest pink just before full sunrise. This was a time she'd always relished at Halderton Manor. The family and servants would still be abed. The birds were just beginning to chirp. She'd always liked to go out for a walk, alone with her own thoughts and safe from becoming the victim of some new trick.

Adam stirred. "Davina?"

"I am here." She sat down on the window seat.

He put on his robe and followed her. "It's early."

"Yes, it's a nice time of morning. A time to think . . . and plan." She smiled up at him.

"What are you thinking?"

She giggled. "A thought just struck me which would make you laugh."

He grinned. "Tell me."

"No, it is silly!" She shook her head. "Pure nonsense."

"Tell me anyway. Didn't we once agree that we should be able to talk about anything with each other?"

Her smile turned wistful. That seemed so long ago, when

they were comporting themselves like irresponsible love-birds. Oh, those days . . .

"Come, love," he urged.

"Very well." She eyed him with shy mirth. "I was remembering growing up in this room and preparing to leave it for my London Season. I dearly hoped to find a gentleman who loved me."

He smoothed her hair. "You did."

"Great lords were beyond even my wildest dreams. I never expected to marry one."

"You didn't."

"Adam," she chided.

"I am not a great lord, Davina. You make me sound equal to men like Nelson or Wellington. It's absurd. I am just a man who loves you and happens to be an earl." He bent to kiss her on the head. "What else were you pondering?"

"Just that. I never imagined I would wed a peer." She reached up to catch his hand. "I merely prayed for an amiable gentleman."

"Am I not amiable, and a gentleman?"

She looked up into his dancing eyes. "Yes, you are, but you are also an earl."

"Somehow I have found that to be a handicap." He pulled her to her feet. "Come, Davina, let us go for a walk."

"The servants aren't even up!"

"Do you believe that, just because I am a grand earl, I cannot dress myself? Or perhaps you, being an exalted countess, are incapable of performing such a feat for yourself," he challenged.

"Ha!" she cried. "I can gown myself just as well as Fifi can accomplish the task. Watch me!"

"I would love to do so."

She blushed. *"Adam,* you have your own clothes to attend."

He chuckled. "I am trying to be amiable."

"Suffice it to say that you are." She hopped from the

window seat and darted to her dressing room. "I shall also attire myself more promptly!"

"We'll see about that."

They were finished at almost the same time, but Davina had to help Adam don his tight coat.

"A poor selection," she observed. "This garment is made for the assistance of a valet."

She stepped back to look at him. His cravat, tied rather haphazardly, bore the sign of haste, but other than that, he looked quite handsome. She nodded her approval.

"Thank you, my dear, and you look as darling as ever." He tucked in a tape at the back of her dress. "Let us go."

They stole down the hall and slowly descended the stairs, tiptoeing to keep from waking anyone. Outside, Davina led him through the rear garden to the gate. Passing through it, they entered a copse. She breathed a sigh of relief. It would have been just her luck to have awakened one of her brothers and ignited his penchant for tricks. They should be safe from such absurdity, for a while.

Davina slipped her hand into Adam's and smiled up at him. They were together and close again, but she must take care not to spoil the delicate thread of accord. She must prevent her family from engaging in their jests. Most of all, she must struggle to retain her newfound Trowbridge sophistication. She had abandoned it last night and behaved like a trollop. This morning, she may have been a bit too playful. This must not happen again.

As if he sensed a change, Adam looked down at her. "What is wrong?"

"Wrong? Nothing. What do you mean?"

"You suddenly seemed tense." He brought her fingers to his lips. "Your hand stiffened."

"I cannot imagine why." She directed his attention to a large oak tree. "Look! A squirrel."

"I'd rather look at you."

"Adam . . ."

"You are vastly more attractive than any rodent." He neatly caught her in his embrace.

Davina tensed.

"My darling, what is it?" he begged. "Please tell me. Have you developed a dislike of me? Davina, I have to know."

"I love you." She bit her lip.

He sighed and took her hand again. "Let us go on."

Relieved, she skipped a step to catch up. She hadn't known what to say to him. How could she complain to him that he caused her desire to overwhelm her so much that she behaved like a trollop? There was nothing he could do about that. She must learn control over those devilish emotions. She had learned to become a refined society matron. She could learn to do this. But, oh, how much harder it was!

She strolled ahead of him. "I will show you a place I dearly loved to visit when I was a child."

"I'd like to see all your childhood haunts," he grinned.

"Only if you will show me yours when we go to Trowbridge Hall," she teased.

He lifted a shoulder. "I really had none. Trowbridge children do their duty. They do not play."

Not my children, she thought. Her offspring, if there ever were any, would run, climb trees, and get dirty. But not the girls. No, it was a mistake to allow a girl to be anything other than a miniature lady. There was too much to change later.

Davina went ahead of him through a brushy area which gave way to a small clearing beside a stream. "This was my special place."

He appreciatively looked around. "It's a perfect spot for a picnic. Perhaps we could do that. Would your family be insulted if we slipped away?"

"We could tell Mother, but we would have to keep it a secret from the others, else they would make mischief." She

walked to the edge of the bank and peered into the water.
"It would be fun, wouldn't it?"

"Let's do it." He followed her. "Did you ever fish here?"

Davina blushed. "Yes. In fact, there are some very big
fish in the stream."

"And here are two more!"

Before she could react to Seth's shout, Davina found herself flying through the air and splashing into the water. She
went under, then pushed herself up, her straw bonnet drooping down her back. Beside her, Adam tread water, appearing
momentarily stunned. On the bank were Seth, Lionel, and
Jeffrey, guffawing and holding their sides.

"Two more big fish!" Jeffrey whooped.

"I hate you!" Davina shrilled, spitting water. From the
corner of her eye, she saw Adam's hat floating swiftly
downstream. She struck off after it.

Her husband caught her arm. "Let the damned thing go.
It's ruined by now."

"I'm sorry," she moaned.

He shook his head. "Let's get out of here."

Davina swam several strokes until she could stand on the
bottom, then slogged ashore, glaring at her unrepentant
brothers.

"I hate you," she repeated. "I really do. If you knew the
extent of my aversion, you would tremble."

"Ooh!" Lionel quivered. "I am so scared."

"You will be," his sister spat. "Oh, yes. Mark my words,
I will get even."

"Excellent!" chortled Jeffrey. "That will add spice to the
game."

Adam came up beside her, shrugging out of his sopping
coat. "Your sister is not a child to engage in juvenile sport.
You owe her an apology," he told Lionel.

"Pure drivel, my lord. Dini is . . ."

No one was privileged to hear the remainder of his
speech. Before more words left his mouth, Adam dashed

at him. Both men wrestled briefly down the bank and fell
into the stream.

"Oh, no," Davina groaned, watching the grapple continue
amid wild splashing.

Adam gained the advantage and held Lionel under water,
the young man's arms and legs flailing. As Lionel grew
more frantic, he jerked him up by the hair. "Apologize!"

"Not to . . ."

Adam shoved him under again and repeated the exercise.

After the third ducking, Lionel came up sputtering, "I'm
sorry, Dini!"

"Do you accept that?" Adam called to her, ready to im-
merse the young man again.

"I do! Let him go."

For a moment, Lionel looked as if he were going to continue the engagement, but thought better of it and waded
ashore. Adam followed, a slight smile playing across his
lips.

"I thought you were a good sport, Adam," Lionel
growled, coughing and spewing water. "It was nothing but
a damned, good joke."

"Of course." Adam laughed, but there was a steely glint
in his eyes. "I suppose it was a good joke. Mine was better
though, wasn't it?"

"You damned near drowned me! My lungs feel like
they're full of water!"

Her husband cocked his head. "That's an interesting state
of affairs. Handy, too, I might add. All you'll have to do
is cough to take a drink. You could go for miles in the
desert, Lionel."

Seth and Jeffrey gaped.

"That's not funny," her middle brother pouted. "I might
get consumption and die."

"Ah well," Adam said. "Unfortunate consequences sometimes happen when jesting gets out of hand.

"I'm probably full of minnows."

"Then you'll have had your breakfast." Gallantly, he picked up his coat and offered Davina his arm. "We haven't, and I confess I'm starving. Come along, my dear."

Giggling girlishly, Davina slipped her arm through his.

Adam sketched a mock bow to her brothers. "You will excuse us? All this fine jesting has made me hungry, but I'll be available again soon."

Seth and Jeffrey merely stared. Lionel, suddenly turning green, dashed behind a shrub and began to retch.

Adam led her to the path. "Apparently, we weren't quiet enough on the stairs."

"Clearly we weren't." She clutched his arm more closely and gazed up at him in awe. "You were magnificent."

"Thank you, my dear."

"They weren't expecting to have the caper turned against them."

He grinned. "I'd have liked to have laundered all three, but Seth is big enough that he might have dunked me."

"You took them by surprise this time," she mused, "but, believe me, they are hatching another plot right now."

"We'll be ready."

Davina wasn't so confident. When they wished, her male relatives could design quite elaborate schemes. Adam might think it was a challenge now, but when his every waking, and sometimes sleeping, hour was engaged in fending off pranks, he wouldn't find it so funny. He had verged on anger this morning. As time went on, he would become furious. He would be sorry he had ever married a Halderton.

She gritted her teeth. She had to convince him to leave Halderton Manor. If they didn't depart soon, he would decide that a young woman from this family could never become a sophisticated countess. He would come to despise her, and that would break her heart.

Sixteen

As the days passed, Davina was surprised to find the Halderton tricks were mild and rather far apart and did not involve her father. Could her family be losing its touch? She was almost afraid to hope! But she thanked heavens nothing too hideous had happened. She simply could not prevail upon Adam to leave.

He couldn't be having a good time. Though he tried to hide it, she knew he became rather irritated by the jokes, especially the one in which unknown parties spread a layer of oats in their bed, and on the occasion when a colony of ants appeared in their dressing room. Whenever possible, Adam immediately turned the jests back on the perpetrator, but he wasn't always successful. He couldn't strike back when Seth put a small hedgehog on his dining room chair, because the beast was too angry and bristly to pick up. Nor could he throw a snake back at Jeffrey, because the reptile speedily slithered away into the shrubbery. But he did surreptitiously manage to transfer a dead spider to Lionel's soup and to stick a pin into Seth's seat at the breakfast table.

Davina remained in a state of horror and tried even harder to appear to be the most poised and elegant countess in England. This attitude drew fire from her brothers, who mocked her refined manners, making her into a caricature of Lady Trowbridge. It seemed the more she tried, the more foolish she appeared.

In private, she attempted to maintain her respectability, but as soon as Adam initiated lovemaking, she was lost. She pleaded headaches, weariness, even an upset stomach, but she always ended up making miraculous recoveries as soon as he gathered her into his arms. Wifely virtue seemed impossible in a shared bed. She could *not* overcome behaving like a trollop. Adam must think her sadly shameless.

More guests arrived, slowly turning the house into a riot of mischief. Davina had not seen most of her relatives for a year, since few of them—thank heavens!—had attended her wedding. She was not overjoyed to see them now. Happily, however, they did not seem to target Adam with their jesting, evidently holding back to size him up first. Davina prayed that fine state of affairs would continue.

It did not, *could* not—not among the Halderton family. On the day of the picnic by the lake, a favored event of the family reunion, the atmosphere was heavy with subterfuge.

In spite of the threatening proximity of Haldertons and water, Davina dressed with care in a fine blue gown, suitable to a Trowbridge countess. Adam, too, was attired in elegance befitting his station. The rest of the company wore old clothes.

"I believe we're overdressed," her husband murmured as they joined the family in the courtyard.

She sniffed. "Perhaps they are *under* dressed. We are wearing what people of quality wear to dine *al fresco* in the country. Maybe they could learn from it."

"Don't be snobbish, darling."

"Me?" she cried, genuinely surprised.

"You can be very pretentious, darling, and it doesn't suit," he dryly observed. "Can't you just be yourself?"

"Oh, you would just love that! Would you have me be like *them?*" She nodded pointedly. "I doubt you would like that."

There was no time for a comeback. Seth approached with

a groom leading Adam's horse. "The men will be riding, but you, my lord, are dressed so grandly that you might prefer to ride in a carriage with the ladies."

"Seth, is that you?" Adam swiftly looked him up and down. "My God, I didn't recognize you in the scarecrow masquerade! You surely fooled me."

Her brother eyed him spiritedly. "Scarecrow, my . . ."

"No, Davina," Adam cut in. "That isn't your brother. It's a tenant farm boy he has called in to serve me."

"This is absurd," Davina murmured.

Her husband snapped his fingers. "Come, lad, give me a leg up."

Seth begrudgingly grinned. "Very good, Adam. You've bested me. But if I were you, I'd be watching over my shoulder."

"Oh, I shall. Never fear."

Before he mounted, her husband escorted her to the carriage in which her mother was riding and handed her over with a bow. "Take care of her, my lady. She is a most precious cargo."

"For me, too." She smiled fondly.

"Mother, I am so worried," Davina divulged as they seated themselves. "Something awful is going to happen."

"For your sake, my dear, I will pray it happens to someone else." She patted her hand. "But do not worry. Adam seems to be a very good sport. I'm sure he will take all in stride."

No, Davina wanted to scream. He wouldn't. He'd survive the event and wish he'd never seen Halderton Manor or *any* Halderton.

"But you, my darling," she went on, "could use a small dose of humility. Why not laugh and enjoy your family's jests?"

"Because they are not amusing! They are totally mortifying and vulgar. I wonder you can live with them." She inched her nose higher.

Her mother laughed. "I'll grant you they are a bit extreme at times, but that is much better than to dwell in an atmosphere of grim propriety. Now loosen your prudishness and have a good time. I hope the fresh air will stimulate your appetite. You are still much too thin." With that, Lady Halderton turned her attention to the guests who were riding with them, leaving Davina to stew in her worries.

Davina irritably nibbled her lip. Her mother was decidedly wrong. The *haute ton* knew what was best, and they condemned the Haldertons. Oh, how she longed to leave this place! Well, the picnic was the highlight of the reunion. After it, she might be able to persuade Adam to depart. If only they could live through this afternoon.

The site of the event was in a meadow, accented by a stand of stately, spreading oaks beside a small lake. Servants had erected long tables groaning with favored picnic foods and drinks, and were waiting to assist the company. Fishing rods were laid along the bank for those who might wish to partake in the sport. Battledore, shuttlecock, and croquet courts had been set up. There were even card tables.

Davina glanced with disfavor upon the croquet venue. Two years ago, during an intense game, Jeffrey had caught up her skirt in his mallet and lifted it above her knees, mortifying her in front of the entire assembly. Games and Haldertons were a lethal combination.

With the aid of a footman, she stepped down from the landau and looked for Adam. The horsemen, who'd followed the carriages to avoid kicking up dust on the ladies, had just reached the scene. Seeing her husband laughing and talking with Lionel, Davina drew a breath of relief. Nothing had happened on the way, or Adam would not have been so cheerful.

Opening her parasol, she strolled toward him, but was intercepted by Great-Aunt Flossie.

"My dear Davina, how grand you have become," she

said, clutching Davina's arm with bony fingers. "I scarcely recognized you."

"I hope my change is for the best, Auntie," she said politely.

"Perhaps. But you still chew your lip too much," she critiqued, "and you seem to have lost your sense of humor. I watched you all last evening, and you looked as though you'd rather be anywhere but here. It is very insulting, Davina."

Davina angrily started to snatch her lip between her teeth, but caught herself and licked it instead. Great-Aunt Flossie had a reputation for plain speaking. The Haldertons thought it funny. So had Davina—until now, when she bore the brunt of that candid tongue.

"A sense of humor is essential in this family." The old lady's nails bit into Davina's flesh. "How can you forget that? You once were lively and devil-may-care. What are you now?"

"For one thing," Davina said tightly, "I am no longer a member of this family."

Her great-aunt laughed. "My dear, you shall always be a Halderton!"

"Not if I can help it! Don't you realize what polite society thinks of the Haldertons?"

"Oh, I don't care!" she chortled. "We have much more fun! Life would be a bore without laughter and people making fools of themselves."

Davina clenched her jaw. "I find it disgusting."

The old lady shook her head. "My gel, you'll become a cold fish if you don't find your lost appreciation of buffoonery. Ah, here comes your lord. He seems like such a good sport. You could learn from him, Davina, and I am not referring to the fusty ways of the *ton!*"

Adam greeted Great-Aunt Flossie and bowed over her hand.

"There you are, you dear boy." The old lady pinched his cheek.

Adam was taken aback. Davina could have dropped into a hole in the ground and pulled it in after her. People just didn't pinch earls' cheeks. Nor was it a simple tweak. Great-Aunt Flossie nipped the flesh between her fingers and shook it at the same time.

"Revolting," Davina said in an undertone.

Adam managed to grin, though his cheek was scarlet and must hurt. "The sun is quite hot, Great-Aunt Flossie. May I escort you to a seat under the trees?"

"The sun does not bother me. At my age, I will soon know enough of shade. But I'll tell you what I would like to do." Her eyes twinkled. "If you'll help me, that is."

"Of course, madam. Anything."

"I want to go wading one last time before I die."

Davina groaned. "Auntie, that is ridiculous. You cannot take off your slippers and hosiery and wade in the water."

"Why not? What is wrong with an old woman's last request?" she demanded.

"It isn't proper," she insisted.

"Fustian!" Great-Aunt Flossie snapped her fingers. "I'll do it even without this young man's help. You are getting above yourself, Davina. I remember you wading just last year."

Davina felt her face grow flushed. "I was just a girl."

"We shall wade!" the old lady proclaimed and pulled Adam toward the lake.

"This is insane," Davina muttered, following behind.

When they reached the bank, Great-Aunt Flossie prepared to sit down to remove her stockings and shoes.

"Get behind the bushes," Davina advised, "else you will show your legs to all and sundry."

"Ah, I am too old to have anything of interest to show!" the old lady cackled. "Isn't that right, young man? Now take off your boots so you may escort me into the water."

Adam looked shocked.

"You can help me, too, gel. Take off your footgear."

"I will not!" Davina gasped.

"Then you will get wet." She plopped down and removed her slippers and stockings, draping them over a bush.

"I have never been so mortified," Davina moaned.

"Help me up!" her great-aunt commanded.

Adam lifted the old lady to her feet. "Hold tightly to me, ma'am."

"You'll douse your boots," she warned.

"I don't care."

"You help me, too, gel!" she ordered Davina.

The scene was gathering onlookers, who began to cheer and shout encouragement to the elderly woman. Supporting her, Adam slogged into the water, while Great-Aunt Flossie dabbled her toes and then boldly stepped in. Davina took her arm and tried to stay dry on the edge of the bank.

"I feel like a girl again!" Flossie shouted.

Everyone applauded.

"Let us go deeper," the old woman asserted, hitching up her skirts.

"No." Davina perched precariously.

"Come on." Great-Aunt Flossie gave a surprisingly strong jerk. "Don't be a namby-pamby."

Water encircled Davina's ankles, soaking her slippers.

"Deeper!" the old curmudgeon cried. She jerked again. "Oh, I am having so much fun!"

Davina lurched into water up to her knees. "Damn it!"

Adam gaped at her. The crowd on the bank roared. Great-Aunt Flossie howled with laughter.

"That washed some of the starch out of that young lady!" she bellowed. "I knew she still had Halderton blood in her!"

"I have had enough!" Davina dropped her arm and floundered toward shore. "You will just have to drown, Auntie, if you are depending on me."

"What a stiff-rumped gel!" Great-Aunt Flossie called after her.

The company laughed and did not part to allow her to gain the bank, forcing Davina to wade around a patch of reeds and get even wetter.

"Ho, sister!" Seth whooped, hastening to the water's edge nearest to her. "I hear it's all the fashion to dampen the petticoats to show off one's figure, but isn't this outside of enough? You've already snared your prize catch!"

Tears of anger and humiliation filled Davina's eyes. She savagely stuck her tongue out at him. "Go to hell!"

"My, what a decorous countess!" he fired back.

With lightning speed, Davina reached underwater, grasped a great handful of muck and weeds, and threw it at him. Not expecting retaliation, he was caught unawares. The slime struck him square in the chest.

Davina gained the shore. "There! How's that for Halderton humor?"

He hooted with appreciation. "I believe our Dini's back! I knew you could not maintain that false front of convention!"

With horror, she suddenly thought of Adam. She had not only behaved like a hoyden, she had even cursed. What could he be thinking of her? How could he ever respect her? His countess had made an awful scene. Cringing, she chanced a glance at him.

Still firmly bracing Great-Aunt Flossie, who was bent double with laughter, he was staring at her, his mouth half open.

Oh, no! Now he would despise her. He would know she could never be trusted to fit in with the *haute ton.*

With a wail, she dashed toward the gentlemen's horses and snatched the reins of one from a groom. In a very uncountesslike manner, she flung herself onto its back and sat astride, kicking it into a gallop. She must escape the awful arena. She must hide. Then she would think of what to do.

Oblivious to the exciting turn of events among their betters, Fifi and Turnbull filled their plates from the servants' table, set up in a grove some distance apart.

"Why don't you go fishing?" Turnbull suggested blithely. "It would be good practice for hooking yourself a man."

"What do I want with a man?" Fifi flicked her fingers at him. "I once had a man. Pah! Worthless! I get rid of him."

The valet's curiosity was piqued. Had she been married? What a miserable life the poor fellow must have had!

"Maybe he got rid of you," he observed. "Who would want a sharp-tongued hussy like you?"

She batted her eyelashes at him. "You."

"You're mad!" He caught her elbow and directed her to a tree where a blanket had been laid. "Who do you think I am? A bedlamite?"

"Yes." She tittered. "You would love having a fine French lady."

"Maybe so, but you aren't fine, and you aren't a lady. You are a particularly noxious pest who seems intent on making my life as miserable as it can be." He watched her pertly sit down. "I suppose you want me to eat with you."

"Ooh la! You may do as you please." She kissed the air. "There are many others who would leap at the chance to sit with me."

"That's a falsehood if I ever heard one." Turnbull peeked behind him. Damn, she was right. The assistant coachman was hovering nearby, watching inquiringly as if waiting to see if Turnbull would remain with the minx. Frowning, the valet plopped down.

"See?" Fifi giggled. "You have competition. Shall I wave him over?"

"You'd best not," Turnbull warned. "Not if we're going to speak of my lord and my lady."

"Oh, are we going to do that?"

"That's what you usually want to do." He sampled a stuffed egg. "Aren't you worried about them, as usual?"

Fifi shrugged dramatically. "They will do. I want some sherry. Fetch it at once."

"I am not your servant."

"Then I shall ask that coachman." She lifted her hand to beckon him, but Turnbull caught it and pulled it down.

"Ooh! We hold hands? I think not." She jerked it away. "Fetch my sherry."

"Fifi, you know the sherry is not for the servants."

"That is no obstacle. Fetch it." She laughed. "Go right to the table and pour me a glassful. Everyone will think you a member of the family."

"No, they won't! Can you imagine what his lordship would do to me if he saw that? I shall fetch ale for you."

She stuck out her lip. "I am French lady, and I want sherry."

"Not even that coachman can perform that miracle," Turnbull scoffed. "No one can."

Fifi bobbed her saucy curls. "Do you care to wager?"

"Half a crown says no one can do it," the valet vowed.

"Just watch!" The abigail hopped to her feet and started toward the guests' table.

Turnbull watched in awe as she joined the crowd of Haldertons. Fifi even nodded to several as if she were greeting old acquaintances. She reached the drinks table, picked up a crystal goblet, filled it, and minced back to him.

"Pay me." She sat down, sipping her wine.

He wonderingly shook his head. "I cannot believe you haven't been fired."

"Where is my half crown?" she demanded.

"You'll get it. I just don't happen to have any money with me."

"I want my money."

"You'll get it," he said through clenched teeth. "Now leave me alone."

"Is that what you truly wish?" she asked coyly.

Turnbull refused to reply. She was a scourge; she was a blight. But, damn it, she was rather fascinating. How did she get away with the antics she enacted? She was amazing.

"Eat," he ordered, although she was already nibbling a chicken wing. "And cease your babble for now."

"Ooh la!" Fifi trilled and sipped her sherry.

Davina did not return to the manor. Instead, she rode into the deep woods to an abandoned woodsman's hut where she and her brothers had played as children.

At first, she had trouble finding it. From disuse, brush had grown high in the narrow path. Saplings had grown higher than the horse's back. She was forced to go slowly, picking her way and making several wrong turns. When she finally sighted the tiny dwelling, she was hot and rumpled and her skirt was torn at the knee.

She paused just outside the weed-choked clearing and surveyed the area to make certain no one was present. The vegetation showed no sign of being trampled, and the door was firmly shut. She rode forward and dismounted, tying the horse to a bush.

Walking through the weeds, her wet skirt slapping against her calves, she listened to birdsong and the humming of insects. It was so peaceful. She almost wished she could repair the little house and live here, away from the Haldertons, away from the Trowbridges, and away from the two families' warring codes of values. She would be happy if she never saw any of them ever again . . . even Adam, who was doubtlessly furious at the scene she had made.

She pushed the door open and hesitated on the threshold,

allowing her eyes to adjust to the cool darkness. The cottage hadn't changed. There was a scarred table and two rough chairs, a cabinet, and a lumpy rope bedstead. A ragged old braided rug lay on the hearth. It had been a perfect place for children to play house. Several times they had even lit fires in the old fireplace and roasted nuts. Those endless days of fun seemed so long ago, and now she wasn't just playing house. It was real.

She sighed and sat down in one of the chairs. Playing the mistress of the woodcutter's hut had certainly not prepared her for being the mistress of Trowbridge House, Trowbridge Hall, and whatever other estates her noble husband possessed. She never should have married Adam. She wasn't the kind of woman he needed. Lady Trowbridge was right. She was a Halderton, and Haldertons had no place in the *haute ton*. She had proved that today. Adam must be perfectly mortified.

She shook her head as if to clear the awful images: saying damn it and go to hell, pelting Seth with muck, leaping onto a horse like a wild Scotsman and riding astride. A proper countess? Ha! She wasn't even a proper wife.

But Adam was saddled with her. Divorces were far too scandalous for a Trowbridge to contemplate. Like many gentlemen who despised their wives, he would settle her on an obscure estate and take pains to assure she never was seen in society again. If she were lucky, she'd bear his children and have some small joy before they were taken far away from her to be raised by nurses, governesses, and tutors. They would hardly know they had a mother, and Adam would forget he had a wife. That was what happened to aristocratic wives who went beyond the pale.

But, oh, she had had that beautiful time of happiness when they had loved and when every day was a honeymoon. She would hold on to that forever. And in the quiet of the night, she would remember Adam's arms. That would be all that was left to her, the memories.

Davina put her head down on the table and sobbed.

Seventeen

Adam solemnly waded ashore, supporting the intrepid Great-Aunt Flossie. Ever since Davina had fled, he had been treated to a critique of her and the Haldertons and himself and the Trowbridges. The old lady had an opinion on everything and everyone, and she did not hesitate to mouth it. At present, it seemed the Trowbridges were taking the brunt of her forthright tongue.

"Too stuffy by half. Too puffed up by their own consequence!" she condemned. "You have attempted to squeeze the very life out of that young lady and make her into a prune like your mother. You are making a mistake, young man. See that it ceases!"

Adam sensed it would be useless to raise a defense. Like the dowager Lady Trowbridge, Great-Aunt Flossie was dictatorial, frank, and set in her ways. Old toad! She had caused him to ruin a good pair of boots in order to behave like a gentleman. Worse than that, she had created a tremendous spectacle that had sent Davina fleeing God knew where. No, she hadn't been alone in that. That dastardly Seth, and indeed most of the Haldertons, had played a role.

"Hoo-ha!" wheezed Great-Aunt Flossie, collapsing on the bank and reaching for her shoes and stockings. "What a day! I did enjoy that, really I did. And when Davina—" She broke off into peals of laughter.

Adam set his jaw. It wasn't amusing. Davina must have

been driven to madness to have enacted such a scene. He cursed himself for bringing her here, denounced himself for allowing his mother to interfere in their lives. Damn it, it was his and Davina's marriage, and they should be able to go on as they saw fit!

"And when Davina flung herself onto that horse and galloped away like a banshee—I wonder if she knew how outrageous she looked? I shall tell her what fine entertainment she provided!"

Adam's temper snapped. "Shut the hell up. Haven't you caused enough trouble?"

It didn't faze the old woman. She laughed even harder. "I see there is spirit behind the Trowbridge milquetoast air. I like that!"

Adam had intended to wait, as a gentleman should, for her to restore herself, then lift her to her feet. Just now he didn't care about that or about the centuries of good Trowbridge breeding and etiquette. He turned on his heel and rudely strode away, leaving her sitting on the bank, one shoe on and one off. Great-Aunt Flossie brayed with laughter.

"Where is that Trowbridge aplomb? Where is the fabled decorum?" she cackled.

It seemed everyone was laughing at him, at Davina, at the incident. There was one serene island in the face of all the boisterousness. He strode toward Davina's mother.

"I am so sorry," she softly intoned. "For yours and Davina's sakes, I beseeched my husband and sons to desist in many of their planned jests, but no one can control Great-Aunt Flossie."

"I believe that, my lady, but just now I do not know what to do. I must find Davina and then . . ." He looked blankly into the distance. "I just don't know."

She linked her arm through his. "Walk with me. A few moments will make no difference in catching up with my daughter."

He led her safely away from the crowd and waited for her to begin the conversation.

"Adam, why did you marry Davina?" she asked.

Didn't everyone know? He'd made a cake of himself in front of the whole *ton*. "I loved her."

"Why?"

He was taken aback. "She wonderful. She's perfect."

She smiled. "Can you not be specific? What do you love best about my daughter? What attracted you to her?"

That was easy. "Her lightheartedness."

She waited, seeming to want more.

"The Trowbridge family is very straitlaced and humorless," he began. "I wearied so of convention and formality. Davina was like a breath of fresh air. In her company, I felt I could relax and be myself, whoever that is."

Lady Halderton patted his hand. "You do not know?"

"I think it's somewhere between the inflexible Trowbridge propriety and the happy, carefree nonchalance of the Haldertons." He shrugged. "Does that make sense?"

"Indeed." She nodded.

"But I don't know what Davina wants," he went on. "I thought she was just like me. Now I'm not so sure. Sometimes I believe she's becoming more of a Trowbridge than I am."

Before she could answer, Adam thought of how he'd encouraged his wife to learn from his mother. He'd told her to pretend to adopt the Trowbridge ways, even if she disagreed with them. On several occasions, he inadvertently expressed doubt as to her ability to rise to the expectations of the *ton*. More than once, Davina had worried about being the kind of countess she thought he wanted and deserved.

"Maybe I have confused her," he said.

"She does seem uncertain about many things," Lady Halderton replied. "She wants to be the perfect countess. She is so anxious to secure your respect."

"She has always had that."

"I'm not so sure she realizes that. Davina feels inferior in many ways." She sighed. "Adam, I don't know how to say this politely, but my daughter feels you look upon her more as a mistress than a wife. That is why she is trying so desperately hard to prove herself the ideal Trowbridge countess."

"Mistress!" He stopped to stare at her. "However could she conceive that?"

She shook her head. "You will have to speak with her about that. I can say no more."

"I will search for her at once. Do you suppose she has gone to the Manor?"

"Probably."

"You will excuse me?" He bent over her hand with perfect Trowbridge manners.

"Go along!" Lady Halderton urged.

Adam hastened to his horse and left the reveling Haldertons at a gallop. Rushing down the lane at breakneck speed, he tried to guess why Davina feared he treated her like a mistress instead of a respectable wife. He drew a total blank. Hadn't he always cherished her, encouraged her to take up the reins as the lady of his household? He'd married her! It didn't make sense.

Only a skeleton staff remained at Halderton Manor, the rest having gone to the picnic. A footman romancing a maid near the front door informed him Lady Trowbridge had not returned to the house. No one there had seen her.

Remounting his horse, Adam circled the house, rode through the garden in true haphazard Halderton style, and leaped the gate into the copse. Davina had doubtlessly gone to her favorite spot by the stream.

The path wasn't made for horseback. Brush whipped at Adam's breeches and limbs swatted his face, altering his appearance from one of damp elegance to soiled disrepute. But Davina's attire wouldn't look much better, so he was glad his clothes wouldn't dominate. He wanted them to be on an equal footing for this meeting.

Pushing through the bushes, he finally reached the stream, but she was nowhere in sight. Disappointment and a mild sense of panic filled his chest. Davina must know of countless places on the estate to go. He knew of nothing else. He'd have to return to the Halderton gathering and beg for help.

As he rode past the manor house, he inquired again, obviously aggravating the amorous footman, but to no avail. Nudging the horse into a canter, he went back to the picnic. Everyone, it seemed, paused to stare at him. Cursing all Haldertons, he spotted Davina's mother and father and went toward them.

"You didn't find our Davina," Sir William stated.

Laughing, Seth joined them. "There are a thousand places she could be. Don't worry. She'll be home by dark. Dini was always afraid of the night."

Adam felt like jumping off his horse and planting Seth a facer.

"She's probably playing a great trick on you," his brother-in-law chuckled.

"I've had it with your damned tricks." Adam vaulted to the ground and started toward him.

"William!" cried Lady Halderton. "Do something!"

Davina's father stepped forward. "Gentlemen!"

Seth backed up, sobering quickly. "Adam, I'm sorry. I didn't mean to provoke you. I—"

Adam, well trained by Gentleman Jackson in the art of fisticuffs, connected his right fist to Seth's nose. His brother-in-law toppled backward and sat down hard on his bottom. He gaped up at Adam, blood running down his chin.

"Tee-hee!" shrieked Great-Aunt Flossie. "Trowbridge etiquette in practice for all to admire!"

Somewhat trembling from the aftermath of anger, Adam

gazed with horror at his victim. Never had he shed his
composure and struck a man with the intent to do harm.
His ancestors must be spinning in their graves at such a
display.

"Seth, I'm sorry." He reached out a hand to help him
up. "Feel free to hit me in response."

"Hell, I had it coming." His brother-in-law clasped his
hand and rose. "I went too far. Of course you're worried
about Davina."

"My dear son!" Lady Halderton scurried up and tried to
wipe Seth's nose with a useless, lacy handkerchief.

"I'm all right, Mother." He took out his own handkerchief to staunch the flow. "I behaved badly, and I got what
was coming to me."

"I must offer my apologies, my lady," Adam said swiftly.
"My conduct was inexcusable."

"No it wasn't!" yelped Great-Aunt Flossie. "I vow I've
never had such fun! You should have seen yourself, Seth.
You simply sat there and—"

"Yah, yah, yah!" growled her nephew. "I'm happy I en-
tertained you, Auntie. C'mon, Adam, I'll help you find
Dini."

"Your nose . . ." he hesitated.

"Devil take it! Jeffrey, stop standing there like a sapskull
and fetch my horse!"

Mounting, they rode from the meadow and into the lane.
From there, they took another trail, which grew narrow
quite promptly, forcing Adam to draw back and allow Seth
the lead. As the trace became fainter, Adam began to wonder if his brother-in-law was enacting another caper.

"This seems awfully remote," he called, as they plunged
even deeper into the woods.

"Not to Dini. Remember, she knows this estate from one
end to the other, and upside down as well." He glanced
over his shoulder. "There's an abandoned woodsman's hut

ahead. We played there as children. Shall we go on, or do you want to go back?"

"Let us try it." He followed Seth's example and leaned over his horse's neck to escape the swat of boughs and briars. As they broke from the undergrowth and into a clearing, he saw Davina's horse. Her brother had chosen well.

"She must be inside." Seth pivoted. "I'll leave you now. And, Adam? Give her my apologies. I've behaved badly to her."

"I will, and thank you."

He slipped from his horse and tied him to the bush beside the other animal. At the door, he was faced with what was becoming an all too familiar dilemma. To knock or to enter? He turned the knob and went quietly in.

"Davina?"

She was sitting at a rough-hewn table, her head resting on her crossed arms. For one terrible moment, he thought she was ignoring him. But as a light sigh escaped her lips, he realized she was sleeping.

"Davina?" Bending, he gently kissed her neck.

"Adam!" She sprang upright. "How did you find me?"

"Seth . . . and he sends his apologies." He sat down in a chair beside her, stroking her back.

"I did not want to be found." Even in the dim light, he could see her deep blush.

"Not even by me?" he asked fearfully.

"Not even by you." She stood and stepped to the window, her back to him. "But I suppose I must hear from you sometime. I know what will happen, Adam. You need make no excuses."

He caught his breath, and his heart pounded with dread. "What are you thinking, Davina?"

She brought her hands to her face. A sob tore from her throat. "You will send me away."

"No!" He swiftly crossed the room to take her into his arms. "Why would you think that?"

"I am beyond the pale. I am an embarrassment. Oh, Adam, I tried so hard to be a proper countess, but I have failed," she sobbed. "Please, please, just lock me away and spare me this anguish!"

"Darling," he whispered, "I do not want to send you away. I want you by my side always."

"I cursed. I behaved as a hoyden," she went on as if he hadn't spoken. "I have degraded the position of countess of Trowbridge. You cannot trust me in polite society. What if I became irate and threw mud at Mrs. Drummond Burrell?"

"I doubt that would happen."

"I disgraced you in front of my family and my relations."

Adam drew her even closer, grinning ruefully over her shoulder. "Actually, I managed to do that quite well on my own."

There was a long pause. "What?" she asked meekly.

"I cursed at Great-Aunt Flossie, and I struck Seth in the nose."

"You?" She drew back, her eyes wide. "You, Adam?"

"I lost my temper. We are even, Davina. We've both shamed ourselves today." He brushed wisps of hair from her forehead. "Can we not forget this day ever happened? Let us go away—not to Brighton, for there are too many people there, but to one of my more remote estates. There we shall resume our honeymoon."

She slipped away from him, stepping out the door. "There is much more, Adam."

He followed her. "Can we not discuss it there?"

Davina hung her head. "I fear nothing would change. I cannot seem . . ." She hesitated.

"Yes?" he prompted.

"It is mortifying to say this, Adam, but I am truly more your mistress than your wife." She wiped tears from her cheeks with the back of her hand. "I wed you under false pretenses. I am not a lady."

He knew that was false. He'd guess he was the only man who'd ever kissed her, let alone done anything else. As to her being more of a mistress, he was just as perplexed as when her mother had voiced that remark.

"I don't understand any of this. You are not my mistress. You are my wife, Davina, and I love you." He tried to take her into his arms again, but she lurched away.

"And I am a Halderton," she continued. "Now you know what that means."

"Davina." He caught her hand and held it firmly. "Please explain all of this to me."

She eyed him tragically. "I don't know how."

"Very well. Let us take it apart, bit by bit. Come sit down." He led her to the stone stoop and drew her down beside him. "Don't you love me anymore?"

"Oh, with all my heart! I am just not suitable."

He felt like shaking her. "Why do you think you are not fitting?"

"I am a Halderton, and the Haldertons are not well received," she said with an edge to her voice. "You know that. Why do you pretend you do not?"

"It seems to me you were on your way to becoming the toast of the *ton*," he observed dryly. "You must have proven your worth to society. The famous Mrs. Drummond Burrell approves of you. Doesn't that put a period to your worries about being a Halderton?"

She stared off into the distance. "Maybe, but you didn't appear to be very happy with my social achievements."

"I don't like the social whirl. I am covetous of your time, my darling, but if you enjoy the parties, there is no reason why we cannot come to a compromise."

She nibbled her lip. "I prefer time spent with you, Adam."

"Excellent!" He kissed her hand. "We will attend only those functions which are absolutely necessary. We don't even have to spend all that much time in London. Being out of town, we would have the perfect excuse."

"It might work," she said softly. Then she stiffened, drawing up her knees and circling her arms about them. "But that is not the only issue."

He perceived some progress, but there was still that knotty problem of the mistress. For the life of him, he could not envision how she could have come to that conclusion, but her thoughts must have been serious enough to cause her to broach the forbidden subject with Lady Halderton. No matter what she thought of herself, Davina *was* a lady. To discuss such a thing would have been very difficult, even with her mother.

"Darling," he said tenderly, "you had best tell me why you consider yourself more of a mistress than a wife."

She squared her shoulders and chewed rapidly on her lip.

He gently placed his fingertip on her mouth. "You'll cause it to bleed. Then I'll be blamed for landing you a facer, too. My reputation is so sadly deteriorating that I doubt I could recover in the eyes of your family."

She managed a smile. "Tell me about Seth."

"Please do not change the topic. We must settle this."

Davina took a deep breath. "It has to do with the breakfast room and our lounging about in the mornings. It is not the thing a respectable wife should do. It is the behavior of a bit of muslin. What makes it even worse is that it was my suggestion. A lady would never propose it."

"Why not? I like it," he enthused. "It is the most perfect start to a day, relaxed and unhurried."

"Too uninhibited," she stated. "Your mother explained a gentleman's thoughts on such conduct. She said——"

"I might have known," he grimly interrupted. "My mother! What does she know of a gentleman's thoughts? Further, what does she know of a wonderful relationship between a husband and wife? She certainly avoided my father whenever possible. Theirs was a marriage in name only."

Davina sent him a troubled glance. "But your mother is all that is proper."

"My mother is a cold fish," he spat out. "I did not—do not—wish for a wife like her. I wanted warmth and cheer. I wanted a wife who loved me. *Me,* not just my wealth and title. I dared to hope I'd found her."

She bowed her head, resting her chin on her knees. "I did not care about your wealth or title."

"I did not believe you did, although I began to wonder when you became so enamored with the *ton.*"

"That was for you," she murmured.

"Well then, Davina," he said happily, "all is well again. Mother is not qualified to judge our morning routine. That is for us to decide, and I definitely do not consider our casual habits to be base."

"There is more. Adam, I . . . I . . . behave like a trollop in bed!" she finished with a rush. "I cannot seem to carry on with dignity. A wife should look upon this as her duty, not as . . . as . . ."

"Pleasure?" he offered.

She nodded miserably. "How can you respect me?"

He wished he could laugh, but that would be a grave error. Davina was terribly serious. She was convinced he thought her a doxy.

He edged closer to her and slipped his arm around her waist. "My darling, when we make love, I am sure I am the luckiest man alive. I have a wife who is not afraid to express her love. Do you realize how many men must search elsewhere for what I have at home? Or do without?"

She gazed hopefully at him. "You do not look upon me as more of a mistress than wife?"

"No! I love you and honor you as the best wife a man could have."

"Are you certain?"

"Absolutely." He took her in his arms, and she did not shrink away. "I don't wish you to change so much as a hair on your head. I love you just as you are."

"You won't send me away?" she breathed.

"Not unless I go with you." He lightly kissed her lips.

"I will always strive to be a good countess!" she vowed. "Today I failed, but . . ."

"There was great provocation." He smiled at her. "I think we are much too influenced by our families. It is our marriage, and we should make of it what *we* want, not what others wish us to be."

She smiled back. "We should listen to our own hearts."

"And just now, mine is telling me . . ." He bent toward her and claimed her mouth.

Looking back at Adam as they rode single file through the woods, Davina laughed happily. "Let us not return to the picnic. Would you not prefer to be alone?"

"If you wish it, too," he called back, grinning. "Shall we go to our chamber and plan our departure?"

"Yes!" she freely replied. Some might judge her a trollop, but Adam didn't, and his opinion was what was important.

When the path widened, he caught up with her. "Race you."

"You will lose!" She nudged her horse into a gallop and outran him to the house, although she suspected he held back.

They gave their reins to a servant and went inside, dashing up the stairs to their chamber.

"Oh, Adam, I cannot wait until we are *really* alone at your estate." She giggled. "Does it have a breakfast room?"

"No, but I'm sure we can create one. However, we are really alone now." He threw open the door.

Standing in the center of the room, locked in a kiss, were

Fifi and Turnbull. The valet leapt back, sending Fifi spinning.

"My lord! Oh, my God!" he cried. "We were only here but a moment! We returned from the picnic to see if you and my lady needed us."

Fifi chortled.

"Shut up!" shouted Turnbull. "You are a pest of the worst sort!"

Adam arched an eyebrow. "Doesn't look much like a pest to me."

"My lord, please allow me to explain further," he begged.

"I think not." Adam grinned. "Go about your own business and leave us to ours. You are released from duty for the rest of the day."

"My lord, I beseech you . . ."

"Come on." Fifi grasped his hand. "Have you no ears? You English! Ooh la, you are dull witted."

Davina closed the door behind them. "So we have a romance brewing in our midst."

"Indeed, my love, and I am feeling very romantical. Can I be lucky enough to discover that you return the sentiment?"

She walked into his arms. "Adam, my darling, I believe you will find I am *always* willing to do my duty. I am setting a new standard of etiquette for the Trowbridge family."

His eyes twinkled. "You are?"

"Yes. And *this* is how it begins." She lifted her chin to be kissed.

Epilogue

A soft scratch sounded at the library door. Adam, cuddling Davina on his lap, barely lifted his lips from hers to reply to the butler's quiet summons.

"We are not receiving, Pinkham."

"You'll receive me!" The door burst open to reveal the dowager Lady Trowbridge, her head flung high and her nostrils dilated in distaste. "Oh, how shocking!"

He grinned. "Mother, you know when you visit us you make yourself subject to mine and Davina's casual style of life."

"Is that what you call it?" she demanded. "It seems to me to be the conduct of a wastrel with his trollop!"

Davina giggled. "Why, Mother Trowbridge, even you have stated Adam and I are quite the models of propriety in Society, and you did agree our private moments should be our own."

"Well," she muttered, "I must have committed that utterance during a weak moment."

"I believe you said that when we were expecting your first grandchild."

"Ha! No wonder! I was enthused about the possibility of an heir, a young man who might restore the family dignity. I was certainly wrong, for *he* is the reason I am forced to invade this . . . this . . ."

"Bordello?" Adam supplied.

"For shame!" Rolling her eyes, the dowager reached behind her back and drew forth the eldest Trowbridge offspring, holding him by the very tip of his ring finger, the cleanest digit on his gummy hand. "I apprehended him as he was fleeing from the service area with your chef in hot pursuit. I ask you, how can the servants prepare for Davina's birthday party with this mischievous imp underfoot?"

Sonny grinned lightheartedly, not one bit remorseful for whatever crime he had enacted.

"Just look at him!" Adam's mother raved on. "And with house guests expected!"

The heir to the Trowbridge dynasty did look disreputable. His hands, face, and the front of his suit were covered with a sticky red substance. His hair was tousled.

"Just like a Halderton," the dowager pronounced.

"Oh, dear," Davina murmured, rising. "I had hoped to strike a pleasing balance in our children's deportment."

"He behaves like a *normal* little boy," Adam contradicted, "don't you, Sonny?"

"Yes, Papa!" The child dashed forward to claim his mother's vacated seat on Adam's lap and promptly smeared some of the gooey mass onto his father's neckcloth.

"Agh!" gasped the dowager.

"What is that?" Davina queried. "Sonny, what have you been into?"

"Cherry pie filling!" snapped Adam's mother. "He has plunged his hands into Chef's pies and ruined every one."

"Go-o-o-od," said Sonny.

"That was too bad of you, young man," Davina scolded. "You will apologize to Chef, and you will never do that again."

"Next time, if you politely ask Chef for a piece of pie, I'm sure he will give you one," Adam added.

"He should be spanked," advised the dowager.

Further comment was prevented by a noisy disturbance

in the hall. Halderton voices rang through the house. Davina's family had arrived for the festivities.

"Grommy! Grampa!" Sonny leaped from his father's lap and ran through the door.

The dowager leaned weakly against the doorjamb. "Why am I here? Why do I do these things to myself?"

"Because you have finally admitted to yourself you love us," Adam guessed, standing, "so you are willing to accept our ways."

"Sentimental rubbish," she claimed, but she actually smiled fleetingly as she turned to enter the hall.

Adam slipped his arm around Davina's waist and moved to follow. "Let us greet your family, darling."

"I confess I am anxious to see them, though this might prove to be a volatile party!" She smiled up at him.

"More hazardous than you might think," he noted, "if Mother realizes she has cherry pie all over the back of her dress."

Davina gaped with horror. "No! This is awful! What shall we do?"

"Pray she doesn't find out. Ah well, I suppose it matches my neckcloth."

"You must hasten upstairs to change."

He shook his head. "I have come to the conclusion that if one wishes happy children, one will become smudged at times."

"At least our daughters are ladies." Davina proudly glanced up the stairs as the girls descended, dainty and pristine in their white ruffled gowns. "Your mother cannot fault them."

"Grommy, Grampa!" Angela, the youngest, suddenly jerked free from Nurse's hand and bolted downstairs, yanking the ribbon from her hair as she ran.

"No!" Davina moaned.

With a sideways glance at her parents, Elizabeth followed

suit, only she vaulted from the last three steps and into her grandfather's arms.

"Just like your mama!" he claimed, hugging her close. "Naughty little minx!"

Davina flushed. "They know better," she said weakly.

"They're excited," Adam said.

"But that is no excuse to forget their manners!" she wailed. "Darling, you of all people know the importance of proper behavior!"

He stopped and turned her toward him. "I know the harm of stifling youthful spirits. My love, haven't we agreed to let them be *children?*"

She nodded ruefully.

"They will be fine. After all, this is family. We needn't stand on ceremony."

Seth lifted Sonny high in the air. "Ho-ho, young man, look at you! You remind me of myself at your age! Yes, you're going to be just like me."

Jeffrey affectionately squeezed the child's leg. "We're going to have fun together, nephew. We'll show you some tricks to play."

Davina and Adam exchanged a horrified gaze.

"Perhaps we should step in and calm things a bit," he suggested.

She bit her lip. "Indeed we must! Oh, Adam, you never should have married a Halderton."

"Balderdash! Think of what I'd have missed."

She pointedly eyed his neckcloth. "I do."

"My love, we've been over this ground before. Can't we put it to rest?" He brought her hand to his lips and grinned provocatively. "Of course, I do enjoy reassuring you of my regard. Shall we slip away to our chamber?"

"With newly arrived guests? Adam, *really!* Where is your sense of dignity?"

"Sadly gone, where you are concerned." He shrugged elaborately. "Very well, darling. I am glad I have you to remind me of proper etiquette. But after our guests are settled?"

"After that, you may reassure me all you wish," she whispered, blushing prettily.

"Then let's be about it!" Clasping her waist, he led her forward into the chaos.

ABOUT THE AUTHOR

Cathleen Clare, the author of numerous Regency romances, lives with her family in Ohio. She loves to hear from readers, and you may write her c/o Zebra Books. Please include a self-addressed stamped envelope if you wish a response.

BOOK YOUR PLACE ON OUR WEBSITE AND MAKE THE READING CONNECTION!

We've created a customized website just for our very special readers, where you can get the inside scoop on everything that's going on with Zebra, Pinnacle and Kensington books.

When you come online, you'll have the exciting opportunity to:

- View covers of upcoming books
- Read sample chapters
- Learn about our future publishing schedule (listed by publication month *and author*)
- Find out when your favorite authors will be visiting a city near you
- Search for and order backlist books from our online catalog
- Check out author bios and background information
- Send e-mail to your favorite authors
- Meet the Kensington staff online
- Join us in weekly chats with authors, readers and other guests
- Get writing guidelines
- AND MUCH MORE!

Visit our website at
http://www.zebrabooks.com

More Zebra Regency Romances

Put a Little Romance in Your Life With
Janelle Taylor